MW00622432

NEVER LET HER GO

ALSO BY A.M. STRONG AND SONYA SARGENT

THE PATTERSON BLAKE THRILLER SERIES

Sister Where Are You • *Is She Really Gone*

All The Dead Girls • *Never Let Her Go*

Dark Road From Sunrise

PATTERSON BLAKE PREQUEL

Never Lie to Me

NEVER LET HER GO

A PATTERSON BLAKE THRILLER

A.M. STRONG
SONYA SARGENT

WEST
STREET

West Street Publishing

This is a work of fiction. Characters, names, places, and events are products of the author's imagination. Any similarity to events or places, or real persons, living or dead, is purely coincidental.

Copyright © 2023 by A. M. Strong & Sonya Sargent
All rights reserved.

No part of this book may be reproduced in any form or by any electronic or mechanical means, including information storage and retrieval systems, without written permission from the author, except for the use of brief quotations in a book review.

Cover art and interior design by Bad Dog Media, LLC.

ISBN: 978-1-942207-44-3

For the real Bill Newport . . .
Keep on reading!

PROLOGUE

LEXIE HURRIED through the midnight darkness. Behind her, the lights of Mackey's Discount Mart, the twenty-four-hour convenience store where she worked the evening shift, receded into the gloom. Further away, a faint rumble of cars carried on the stirring breeze—a constant soundtrack courtesy of Interstates 40 and 27 that pinned downtown Amarillo in their crosshairs.

Pulling her coat closed and zipping it up, she pressed on. The day had been hot—ninety degrees—but an unseasonable cold front was moving through, and the overnight temperature was forecast to dip into the mid-fifties. Not exactly Arctic conditions but nippy enough for residents of the Texas Panhandle, especially in August.

Not for the first time, Lexie wished she had a car. The walk to her accommodation from the convenience store was twelve blocks and took twenty minutes. That was too long for a twenty-six-year-old woman to be walking alone at this time of night when the streets were empty. But she had no choice, at least right now. Maybe when her situation improved, something she expected to happen soon, Lexie would buy a car.

She might even quit the convenience store and find an apartment in a safer part of the city. For now, though, her options were limited.

She reached an intersection, glanced around, stepped off the curb, and hurried across. As she reached the opposite side, a movement caught her eye. A man appeared. He stumbled out of an office building doorway, clearly homeless. A shopping cart was pushed against the wall, it's wire framed interior loaded with bulging plastic bags and dirty clothing. She saw bedding arranged inside the doorway and suddenly felt lucky. Her situation might not be great, but at least she wasn't sleeping rough on the streets.

The homeless man moved into a pool of light under a streetlamp, and she got a better look at him. Wild and tangled hair. Ragged clothing. Ratty beard. A piece of nylon rope wound through the belt loops of his pants. He carried a liquor bottle in a brown paper bag. Two more bottles sat by his makeshift bed, both of them empty.

When he noticed Lexie coming toward him, the man took a swig from the bottle and shuffled forward. His intent was clear.

She changed course and crossed the road, then picked up the pace, eager to get past before she was forced to engage with him.

He stopped at the curb and watched her as if the road were a boundary beyond which he could not venture. His meager possessions, the tattered bedding, and assorted junk stashed in his shopping cart were too valuable to leave unattended, even for the few moments it would take to hassle her for a dollar or two.

A car sped past, briefly catching her in the glare of its headlights before darkness swallowed the vehicle up to leave nothing but a pair of twin red pinpricks, swiftly fading, to mark its passage.

With the homeless man behind her, Lexie crossed back over and continued her journey.

Nine blocks to go.

She passed a vacant lot ringed by chain link. Until a few months ago, it had been an abandoned discount beverage store with empty apartments above, their windows broken out, but now it was slated for redevelopment. A sign on the fence announced new luxury condos coming soon. The sidewalls of the buildings on both sides still bore ghostly impressions of the demolished structure in a patchwork of faded brick and plaster squares separated by the skeletal imprints of walls and a roof that no longer existed.

As she reached the corner of the lot, another set of headlamps flared ahead of her, turning out of a side street. The car crawled along at several miles under the speed limit. It was an older model sedan that sent the hairs on the back of her neck prickling. Was it the same one that had driven past a few minutes ago, moving in the other direction?

She couldn't be sure.

Lexie watched warily as it approached, the driver nothing but a black shape sitting behind the wheel. She was relieved when it passed by without slowing further.

Lexie glanced over her shoulder.

The car was eighty feet away and making another turn onto a side street. She watched it disappear from view, then looked forward again, hurrying down the block.

At the next road, Lexie stopped to catch her breath, then pressed on.

Six blocks to go now.

She didn't see the shape separate itself from the shadows of an alley running next to a shuttered grocery store until it was too late. Unlike the homeless man a couple of blocks to her rear, this one moved with serpentine precision.

A hand clamped over her mouth. The point of a knife pricked against her neck.

"Struggle, and I'll cut you open," said a rasping voice in her ear as she was dragged back into the darkness.

Lexie's eyes flew wide.

There was a car parked near a shuttered loading bay. It was the same car that had cruised past her twice already. It must have circled around and entered the alley from the other end, then laid in wait.

The trunk was open.

If Lexie ended up in there, she would be dead. She bucked and twisted, ignoring her assailant's instructions. The knife sliced across her throat, drawing blood even as she tore free.

Then Lexie took off running.

She fled toward the alley entrance, a scream welling in her throat. If only she could get back to the road, there might be another car. Someone she could flag down for help. Or maybe even that homeless guy.

She was going to make it, too. She was almost there. Just a few more steps and—

The roar of an engine filled the alley.

She glanced back over her shoulder a second before three thousand pounds of steel slammed into her. She rolled up onto the hood then tumbled back off as the car came to a shuddering halt. Her head slammed into the concrete.

The car door opened. The man stepped out. He walked toward her even as she pushed herself up and tried to crawl away, crying out in pain as the bones of her shattered hip shifted like marbles in a bag.

"You should have done as I told you," said the man, grabbing her arms and dragging Lexie back toward the car's trunk. "Now it's going to be all the worse for you."

"Please," Lexie gasped, tears running down her cheeks. "It hurts."

"Nowhere near as much as it will," the man said. He lifted her from the ground and dumped her into the trunk.

White-hot tendrils of pain exploded through Lexie's shattered body. She tried to scream but could draw no breath into her lungs. Twinkles of light sparkled at the edge of her vision.

Then the trunk lid slammed down, and Lexie was plunged into blackness.

ONE

PATTERSON BLAKE SAT in the outer office of a suite in a nondescript commercial building on the east side of downtown Amarillo. It was the first place she had visited in the city after checking in to her hotel two hours earlier. She browsed emails on her phone while an administrative assistant with light blonde hair pulled back into a ponytail and soft hazel eyes tapped away on a laptop without giving her a second glance.

After ten minutes, the admin looked up and cleared her throat to get Patterson's attention. "Special Agent Ricketts will see you now."

Patterson thanked the woman and made her way to the suite's only other office, slipping the phone back into her pocket before knocking on the door. Two quick raps of her knuckles.

A baritone voice bade her enter.

On the other side of the door was the resident agency's only full-time FBI agent. Duane Ricketts was fifty-six years old with slicked-back silver hair and a square jaw. A veteran agent of twenty-seven years, he had spent much of that time in the Miami Field Office battling drug cartels, fighting organized crime, and heading a terrorism task force responsible for foiling two major plots. Now he was taking the off-ramp to retirement with a less strenuous posting.

"Special Agent Blake. It's nice to meet you." Ricketts leaned back in his chair. "Have a seat."

"I won't take up much of your time," said Patterson, settling into a chair on the visitor side of the only desk in the office. "This is merely a social call to advise you of my presence in town."

"Which I already knew about thanks to a heads-up from SAC Harris down in Dallas. You've made quite the impression in the last two cities you've visited. I hope this visit to Amarillo will prove less eventful."

"That's my intention." I don't expect to be here long. I'm just following a lead related to my sister's case."

"Julie. Missing since you were a child."

"That's right."

"And now the FBI has taken an interest in the case and given you the resources to pursue it."

"Yes."

"Even though you have a personal stake in the outcome."

"Yes."

"Curious." Ricketts leaned forward. "Is there something I should know? Since you're playing in my sandbox."

"I don't believe so," Patterson said, her eyes falling onto a manila folder on Ricketts' desk. "Especially as you've already familiarized yourself with the circumstances surrounding my sister's disappearance and my progress so far."

"Which is the same thing you would have done in my position." Ricketts tapped the folder. "You have a habit of causing a stir wherever you land. I won't beat about the bush. That concerns me."

"I already said I have no intention of causing trouble while I'm here. I'm following up on a lead. Nothing more."

"I bet that's what the field office in Oklahoma City thought when you breezed into town. Not to mention Dallas."

"I'd hardly call catching a serial killer operating with impunity for decades causing a stir. And as for Dallas—"

"I'm not disputing that your presence was useful in both locales, but this is Amarillo. It's small and quiet. I'd like it to stay that way during your visit."

"Your implication is that I was somehow responsible for the events in Oklahoma City and Dallas." Patterson kept her tone light even though the insinuation that she was disruptive prickled her.

"That wasn't my intention. The resources of my office are available to you as per SAC Harris, but this isn't New York or Dallas. I don't even have a desk to lend you. All I'm asking is that you keep things simple."

"I can work out of the hotel." Patterson would have preferred such an arrangement in Dallas but had instead ended up mentoring a newbie partner and being assigned to an unrelated case that had almost gotten both of them killed. She anticipated no such diversions in Amarillo. She was only in town because a couple of the band members Julie had tagged along with had gone there after playing at the festival in Dallas. One of them still lived in the city, and she hoped he would provide a clue regarding where Julie went next. She expected her business to take only a day or two, and then she would be gone, following her sister's trail wherever it led next. "I'll stay out of your hair."

"I'll hold you to that." Ricketts moved the folder aside to reveal another underneath. He opened it and looked at the top sheet of paper before turning his attention back to Patterson. "The man you're here to see. Mark Davis. There is something you need to know about him."

Patterson stiffened in her chair. She had wondered why Special Agent Ricketts was so concerned she would cause a problem in his jurisdiction. She had a feeling he was about to tell her. "What about him?"

"See for yourself." Ricketts slid the file across the desk toward her.

Patterson studied the topmost document in the file with a growing sense of alarm. After reading it twice, she looked up. "Is this for real?"

"Now you understand why I was worried," Ricketts said. "I'm sure I don't need to tell you the implications this has on your search for Julie."

"No. You don't." Patterson picked up the file and leafed through the pages. Mark Davis, former bass player for the now-defunct band Sunrise, was in a whole heap of trouble.

"As you can see, the evidence is overwhelming."

"It does look that way." Patterson thumbed through statements from the victim and witnesses, an interview conducted with Mark Davis after his arrest, and most damning —a report outlining the results of a DNA test. She closed the file and dropped it back on the desk. "He's a rapist."

"Yes. Although the case hasn't yet gone to trial, making him an alleged rapist. Innocent until proven guilty and all that. But . . ."

"If he did it once—"

"He might have done it before."

Patterson said nothing, pondering on the enormity of what she had just found out. The man she had come here to see, hoping he would provide a clue regarding her sister's movements all those years ago, had just become the number one suspect in her disappearance.

TWO

THIRTY MINUTES after discovering that Mark Davis had jumped to the top of her admittedly small suspect list in the disappearance of her sister, Patterson Blake left Amarillo's FBI office with a copy of his file under her arm and more questions than answers.

On the face of it, the ex-bass player had led an unremarkable life since his college days. A wife of seven years and a five-year-old son. With a degree in environmental engineering, he had worked for the local EPA for almost a decade, before leaving to start his own company performing preliminary assessments of brownfield sites to determine if the land could be developed or was too polluted. That was five years ago. It was a small operation, just him and a secretary, but it paid the bills. Until one night on his way home from work, he had stopped at a local bar, picked up a woman by the name of Alexandria Rowley, who was ten years his junior, drove her to a secluded spot outside of town, and viciously raped her. Now he was sitting in the Potter County Correctional Facility awaiting trial.

As she crossed the parking lot, car keys in hand, her phone rang. It was Marcus Bauer, the temporary partner assigned to her back in Dallas.

"Hey. Just checking to make sure you got to Amarillo," he said when she answered.

"U-huh. I just checked in with the local RA." She unlocked the car and climbed in, slamming the door. "It didn't go exactly as I expected."

"You haven't been in town for a day yet. You're in trouble already?"

"Not me. Mark Davis. He's sitting in a jail cell awaiting trial for rape."

"You're kidding me."

"I wish. A woman he picked up in a bar on the way home from work." Patterson laid the file on the passenger seat next to her. "I've already put in a request with the prison to visit him."

"How strong is the case?"

"Pretty airtight. They have the victim's testimony, surveillance footage of them leaving the bar together, a hospital report showing trauma, and DNA evidence that points squarely at Davis."

"What does he have to say for himself?"

"What do they always say? Claims he's innocent. Says he never touched her. I haven't had time to read through the interview transcripts yet, but I don't see him getting out of this. The evidence is pretty damning."

"You know what this means, right, Patterson?"

"Yeah. I know. Maybe this isn't the first time he's done this. Maybe he's more than just a witness in Julie's disappearance." Patterson's throat tightened. She paused for a moment, waiting for the sudden wave of emotion to pass. "Ever since I started this, I've been preparing myself for the worst. I knew that finding answers could mean discovering that my sister is dead.

Probably would, in fact. I know the statistics. The odds of her still being alive . . ."

"Practically nil," Bauer said in a soft voice. "But there's always that sliver of hope. It's human nature."

"Now that I might be close to getting that answer, I'm not so sure I want to know. Maybe ignorance really is bliss."

"You're afraid of what he might tell you."

"Terrified. Maybe following Julie's trail wasn't such a good idea."

"Learning what happened doesn't change the reality of it, but it might bring closure to your family."

"That's what I thought when I started, but is that really true? A sliver of hope might be better than no hope at all."

"You don't mean that. You've worked enough cases to know that closure is better than false hope. Putting the ghost of Julie's disappearance to rest will let your family move on and heal. You've lived with this hanging over you all for long enough."

"I know." Patterson glanced down at the passenger seat. Laying there, next to the folder on Mark Davis, was a faded blue T-shirt with the phrase 'live your best life' printed across it. It had come from Claire Wright, sister of the band Sunrise's lead singer. Julie had traveled with the band all those years ago and gifted it to Claire as a memento of their brief friendship before leaving town. Remembering that she still had it, Claire had called Patterson that very morning before she left for Amarillo and returned the T-shirt. For what felt like the fiftieth time in the last eight hours, Patterson laid the phone on the dash and picked up the T-shirt. She held it to her face, trying to detect any lingering scent of Julie even though she knew there would be none after so many years. She swallowed, overcome by a sudden sense of resounding loss.

"Hey, you still with me?" Bauer's voice sounded small and tinny through the phone speaker.

Patterson placed the T-shirt back on the passenger seat and lifted the phone again. She cleared her throat. "Yes. Sorry."

"You okay there, partner?"

Patterson took a deep breath. "I'm fine. Just indulging my emotions. Seeing if Julie's ghost wants to tell me anything."

"You know, if you're struggling with this, I can take a personal day and drive up there. Tag along when you visit the prison. It's not like I'm doing anything exciting here. Just stuck behind a desk until they let me back in the field."

"That's a sweet offer," Patterson said. "But unnecessary. I'll be fine. Besides, you've just gotten rid of me."

"Maybe I miss the excitement. You are kind of like a whirlwind."

"A whirlwind who got you shot on our last outing. You're still recovering. I can't imagine Phoebe would be too happy with you dropping everything to run up here and get involved in my mess all over again."

"Probably not. But luckily, she isn't my boss."

Patterson wondered if that was a reference to her own boyfriend, Jonathan Grant, who actually was her boss at the New York Field Office. Either way, she let it go. "How about I agree to keep you informed on my progress, so you don't go completely bonkers behind that desk."

"Sounds like a fair compromise." Bauer chuckled. "When are you going to see Davis?"

"As soon as they process the visitation request. Since it's the FBI asking, it shouldn't take long, so hopefully tomorrow."

"That gives you some time to put your feet up and think about what you're going to ask him."

"I know. I'm going to pick up an early dinner and head back to the hotel now. After the drive up from Dallas, I'm beat."

"I bet you are. Keep me in the loop, okay?"

"Sure."

"Take care, Patterson."

"You too." Patterson ended the call and placed the phone on the center console. She sat with her hands on the wheel and looked out through the windshield at the mostly empty parking lot. Soon she would be sitting opposite Mark Davis, a man who might hold the answers she had been looking for. She only hoped she was ready to hear them.

THREE

THE AUTHORIZATION TO visit Mark Davis was already waiting in her inbox when Patterson arrived back at the hotel that evening, along with a brief message from Special Agent Ricketts saying she could pick up a hard copy the next morning at the FBI office before making the drive ten miles out of town to the correctional facility.

She read the message while sitting at a table near the hotel room window eating takeout Chinese food. Afterward, she turned her attention to the file Ricketts had given her.

The interview transcript portrayed a man confused by his circumstances and adamant that he was not responsible for the crime of which he was accused. Sure, he'd stopped at the bar for a drink on the way home, just like he often did on a Friday night. Yes, he had been approached by a young woman many years his junior who had shown enough interest in him that at first, he assumed she must be looking for a John, as women of a certain profession liked to call their clients.

But nothing happened.

He had politely turned her down. After all, he was a decent man and had no interest in straying outside the bounds of his marriage. Instead of walking away, she had set him straight—she was not a prostitute—and settled on the stool next to him, where she proceeded to engage in lively conversation despite his obvious disinterest. She had even bought him a beer while cautioning that it should not be interpreted as a come-on. Her only interest was in not drinking alone.

Even though he only drank one more beer after that, things became a little hazy, but at some point, he had left the bar and must have walked the mile and a half home, which was something he often did if he had drank more than one beer.

He returned to the bar on Saturday morning to pick up his car from the small rear parking lot. Except it wasn't there. He spent an hour searching the streets around the bar, even though he remembered parking in the lot, then decided to report the vehicle stolen. He never got the chance.

The police were waiting when he got back home.

That was when he found out about the accusation of rape.

He vehemently denied it. Sure, his memory of the previous evening was full of holes—strange after only three drinks—but he was sure of one thing. He was neither a cheater nor a rapist. He had not touched that young woman who sidled up to him at the bar, let alone violated her.

Unfortunately, DNA evidence in the form of a vaginal swab and a damning trauma report from the hospital begged to differ. With the addition of a graphic and detailed statement from the victim—who claimed he had offered her a ride home, then driven to a vacant lot on the edge of downtown and raped her—Mark Davis was in it up to his neck.

Patterson closed the folder and sat for a few minutes in silence, letting the information sink in. Was this just a one-off crime of opportunity committed by a man bored with his humdrum existence, or was Mark Davis something more? A dangerous serial rapist who had so far gotten away with his crimes. If the latter were true, her quest might be over. And if

Mark Davis really was responsible for Julie's disappearance, it made him so much more than a rapist. It made him a killer. Maybe even a serial killer.

Patterson leaned on the table and rubbed her brow. The thought of Julie dying at the hands of such a depraved individual sickened her, but tomorrow, hopefully, she would find the truth. She straightened up and stared out the window toward the back of the parking lot, where a ridiculously large RV was making a hash job of parking sideways across six spaces.

Her gaze drifted to the battered Corolla she was driving on loan from the Chicago Field Office, then back to the RV.

Despite his obvious lack of skill at parking the behemoth, the old guy behind the wheel might have the right idea. If she had an RV, there would be no more cheap motels next to the highway. No more nights sleeping on sheets that may not have been properly laundered over a mattress that was probably older than the car she was driving. She wouldn't want anything like the monstrosity out in the parking lot—it was too big—but the idea was appealing. And not only because she would always fall asleep in familiar surroundings and on clean sheets. The RV would become her office on wheels. A mobile command center dedicated to finding Julie. She wouldn't have to pack up all her files and evidence—all the stuff relating to her sister that wasn't stored on her laptop—bundle everything into the back of the Toyota and haul it out again at the next place.

On the other hand, the guy driving the RV was at a hotel, meaning he obviously didn't find much benefit to his bedroom on wheels. Unless the hotel was letting him park there for a fee, of course, which was also possible.

Patterson watched the RV for a few moments longer, then stood and went to the compact fridge nestled in a cabinet underneath a flat-screen TV. She took out a bottle of water and twisted the top off, then took a large gulp. When she returned to the table, the old guy had the RV's side door open. A set of metal steps extended down to the ground. He was walking a medium-sized dog that looked like a cross between a Labrador and a golden retriever along a strip of grass between the parking lot and the road beyond. The man's wife, in her sixties and wearing bright blue sweatpants and a floral blouse, stood in the RV's doorway with a can of soda in her hand. She looked up at the hotel window, appearing to stare directly at Patterson. It was not yet dark, which meant the woman could not see inside the hotel room, but even so, Patterson looked away quickly. At that moment, her phone rang.

FOUR

THE CALLER ID read Jonathan Grant.

Patterson was surprised that he was calling so early. It was only seven-thirty. Grant often worked until well past eight at night and sometimes even longer. She picked up the phone and answered.

"Hey, you. This is unexpected," she said.

"Wanted to make sure you got to Amarillo," Grant replied. "Did you visit the RA?"

"Ah. You're checking up on me." Patterson had texted Grant that morning as she was heading out of Dallas. He had replied telling her to drive safely and visit the local FBI office to confirm her presence when she arrived in Amarillo.

"Not in the least. Can't a guy miss his girlfriend?"

"I'd be hurt if you didn't." Patterson looked back out the window. The old guy with the dog was gone now, and the RV's door was closed. "I miss you, too." She paused. "But I might be close to finding out what happened to Julie, and then I can come home."

"Really?" Now it was Grant's turn to sound surprised. "You only got there a few hours ago."

"And there was a surprise waiting for me when I did." Patterson filled him in on the information Special Agent Ricketts had given her about Mark Davis.

He listened in silence, then sucked in a long breath. "You think Mark Davis might have something to do with Julie's disappearance?"

"I think the odds are good considering what he's sitting in jail for right now. After all, she traveled up with him from Dallas. I already know that much. The question is— what happened after they got to Amarillo?" The sun was slipping down below the horizon. Long shadows stretched into the room. Patterson reached up and turned on a floor lamp standing behind the chair. "I have an appointment at the correctional facility tomorrow."

"He's claiming innocence. You realize he isn't going to confess to a cold case crime if he won't even admit to one he committed a week ago."

"I know. But I don't need a confession right now. His reaction when I mention Julie will be enough to tell me if I'm on the right track. Once he realizes the magnitude of evidence against him—how hopeless his situation is—he might be willing to cut a deal in exchange for information about other crimes he may have committed in the past."

"I guess it's worth a shot." Grant fell silent for a moment. "In other news, I had dinner with your father last night."

"Really?" Patterson was momentarily stunned. "How did that happen?"

"I called to see how he was doing, and it just sort of happened. Figured he was missing your weekly dinners since he's all alone now. I also figured you haven't been calling him as much as you should."

"I speak to him now and again," Patterson said, realizing that Grant was right. She was so preoccupied with work and following Julie's trail that she hadn't made enough time for those who were still in her life. And not just her dad, but Grant, too. "How is he?"

"If you spoke to him more often, you'd know."

"All right. I don't need a lecture." The words came out snippier than she intended. "Sorry. I guess you touched a nerve."

"It's fine. And so is he, other than being a little lonely."

"Now you're really making me feel bad." Patterson made a mental note to call her father later that evening. "Where did you go?"

"Hole in the wall called Park Pizza. He said it was the last place the two of you went before the whole Julie thing."

"I remember. That was the night he showed me those postcards. The ones I didn't know existed."

"He said as much. I have a feeling he regrets mentioning them. Thinks you're setting yourself up for disappointment by following in Julie's footsteps."

"I know." That was part of the reason she didn't call her dad more often. She sensed his fear of reopening old wounds. She also suspected he preferred the glimmer of hope he could cling to by not knowing the truth—that Julie was still alive and might walk back through his front door one day. Changing the subject, she said, "What did you think of the place?"

"Wasn't bad. Bit of a dive. Your dad sure loves his pizza."

"Yes, he does." Patterson laughed. Her thoughts briefly turned to Bauer, who was also something of a pizza aficionado. The two of them would get along great. Grant and her father, on the other hand, were more like chalk and cheese, at least in the culinary department. Her boyfriend preferred upscale establishments with fancy names and even fancier chefs. A week before she hit the road, he'd taken her to a French restaurant in Manhattan. The prices were ridiculous, and she didn't understand half the dishes on the menu, let alone the wines, but Grant was in his element. The thought of him eating in a divey neighborhood pizza joint made her grin.

"You should make an effort to call him," Grant said suddenly. There was a note of recrimination in his voice. "He did nothing but talk about you the whole time we were there."

"He did?" Patterson's throat tightened.

"You're all he has left."

"I know." Patterson squirmed in her seat. "Maybe I've been a little too single-minded in my pursuit of Julie. Sometimes I forget that I'm not the only one with a stake in this."

"Pleased to hear you admit it." Grant coughed lightly. "While we're on the subject, you could call me more often, too."

"You can't blame me for that one," Patterson said. "You're always working. How many times have you sent my call to voicemail or failed to return a text?"

"All right. I guess we're both guilty of putting work ahead of our personal lives. I don't mean to do it. It's just that—"

"Yeah. I get it." When they were both working in the same field office, it was easy to maintain a relationship, even when they were busy, which was most of the time. They could snatch a few minutes in the hallway. She could drop by his office. They could go home together after a long day and spend the night at her apartment or his. The concessions they made to their work felt more like a way of life than a bad compromise. Now, though, separated by so many miles and out of each other's daily routines, they were floundering. On a whim, she said, "You should take a few days off and fly out to see me. I'll put Julie on the back burner for a weekend, and we'll book a romantic B & B. There must be some great places out here. What do you think?"

There was a moment of silence on the other end of the line.

Patterson's breath caught in her throat. Had she said the wrong thing? Maybe their metaphorical ship wasn't floundering but had already wrecked on the shore. She was about to tell him to forget the idea when he spoke up.

"I'd like that. It might have to be next month, though. I'm knee deep in a task force and at least three major investigations."

"That long?" Patterson deflated.

"You could take a weekend and fly back here."

Now it was Patterson's turn to deflect. "I don't want the trail to go cold."

"Your sister's been gone for a decade and a half. Her trail's not getting any colder. You can afford a weekend."

"I know. But there's Mark Davis. If he really is a serial rapist and killer—"

"Then it might take months for him to admit it. Or he might never admit it."

Patterson sighed. "You're right. I'll go to the prison tomorrow and see what he has to say for himself. After that, I'll have a better idea where this is heading."

"Then you'll take a weekend off to fly back and see me?" Grant hesitated. "And your father, too?"

"I'll try. It depends."

"Dammit, Patterson. The man's in jail. He's not going anywhere anytime soon. Whatever he knows will still be in his head when you get back. I doubt he'll even tell you anything useful. He's hardly likely to admit Julie's murder and dig an even bigger hole for himself."

"Hey. You just got done telling me how you're too busy to fly out here. But you expect me to drop everything and run there. I guess what I'm doing is less important."

There was another pause. When Grant spoke again, the edge was gone from his voice. "I never said that. And you're right. I'm just as stubborn."

"What are we going to do?" Patterson wondered if the distance between them was highlighting a fundamental flaw in their relationship. "If we're both too busy to make time for one another, there's no hope."

"Then we make the time. I'll see if there's an opening in my schedule to sneak a few days away. How about that?"

"Sounds great," Patterson replied, aware that her reply came across as less than enthusiastic. She hoped he wasn't just saying what she wanted to hear.

"I don't want to lose you, Patterson."

"Me either."

"See. We agree on something."

Patterson laughed. Ten minutes later, when Grant wished her luck the next day and said goodbye, she hung up the phone, feeling only slightly better than during the conversation. She sat for a while at the table, staring out the window at the dark landscape beyond and the faint reflection of her face caught in the glass. She had become so wrapped up in her search for Julie that nothing else mattered. Now she wondered if the cost was too high. But deep down, she knew the answer wouldn't make a difference. Regardless of whether it wrecked her relationship with Grant or caused a rift with her father, Patterson was going to see this through because, after coming so far, giving up would feel like a failure. And Patterson Blake hated to fail.

FIVE

THE POTTER COUNTY CORRECTIONAL FACILITY was about as bleak a place as Patterson Blake had ever seen. A dull gray concrete and metal three-story building with bars on the windows and razor wire circling the roof, it sat inside a twelve-foot perimeter fence crowned by more loops of razor wire. This was, in turn, circled by yet another outer fence, between which ran a cracked and weed-choked ribbon of dirty asphalt. At each corner was a tower manned by an armed guard with a high-velocity rifle. If anyone breached the fences, inmate or otherwise, and made it to the no-man's-land in between, the guard would shoot first and ask questions later.

Patterson approached the perimeter entrance from the direction of the secure parking lot and stopped in front of a full-height metal turnstile next to a security booth. Inside was a guard wearing a tan uniform. A gold shield hung on his shirt, under which was a name tag that read 'Peterson'.

"ID and paperwork," the guard said, even as he looked Patterson up and down, making sure her attire was suitable and did not violate any of the prison's dress code rules. No skirts or dresses. No blue denim, chambray, or orange-colored clothing, or any garments that could lead her to be mistaken for an inmate or guard. Nothing revealing or tight-fitting. No stilettos or raised heels. And absolutely no jewelry. She was also prohibited from wearing an underwire bra, but the guard would let the metal detector figure that out.

Patterson ignored the unabashed inspection. This was not her first prison visit. She handed over her credentials and a folded sheet of paper containing her authorization to enter the facility.

The guard studied both documents, held the ID up to check her face against the photograph, then consulted his computer to make sure she was on the authorized visitor manifest.

He handed the credentials and paperwork back to her. "Weapons?"

"Just the one," Patterson said, pulling her jacket open to reveal the Glock service pistol in a holster at her hip. Her backup, a subcompact that sat in an ankle holster, was stashed in the trunk of her car.

The guard nodded toward a door beyond the perimeter fence. This was the sally port—a one-in, one-out, secure room at the entrance to the facility that acted like an airlock. "Leave your gun in the safe box, along with any other prohibited items. Cell phones and pagers, too."

Patterson nodded. She wondered who still carried a pager.

The guard observed her a moment longer, then pressed a button in the booth. There was an electronic whir from the turnstile, and a light above changed from red to green.

"You can enter," said the guard.

Patterson pushed through and made the short walk, under a covered path, to the sally port. Once inside, she went to a row of lockers on the wall to her left. She put her gun, car keys, and cell phone into one and closed it, then took the key. She would retrieve her belongings and gun on the way out. Beyond this point, not even the guards carried weapons, relying instead on

OC aerosol—basically pepper spray—and an expandable baton. It was a rule in every prison she had ever visited. Absolutely no guns anywhere near the inmates. Ever.

Patterson made her way to the metal detector, put the key into a small plastic dish, along with her credentials, and stepped through. Above her and angled down was a security camera, its cycloptic wide-angle lens taking in the entire room. Somewhere nearby, beyond the sally port, she was being observed.

She retrieved her credentials and the locker key, slipping both into her pocket. After a few seconds, deadbolts retracted, releasing the inner door. A buzzer sounded.

Patterson pulled the door open and stepped into the prison.

A guard waited on the other side.

"Follow me, please, Special Agent Blake." The guard turned and retreated down a tiled corridor bathed in cool fluorescent light.

At the end was another door, which he buzzed them through using a proximity card reader, then led her to the visitation room. She settled onto a metal bench facing a plexiglass partition with a grill set into the center at shoulder height. Beyond the partition was a similarly appointed space with another metal bench for the prisoner to sit on.

"You good here?" The guard asked.

"Yes, thank you."

"I'll be outside." The guard retreated and pulled the door through which they had entered closed.

No sooner had the guard stepped from the room than another door opened on the other side of the partition. A second guard appeared, flanking a man in his mid-thirties. He wore an orange jumpsuit that hung loose on his wiry frame. A three-day shadow darkened his chin beneath a pair of black-rimmed glasses. His hair was unkempt, like it hadn't seen a brush in a week.

The guard told the prisoner to sit on the bench opposite Patterson and then retreated to the door, where he stood with folded arms.

Patterson noticed the bulge of muscles under his shirt and the breadth of his shoulders. He was tall enough that another few inches and he would have been forced to stoop through the door.

The prisoner facing her, the person she had come here to see, was the exact opposite of the guard. Mark Davis was small and fragile, like a mouse caught in a trap. When she met his gaze, she saw not a hardened criminal, but a man bewildered and frightened by his circumstances. That didn't mean he was innocent, of course. In a place like this, it was easy to be guilty of a heinous crime and still be terrified. Especially if it was your first time inside, and in this case, Patterson knew that it was.

Davis fidgeted on the other side of the plexiglass. He would have been informed that an FBI agent wanted to talk to him, but he wouldn't know why. The crime he was accused of—his case hadn't yet gone to court—was a local matter with no reason for federal involvement.

Patterson placed her hands on the ledge in front of her, palms down, arms apart. A disarming gesture meant to telegraph openness. She counted off several seconds in her head, giving Davis time to ponder why she was there. Then she leaned forward and got right to the point.

"Tell me about Julie."

SIX

MARK DAVIS STARED BACK at Patterson with a blank expression. "Who?"

"Julie Blake. Have you forgotten her name so easily?"

"This is why you wanted to see me?" Davis leaned forward so that his face was inches from the plexiglass. "To ask about some woman I've never heard of."

"I don't believe you." Patterson kept her tone neutral. She watched Davis. His tics. His mannerisms. So far, she saw no evidence he was deceiving her. What she did see was fear, which was not surprising considering where he was and why. "Tell me about Julie."

"Look. If you're trying to pin some other crime on me, forget it. I never raped anyone in my life, and that goes for the woman who put me in here. When this goes to trial, y'all will have some apologizing to do."

"Your lawyer must have told you the situation—the charges you're facing. The evidence against you," Patterson said. "What makes you think anyone on this side of the glass is going to apologize?"

"Because I'm innocent. You can throw all the evidence you

want at me, but it doesn't alter the truth." Davis narrowed his eyes. "Should my lawyer be here right now?"

"Do you want him to be?"

"If you're accusing me of another crime, then yes. But, even if you're not, I suspect he would want to be present. I can't imagine that FBI agents stop by to visit people in prison just to be friendly."

"Would you like me to leave and come back when your lawyer is here?" Patterson had known there was a chance Mark Davis would refuse to speak to her. She didn't expect him to be any chattier with a member of the legal profession at his side.

Davis shook his head. His shoulders slumped. "What's the point? I'm stuck in here either way, and my lawyer isn't exactly on my side, despite his claims to the contrary. He thinks a not-guilty plea will only make things worse. Wants me to cut a deal. Admit I raped that woman in exchange for a plea bargain."

"Sounds like he's giving you good advice," Patterson said. "Don't interpret this as legal advice because it isn't, but you're not in the best position to claim innocence, at least from what I've seen of your case file."

"Even if it's true?"

They were getting off track. "Look, I'm not here to discuss your current situation. I didn't even know about the rape accusation when I came to Amarillo. I only found out about it yesterday."

"Lucky you." Davis grimaced.

"I'm here about Julie Blake. I want to ask you some questions, that's all."

"I already told you I don't know who she is, so it looks like your trip was in vain."

"Are you sure about that?" Patterson still didn't see any sign of deception in Mark Davis's body language. It appeared he really didn't remember Julie. Was that because he had more pressing things on his mind, like being locked up for a crime he claimed not to have committed, or because there had been so many victims over the years? "You met her sixteen years ago. She traveled from Oklahoma City to Dallas in your van when the band you were in played TexFest."

"Sunrise." A smile creased his lips.

"That's right. After the festival, she accompanied you to Amarillo."

"Julie Blake. I remember now. She was kinda cute." The years had apparently melted away for Davis. "If Trent hadn't been all over her, I probably would have asked her out myself. But they were inseparable. Even kicked me out of the van a couple of times so they could . . . Well, you know."

Patterson stiffened. Trent Steiger was the band's lead singer and had traveled up to Amarillo with them after the festival. It sounded like her sister was in a pretty heavy relationship with the guy. It made her theory of Mark Davis being a lone wolf serial rapist and killer harder to justify. When would he have had the time or opportunity? Then again, Davis could be lying to cover his ass. "What happened to them after you got to Amarillo?" she asked. "Where did Julie go next?"

Davis folded his arms. "You really aren't here about the rape, are you?"

"No." Patterson shook her head.

"Why the interest in some groupie from so long ago?"

"She wasn't a groupie."

"If you say so." Davis met Patterson's gaze. "What's the deal with her?"

Patterson decided it was time to bring out the big guns. She was curious to see how Davis would react. "She's been missing for sixteen years. Never came home from that road trip."

Davis said nothing for several seconds. "Sorry to hear that. I didn't know."

"You don't seem very surprised."

"No offense, but I've got bigger issues than someone who

32

went missing sixteen years ago." Davis suddenly looked alarmed. "You don't think I had something to do with her disappearance?"

"Did you?"

"No!" The alarm had turned to indignation. "I didn't touch Julie Blake sixteen years ago and did nothing to that woman in the bar. I'm innocent and damned if I'll agree to a plea deal for a crime I didn't commit."

"How do you know you're innocent when you remember nothing after leaving the bar until the next morning?"

"Because I'm not that kind of person. I can't explain my memory loss. I had three drinks—light beer. The receipt from the bar backs that up. I bought two beers for myself, and that woman who came up to me bought a round. Check it out if you don't believe me."

"It's in your file," Patterson said.

"Then you are investigating me." Davis shifted on the bench. "I think any further questions should be asked in the presence of my lawyer."

"I'm not investigating the crime you're accused of. I want to know what happened to Julie Blake after she traveled to Amarillo with you. Tell me that, and I'll leave."

"What do I get in return?"

"I beg your pardon?"

"You heard me. I'm sitting here for a crime I didn't commit, and you want me to give you information about some old cold case. I'll tell you everything I remember about Julie Blake, but not from inside this place. Find out what really happened that night after I left the bar, and then we'll talk."

"I already told you; this isn't my case."

"And I told you that I'm innocent. The police don't believe me. My wife doesn't believe me. Hell, I'm not even sure if my own lawyer believes me. Everyone is ready to lock me up and throw away the key. There's no one in my corner. Just promise me that you'll look into it. If I really committed this crime and don't remember doing it, I deserve to be in jail. But I know in my heart that nothing happened that night between me and that woman other than sharing a drink."

"I'm not sure I can—"

"Do you want to hear what I have to say about Julie Blake or not?"

"Yes." Patterson lowered her head.

"What was your name, again? The guard told me, but I wasn't exactly paying much attention. Too wrapped up in wondering why an FBI agent wanted to interview me."

"Patterson."

"Surname?"

Patterson hesitated. She had wondered if Davis would make the connection when she said Julie's name. It appeared the penny had dropped. "Blake. Patterson Blake."

"Ah. Now it makes sense." Davis nodded slowly. "She was your sister?"

"Older sister. I was still in high school when she went missing."

"I'm sorry. It must've been tough on you."

"It was."

"This an official FBI investigation, or is it personal?"

"Both," Patterson admitted. "I would appreciate anything you can tell me about my sister."

"Then we have a deal?"

"I'm not authorized to make deals with you."

"Then think of it like a quid pro quo. You review my case and see if anything jumps out, fill in the missing hours and let me know if I'm a monster like they say, and I'll tell you everything I remember about your sister and the time we spent together."

"I'll take a look," Patterson agreed. "But I can't guarantee you'll like what I come back with."

"Just be fair and open-minded. Consider the possibility that I didn't do this. That's all I'm asking."

"That much I can do."

"Thank you." Davis looked genuinely relieved. "When you come back, I'll tell you what I can. In the meantime, I'll put your mind at rest regarding the suspicions you came in here with. I didn't raise a finger toward your sister. The last time I saw her, Julie was alive and well."

SEVEN

ON THE DRIVE back to Amarillo, Patterson replayed the conversation with Mark Davis in her mind. She was good at reading body language. More than that . . . she considered herself an expert. Nothing in the way Davis carried himself, or his mannerisms, suggested he was deliberately deceiving her with regard to either the crime he stood accused of or his recollections of Julie. He displayed none of the usual tells associated with deceit or misdirection. What did come across was genuine fear mixed with bewilderment about his predicament.

That didn't mean much, of course. He could simply be a good liar and an even better actor. But she didn't think so. Patterson's gut told her that Mark Davis genuinely believed he was innocent. Unfortunately, he couldn't remember the hours between leaving the bar and waking up the next morning at his home. That presented a problem. Especially with the overwhelming pile of evidence stacked against him. DNA didn't lie. Mark Davis had engaged in unprotected sexual activity with Alexandria Rowley that left more than enough genetic material inside her to quell any doubts. That intercourse had been violent enough to leave bruises on her body and evidence of forced intimacy, quashing any question of consent. If he kept up his protestations of innocence in court, he would likely be convicted anyway, and without a plea deal, he could be looking at decades behind bars.

Patterson wasn't sure what Davis hoped she would find by poking around in the case, and she also knew there was a question of jurisdiction. The locals had not asked for FBI help because as far as they were concerned it was a one-off crime, and Davis was the perpetrator. Maybe if she could make the link to her sister's case and paint Davis as more than just an opportunistic predator, it would be different, but she had no evidence that he ever laid a finger on Julie, let alone murdered her. Not only that, but Davis was sure to clam up if he thought Patterson was trying to prove him guilty of more crimes instead of reviewing the one he was already accused of with an open mind.

She picked up her phone and made a call, putting it on hands-free, then laid it back in the center console.

The call was answered after two rings.

"Federal Bureau of Investigation, Amarillo office," said a voice Patterson recognized as the same administrative assistant she had met the day before. "How can I help you?"

She introduced herself and said, "Put me through to Special Agent Ricketts."

"Good morning, Special Agent Blake. He's on a call right now. I don't know how long he'll be. Would you like to hold, or shall I have him ring you back?"

"I'll hold, thank you."

The line clicked, and classical music floated from the speaker. Patterson was approaching the outskirts of Amarillo. It was almost noon, and she was hungry, having skipped breakfast. She pulled into a fast-food restaurant and ordered a burger and fries, then sat in the drive-through lane as the cars ahead of her inched forward. As she reached the service window and leaned out to take a brown bag containing her food and a medium soda, the line clicked again, and Ricketts' voice filled the car.

"Special Agent Blake, I was just talking about you."

"That sounds ominous." Patterson dropped the bag onto the passenger seat and placed the drink in a cup holder. She rolled up the window and drove forward, parking in an open space at the side of the restaurant to eat. "Let me guess. SAC Harris in Dallas."

"Actually, no. Your supervisor in New York. Jonathan Grant."

"Huh. What did he want?" Patterson hoped Grant wasn't checking up on her. Their testy conversation the previous night was still fresh in her mind.

"To remind me that I should afford you all the help you need, and your investigation has the full backing of the Bureau's upper echelons. Namely SAC Khan, who is apparently in the mix for promotion to Executive Assistant Director."

"You're kidding." Patterson was reaching for the food, but now she hesitated, her appetite gone.

"I most certainly am not."

"Wow." Why hadn't Grant mentioned this to her? If Khan was promoted up the ladder, he would be in line to become Special Agent-in-Charge of the Criminal Investigative Division. No wonder he was working long hours and loath to fly out to see her. She wondered what that promotion would mean for their relationship. Right now, he was her line supervisor, but if he became the SAC, he would truly be her boss, and the conflict of interest was clear. She wondered who would fill his current position. One thing she knew—it wouldn't be her.

"Did you get what you needed from Mark Davis?" Ricketts asked, cutting into her train of thought.

"Not so much," Patterson answered, still distracted by what Ricketts had just told her. But at least Grant's call was well-timed. "I need a favor."

"To quote what you just said to me, that sounds ominous."

"I told Mark Davis that I would look into his case. Do some digging."

"Why on earth would you agree to that? You realize it's nothing to do with us."

"I know. But it was the only way I could get his cooperation. He swears he didn't do it. Claims no one is on his side, and it's probably true. Even his lawyer is pushing for a plea deal."

"I don't doubt it. The evidence is conclusive and overwhelming. It's a slam dunk for the DA. Honestly, Patterson, if we believed their protestations of innocence, we'd have to set free ninety percent of the country's prison population."

"I'm not saying he really is innocent. I just agreed to look at the case with fresh eyes. I already told him it probably won't change anything."

"Good. The last thing we need is the DA mad at us for giving his lawyer an opportunity to sow the seeds of reasonable doubt without merit. I can't imagine SAC Harris is going to be happy with this. Cutting a deal with the defendant? Yikes."

"I didn't cut a deal. I made it clear to him this was not on the books. I'm doing Davis a favor, and in return, he'll tell me what he knows about Julie." Patterson hesitated a moment. "I figured we didn't need to run this through Harris. You can reach out to Amarillo PD's Special Victims Unit and say that a parallel investigation intersects with theirs. Tell them we don't want to step on any toes or undermine what they've already done, but we would like to conduct our own inquiries. If we dig up any fresh evidence, we'll share it."

"I don't know about this."

"Didn't you just get a phone call saying you should afford

me all the help I need?"

"Yes, but—"

"Look, this won't spoil the DA's case. If Mark Davis is guilty —and all the evidence points that way—then my inquiries won't change anything. In fact, they may even bolster the case. But if this guy is somehow innocent, like he claims, then we'll be averting a miscarriage of justice. Either way, it's a win unless the DA is just out for blood and doesn't care whose it is."

"I'd be careful, saying things like that," Ricketts cautioned her.

"All I'm pointing out is that a thorough review of the case won't do any damage. He's already been arraigned. He isn't going anywhere. There's plenty of time before this goes to trial. I'm asking for a few days. A week at most."

"All right. I'll call Amarillo PD and let them know of our interest. But remember, you promised to keep things simple while you're here."

"And I intend to keep that promise," Patterson replied.

"Give me the rest of the day. All things being equal, you should be good to go by morning."

Patterson thanked Ricketts and hung up.

She sat staring through the windshield at a bank parking lot adjacent to the fast-food restaurant. Marilyn Khan would get that promotion because the woman always got what she wanted. Patterson's own previously unofficial investigation into Julie's disappearance had been hijacked as a pawn in the SAC's machinations back in Oklahoma City. Now Grant would probably be promoted, and she feared how that would impact their relationship. A knot twisted in her stomach. She reached for the bag of food, opened it, and pulled out the fries. Then she dumped them back in, threw the bag onto the passenger seat, and reversed out of the parking space. She wasn't yet sure what this meant for her future, but she knew one thing: her life had just gotten a whole lot more complicated.

EIGHT

THE YELLOW CACTUS BAR AND GRILL sat on the edge of Amarillo's downtown, about a mile from the patch of waste ground where Mark Davis had allegedly driven his victim and assaulted her. Patterson had stopped there after leaving the fast-food restaurant but found nothing of interest. The car was long gone, no doubt sitting in an impound lot, and all she saw was cracked and dirty concrete with weeds pushing up through under a billboard advertising injections to get rid of facial wrinkles and crow's feet.

The conversation with Ricketts, and the revelation that her boyfriend might soon be Special Agent-in-Charge of the Criminal Investigative Division at the New York Field Office, was fresh in her mind as she stepped into the bar.

The place looked like every neighborhood watering hole she had ever set foot in. The interior was gloomy, the lighting low, possibly to hide the establishment's general shabbiness. Neon signs advertising domestic beer hung on the dark green colored walls. There was a pool table near the back. Booths lined the walls, barely illuminated by hanging light fixtures in red and green stained-glass shades. High tops dotted the middle of the space.

Patterson walked through the mostly empty saloon and approached the bar where a bartender with a buzz cut and too many muscles pushing back against his black T-shirt stood, arms folded, watching a sports show on a wall-mounted TV.

At her approach, he looked down, his gaze lingering on her black pants, white shirt, and light jacket, which were probably a cut above the usual attire worn by his customers. "What'll it be, Honey?"

"How about a Diet Coke and a chat," Patterson said, prickling at being called Honey but containing her annoyance.

"Yeah?" The bartender grabbed a glass, scooped ice into it, and poured soda from a dispenser. A salacious smile lifted the edges of his lips. "What would you like to talk about?"

"An incident that started at this bar and ended with an alleged rape." Patterson didn't flash her credentials. Until Ricketts spoke with Amarillo PD and advised them of her interest in the case, she needed to keep a low profile or risk skewering their investigation. That was why she was in the Yellow Cactus making discreet inquiries instead of interviewing the family of Mark Davis or the victim.

The bartender looked like he'd received an unexpected slap on the face. "You a detective or something?"

"Something like that," Patterson replied vaguely. She had clipped her shield to her belt prior to entering the bar, and now moved her jacket aside in a swift movement to reveal a flash of both the shield and her Glock service weapon in its holster. She let the jacket fall back in place. "You working on the night of June 24? It was a Friday."

"I work every Friday."

"What do you remember about that night? Specifically, a man sitting at the bar drinking alone who was approached by a younger woman, who he subsequently left with."

"I already told the detectives everything I could, which wasn't much, when they came in a couple of weeks ago."

"You didn't tell me."

The bartender sighed. "Look, I served at least a hundred guys that night. Fridays are busy. Like I said to the other detectives, unless there's an incident—like a fight or something—they're just another face in the crowd. I don't remember what half the guys who came in here yesterday did or didn't do, let alone weeks ago."

"What about the woman?"

The bartender shook his head.

"Nothing happened that stood out to you, then?" Patterson asked.

"That's what I just said."

Patterson's gaze lifted to a small camera sitting on a high shelf behind the bar, its wide-angle lens pointed downward. "That thing record continuously?"

The bartender nodded. "There's a hard drive in the storage room. Backs up each night to the cloud. The other detectives already took a copy of the file for the night in question."

Patterson was tempted to ask for her own copy, but she didn't. If Amarillo PD agreed to let her review the case and make her own inquiries—which they almost certainly would since it was the FBI asking—then she would have access to their copy. Stepping on their toes now and gathering unauthorized evidence would only make things more difficult.

"There any other cameras around this place?" she asked.

"There's one by the door and another in the parking lot out back. You'd be surprised how many altercations happen in the parking lot."

Patterson wouldn't, but she didn't say as much. "Did the detectives take those recordings, too?"

"Sure. Far as I know."

"You had any trouble like this in the past?" Patterson asked.

She wasn't expecting the bartender to admit it, even if he had, but you never knew.

"Never. We might not be as fancy as those places downtown, but we run a safe establishment. We don't tolerate that sort of behavior. If a customer starts hassling another patron or picks a fight, they're out on their ear and won't be coming back. That rule stands regardless of who you are. No exceptions."

"Pleased to hear it." Patterson was getting nowhere. The bartender clearly didn't remember anything about Mark Davis or the young woman who had come up to him, and in fairness, he had no reason to. As the man said, hundreds of people came through his bar every week, and the assault had not taken place on the premises. Men left bars with women all the time. It was hardly unusual. Unless Davis or the woman had done something to draw attention to themselves, they would just be another pair of customers no different from any other.

"You got any more questions?" The bartender asked. There was a cloth in his hand now and he was wiping down the bar top in slow sweeps.

"No." Patterson thanked the bartender for his cooperation and pulled out a five-dollar bill, which she put on the bar to cover the diet soda that she had not touched. "Keep the change."

The bartender scooped up the cash as Patterson turned toward the door. When she got outside, she turned right and wandered down the side of the building to the rear parking lot. There were only three cars. The one parked closest to a rear door marked 'staff only' bore a bumper sticker that read 'A Bartender is just a Therapist who Works Nights'.

It didn't take a genius to figure out who that car belonged to. She glanced up at the door to a second security camera angle to cover the parking lot. If Mark Davis had parked here, the footage from that night would show him leaving with

Alexandria Rowley and driving off. But she would have to get those files from Amarillo PD, and that wouldn't happen today.

She walked back to the front of the building, climbed into her car, and started toward the hotel. Despite her sour mood, she was hungry again. The fast-food fries and cheeseburger were still sitting in a bag on the passenger seat. She couldn't be bothered to stop for more food, and there was a microwave at the hotel. It would do. If only her other problems were so easily solved. She still wasn't sure what to do about Grant. He had mentioned nothing about Marilyn Kahn, or his own potential slide up the ladder when they talked the previous evening, and that worried her. Was he having second thoughts about their relationship and how it would affect his career? Or maybe he was just waiting for the right time to tell her. But then, why mention it to Special Agent Ricketts? He must've known it would get back to her, and maybe that was the point.

Patterson gripped the steering wheel tight enough that her knuckles turned white and pushed the accelerator an inch lower. The Corolla jolted forward, tires biting the asphalt.

By the time she reached the hotel, her mood was black, and her appetite was gone again. She pulled into a space close to the room and grabbed the fast-food bag, dumping the now cold and soggy meal into a trashcan near the stairs leading up to the second floor. Then she climbed up to her room, removed her gun and holster, and flopped down on the bed where she stared, despondent, at the ceiling. Maybe she would call Grant later that evening and ask him what was going on. Find out where she stood. But even as the thought crossed her mind, Patterson knew she wouldn't . . . Because she might not like what he had to say.

NINE

PATTERSON SPENT the rest of the night in the hotel room and ate the now hours-old burger and fries. The next morning, with the revelations of the last forty-eight hours lingering in the back of her mind, she headed to the one-agent FBI resident agency office downtown. Special Agent Ricketts wasn't there—he was following the trail of a money laundering operation in Lubbock—but his administrative assistant was behind her desk when Patterson walked in.

"Special Agent Ricketts spoke to Amarillo PD yesterday afternoon," she said after greeting Patterson with a smile. "They finally got back to us. You're good to go. I was about to call and let you know."

"Guess I saved you the trouble," Patterson replied.

"U-huh. All they ask is that you pass on any new information and let them know if your case has any relevance to theirs."

"Shouldn't be a problem." If Mark Davis was lying about Julie being alive the last time he saw her, then it wouldn't just have relevance; it would turn a sexual assault case into a murder investigation spanning more than a decade. On the other hand, if she found a glimmer of reasonable doubt that bolstered his claims of innocence—a scenario she found unlikely given the evidence—it would be a gift for his defense lawyer. "I need something from them, too. They took copies of surveillance video from three cameras at the bar. I'd love to see them."

"Got it." The assistant scribbled Patterson's request on a notepad next to her computer keyboard. "I'll ask them about the surveillance files. See if they can email copies to you. Anything else?"

"Not so far. I already have the case files and interview transcripts, courtesy of Special Agent Ricketts. I'm going to conduct my own interviews, though. Speak to Davis's family and the victim."

"I assume you will keep us informed of your progress." The admin assistant fidgeted in her seat. "Special Agent Ricketts was most adamant that I make that request. I think he's worried that you'll . . ."

"Cause ripples in his little pond?"

"I wouldn't phrase it quite like that." She gave Patterson a sympathetic smile as if to say, *I know what he can be like*. "But it's close enough."

"I'll behave myself," Patterson said, returning the smile. "And I'll be sure to check in with him regularly."

The administrative assistant looked relieved. "I'll pass along the message."

Patterson stepped toward the door. "Let me know about those surveillance videos, okay?"

"Sure thing. I can't guarantee that Amarillo PD will send them today. The wheels of bureaucracy move slowly over there, but I'll do my best."

Patterson thanked the woman and headed for the parking

lot. Once in her car, she entered Mark Davis's home address into her phone's GPS and headed in that direction. She also wanted to speak with the victim, Alexandria Rowley, but first she wanted to get a baseline impression of him from those who knew Davis best.

Thirty minutes later, she pulled up outside of a nondescript single-story house in a sprawling subdivision surrounded by similar dwellings. It was obvious the entire development had been constructed by the same builder. Each home sat on a thin sliver of land with barely enough room between them to push a mower and stay on your own side of the property line. A small tree out front struggled to survive mere feet from the road and flanked by driveways on both sides that surely cut down on the amount of groundwater available to its roots. The patchy brown grass surrounding it was further proof of the soil's arid condition.

Patterson sat in her car for a few moments, studying the house and taking in the surrounding neighborhood to get a better idea of where Mark Davis lived and what his life was like when he wasn't sitting in a jail cell. The houses were hardly high end. Cookie-cutter facsimiles of each other, arranged in neat rows along the arrow-straight street. Affordable dwellings for middle-class suburbanites who wanted to get on the property ladder and couldn't afford the lofts, condos, and McMansions occupying Amarillo's downtown and wealthier neighborhoods. The cars sitting in the driveways out front of each home were similarly middle-class. There were pickup trucks, family sedans, and minivans with bumper stickers proclaiming their political affiliations and the fact that their kids went to one local school or the other. Noticeable in their absence were higher-end marques like BMW, Mercedes, and Lexus.

Nothing about her surroundings would have led Patterson

to believe that a dangerous predator lurked among the soccer moms and lower-echelon white-collar workers who had carved out their piece of the American dream from a dusty patch of ground in the Texas Panhandle. On the face of it, Mark Davis was just an average guy living in an average subdivision in an average city—except for the horrific crime he was accused of. But then again, thought Patterson as she opened her car door and climbed out onto the sidewalk, if rapists and murderers looked like the monsters they were, it wouldn't be so hard to catch them.

Slamming the driver's side door closed, Patterson made her way up the driveway, stepping around a dark green older model Ford Mustang backed close to the garage door with its nose facing the road. The wife's car, no doubt, because the vehicle within which the crime allegedly took place was almost certainly still in police custody.

She pressed the doorbell and took a step back, slipping the credentials wallet from her pocket as she did so.

The door opened a few inches; its swing stopped by a security chain. A female face appeared in the narrow gap between the door and the frame. "If you're a reporter, I have nothing to say."

"I'm not with the press," Patterson said quickly, opening the wallet and holding it up. "FBI. Special Agent Blake."

There was a brief silence before the face disappeared and the door closed. A moment later, Patterson heard the chain being removed, and the door swung wider to reveal a woman in her mid-thirties with brown hair that fell below her shoulders and matching brown eyes. She wore a white T-shirt and blue jeans. Her feet were bare. Her toenails were a bright fuchsia, but one was chipped, indicating she hadn't been to the nail salon recently.

"Mrs. Davis?" Patterson asked.

"Call me Carol." The woman attempted a smile, but it lacked warmth. She stepped aside and motioned. "You'd better come in. Don't want to give the neighbors any more to gossip about. Heaven knows it's not like they don't have enough already."

TEN

THE HOUSE HAD PROBABLY BEEN neat before Mark Davis brought a metaphorical wrecking ball to his home and those that dwelt within, but now it was anything but. A pile of dirty laundry sat in the front hallway next to a door that Patterson assumed led to the garage and the washer and dryer. More clothes were piled on the stairs in a haphazard fashion, some of which looked like they had been folded and then abandoned to be picked at as needed. A couple of empty delivery boxes sat near the door next to another box that contained what looked like recycling that had not been taken out.

Carol Davis led Patterson down a short hallway to the kitchen. She ignored a sink full of dishes and went to the coffeemaker, pulling out the carafe and emptying the contents before turning back to Patterson. "Can I get you something to drink? I can brew a fresh pot."

"No, thank you."

Carol replaced the empty carafe and turned back to Patterson. "Alright, let's hear it. What has my husband done to attract the FBI's attention? Please don't tell me he's in even more trouble."

"Not as far as I know," Patterson replied. "I went to visit him in prison yesterday because he might have information on an unrelated case."

Carol's face fell. "I don't like where this is going." She glanced toward a bottle of wine sitting on the counter with a stopper pushed into the neck. "You know, I never used to drink that much. But since Mark got himself arrested . . ." She sighed. "You think you know a person. Live with them all those years. Raise a child with them. Then something like this comes at you out of the blue, and suddenly you realize they were a stranger all along."

"That's why I'm here," Patterson said. "A young woman vanished sixteen years ago. Mark was one of the last people to see her alive. It's a cold case I'm working on. I wasn't aware of your husband's current legal troubles and had hoped he could shed some light on the young woman's movements."

"And did he?"

"No." Patterson didn't mention that he had all but blackmailed her into looking into his current situation in exchange for information on Julie.

"Do you think he had something to do with her disappearance?"

"I don't know," Patterson admitted. "If he did, it isn't something he's willing to admit."

"Tell me about it." Carol rubbed moisture from her eyes. "He won't even admit what he did to that poor woman a few weeks ago. Claims he's innocent."

"You don't believe him?"

"I did at first. Still want to. He's my husband, and I love him. But the evidence . . . I don't see how he can be innocent when they have DNA that proves he did it. Surveillance video of him leaving with the woman." Her shoulders slumped. "This is a nightmare I can't wake up from."

"What was he like as a husband?" Patterson asked. "Before all this happened, did you ever have any misgivings about him?"

"You mean, could I have imagined in my wildest dreams that Mark was capable of raping someone?" Carol shook her head. "The answer is no. I'm not saying he was perfect. He'd leave dishes out instead of putting them in the sink. Drop dirty laundry on the floor in the bedroom instead of putting it in the laundry basket. But he was a good husband and a fantastic father. We had the occasional disagreement like all married couples, but he never once did anything to make me believe he was violent or dangerous. He never raised a hand against me or our son."

"Your boy. He's five, right?" Patterson asked.

"Tyler. He'll be six in October. He doesn't know about his father. I told him daddy was away on business, although goodness knows how I'll keep up that pretense. He's in kindergarten, so all it will take is one of the other kids to overhear their parents talking and say something to him. Thankfully, he's on summer break, so I have a while to figure out what I'm going to say when and if he finds out."

"Where is he now?" Patterson asked.

"Staying at his grandmother's. He likes it there and thinks it's a treat. I thought that was best, at least until this all dies down, and people stop coming to my door."

"Makes sense." A thought occurred to Patterson. "Does your husband have a computer?"

"A laptop, but the police took it the day they arrested him. I don't know why."

Patterson knew the answer to that. They wanted to check his search history and see what he'd been up to online in the weeks and months prior to the crime. It was the same thing she wanted to check. She didn't say this to Carol Davis, though. The woman must already be second-guessing how she could live with him for so long and not know her husband was capable of such an awful act of violence. She must also be wondering if he'd gotten away with doing it before. "Are there any other computers in the house?"

"I had an iPad, but they took that, too, along with both our cell phones." Carol grimaced. "Still haven't told me when I'll get any of them back. I had to go buy another phone just to answer calls from the same people who took my first one."

"They're just doing their job," Patterson said. She made a mental note to request the digital forensics report regarding the computers and phones. It would tell her more than her own investigation could, anyway. All Patterson could have done was check the search history on the browsers and do some basic snooping around on the machines, but Amarillo PD would be able to recover all sorts of things, including deleted files, search results, and even searches performed in private browser windows, which were not as secure as most people thought. The device still remembered what you were doing; it just didn't display it in the search history. When it came to electronics, the only way to be safe if you were afraid of what someone might find was not to use them.

"Is there anything else I can help you with?" Carol asked, looking defeated.

"Just one thing," Patterson said. "What time did your husband come home the night of the crime?"

"It was late," Carol answered. "After eleven. He stops at the bar on a Friday evening after work because mom takes Tyler and I go out with the girls that night. But we're usually both home by nine-thirty or ten at the latest. He's often back before I am. I was surprised when he wasn't there already when I came back that night because I was later than usual. One of the girls had gotten a promotion at work and wanted to celebrate."

"What time did you arrive home?"

"About ten-fifteen. Maybe a little after. I called to see where he was, but there was no answer. By eleven, I was getting worried, so I called again. It went to voicemail. I was about to phone the bar and ask if he was still there when he came stumbling in. He was sweaty, and his clothes were disheveled. His shirt was partly untucked. It looked like he'd been walking."

"Which he often did if he'd had more than one beer, right?"

"But he never came in like that. He always keeps it to three beers or fewer. That night, he looked out of it. His eyes were glazed. His speech was slurred. The next morning, he couldn't remember anything when I asked him. He went back to the bar to get his car. The police showed up not long after that and arrested him when he came home."

"You think he was acting out of character that night?"

"Very much so. I've never seen him like that before."

"Thank you," said Patterson. "You've been very helpful." She turned toward the hallway and the front door beyond, then paused and looked back. "One more thing."

"Yes?"

"What does your gut tell you?" Patterson asked. "I mean—if you set aside the evidence and everything else and talk straight from the heart purely based on your knowledge of the man you married."

Carol thought for a moment. "I'd say he wasn't capable of doing what they all say he did. Just simply not capable. That's what makes this so hard."

ELEVEN

AS PATTERSON DROVE AWAY from the Davis residence, she mulled over her conversation with the accused man's wife. She wasn't sure what she had expected Carol Davis to say, but the interview had done nothing to move the needle either way on Mark Davis's guilt. If Carol had said Davis possessed a temper or that he often stayed out late without explanation or came home acting cagey, it would be different. But the woman had painted her husband as a loving spouse and father. Up until the police showed up on her doorstep, Carol had never even considered the possibility that Mark Davis was anything but what he seemed. She loved him. That much was obvious. And as they said, love was blind. But was it really that blind? Even if she didn't want to admit it, Carol couldn't possibly have lived with a sexual predator for so many years without noticing something, could she? Certainly, there were other cases where women had lived with sexual predators or killers and claimed they had no idea until the crimes were exposed. And serial killers were certainly good at blending in. Sociopaths made great actors and could often fool even their families and friends. But was Mark Davis in that category?

Patterson had her doubts.

The crime was sloppy and ill-conceived. He picked the woman up in a bar under the gaze of surveillance cameras. Left his DNA behind. Abandoned the vehicle within which the crime had taken place for the police to find. Lastly, he let the victim live. Those were not the hallmarks of a man who had planned his crime or even expected to get away with it. What were the odds he was a serial offender capable of evading capture? Perps normally got better at covering their tracks, not worse. Which all pointed to this being his first offense. A crime of passion. But why? If Carol Davis was to be believed, their marriage was good, and they loved each other. They hadn't been fighting, and there was no indication anything was wrong in his life. On the night in question, he followed the same routine as every other Friday night, right until the point when he convinced a younger woman to get into his car, drove her to a remote location, and raped her.

Patterson felt like she was missing something, but she didn't know what. The evidence against Davis was overwhelming, and from a practical standpoint, she knew it was more than enough to convict. Open and shut. But she wanted to understand his motivation for committing such a brazen and ill-planned assault out of the blue on a night no different from any other in his life. Had he just become fed up with the monotony of his humdrum existence and snapped? Was there something Carol Davis wasn't saying? Was it even possible that he was innocent, given the circumstances?

Patterson knew where she had to go next. The victim. She had read the statement Alexandria Rowley had given the police, but Patterson wanted to hear it with her own ears. Sometimes a question asked a different way, or perhaps even a question that had not been asked before, would provide clarity or even open up a new line of inquiry.

For example, the police had asked if Rowley knew the

defendant prior to that night—to which she said no—but they had not asked how many times she had frequented the Yellow Cactus Bar and Grill on evenings when Davis might have seen her there even if they had never spoken to each other. The answer to that question might let Patterson know if Davis had targeted the young woman . . . Except that Rowley had come up to him, not the other way around. She had made first contact. On that point, the statements of both the victim and defendant agreed. Still, it was worth asking, among other questions.

Patterson pulled up to the curb and stopped on a street south of downtown lined with businesses such as auto repair shops, liquor stores, and pawnbrokers. The building she had parked beside was none of those things. It was a women's shelter. Patterson had asked her phone for directions after reading Rowley's address in the police report. Apparently, the woman was down on her luck but was trying to claw her way back with night shifts at a local convenience store. Which meant she would probably be home now since it was only midday—if you could call such a place home.

She exited the car and headed straight for the shelter's front door, soon finding herself inside a drab, gray-painted lobby. There was a counter to her left and another door to her right, upon which was fixed a sign that read 'residents and staff only beyond this point'. The only furniture in the room was a row of four hard plastic chairs against the wall opposite the front door.

Patterson approached the counter and rang a bell fixed to the wall. For a minute, no one responded, but then an African American woman in her sixties with graying hair and a lean figure appeared.

"Can I help you?" she asked.

Patterson flipped open her creds and introduced herself, noting the brief flash of alarm on the woman's face when she saw FBI printed in blocky blue lettering.

"I'm looking for a resident here," Patterson said. "Alexandria Rowley."

"Lexie." The woman nodded, recognizing the name. "Is this about the incident?"

There was only one incident she could be referring to. Patterson nodded. "Yes. I'm just following up on the statement she gave the police."

"That might be easier said than done. Lexie took off last week. Quit her job, too. Or at least stopped showing up for it, which amounts to the same thing."

"Are you telling me she's no longer a resident here?"

"There's still a bed for her should she decide to return. She didn't clean out her locker, so she'll probably show up again at some point. They often do."

"Locker?"

"Each resident gets a locker to store their personal items in. Anything they deem valuable. It's safer than leaving stuff lying around."

"I see." Patterson was overcome by a mild unease. "When did she leave? What day exactly?"

"Thursday. She worked her shift Wednesday night, but was gone by the next day."

"Did she tell anyone where she was going, or why?"

The woman shook her head. "Not so far as I know."

"Is that usual?"

"It's not *unusual*. What you have to remember, Special Agent Blake, is that the women who stay here are often down on their luck and running from bad situations such as domestic violence or homelessness. Some of them have psychological issues or substance abuse problems in their past. These women are looking to make a better life for themselves or avoid the problems that led them here in the first place. Many of them hold jobs, just like Lexie, and are saving money to set themselves up in a new life. Others just need a port in the storm. They come and go."

"You don't require them to let you know when they're leaving?"

"This isn't a hotel, Special Agent Blake. Nor is it a prison. You must remember that many of our residents are struggling to get back on track, and sometimes they veer from the path. Lexie isn't the first to make a dubious choice, such as quitting her job and walking away."

"Doesn't that concern you?" Patterson asked.

"How could it not?" The woman sighed. "I'm worried for her, but there isn't much I or the other staff who work here can do. She's a grown woman who came to us voluntarily and is free to leave whenever she wants."

"What if something happened to her?"

"That is a concern, but as I said, we can't keep people locked up here. Hopefully, she'll show up again of her own free will, but given the circumstances, we notified Amarillo PD. We avoid invading our resident's privacy, but it seemed like the prudent thing to do."

"Really?" Patterson was surprised that Rowley's disappearance was not in the case file she had been given. "What did they say?"

"Not much. Lexie is one of our longer-term residents. She's been here on and off for several years, and this isn't the first time she's walked away. She's led a hard life. Been through some stuff. The job at the convenience store was a step in the right direction. We hoped she would finally get on her feet and put her problems behind her. But crazy as it sounds, that can be scary. She was doing better than ever before, despite what happened to her. She probably got scared. It wouldn't be the first time someone has self-sabotaged their own success."

"How many times has she gone missing in the past?"

"Two or three. She usually comes back in a few days. It's

been longer this time, which is what concerns me, but I've done what I can."

"It must be a hard job, working here," Patterson said.

"It is. But rewarding, too. We make a real difference in the lives of the women who walk through our doors. At least, most of them."

"Could I see that locker you were talking about?" Patterson asked. "And also, where she sleeps?"

The woman hesitated. "I can't do that. Part of the promise we make to our residents is respect for their privacy. I hope you understand."

"Of course." Patterson thought about threatening to come back with a warrant, but she doubted it would have the desired effect, and she had no valid reason to go before a judge. Alexandria Rowley was a victim, not a criminal. Moreover, she didn't want to give Mark Davis's defense the means to sow unfounded doubt. A warrantless FBI search of the victim's possessions could do just that. Hopefully, Rowley would come back, but until then, all Patterson could do was wait.

TWELVE

WITH NOTHING else to do and no more leads to follow, Patterson drove back toward the hotel. Where had Alexandria Rowley gone, and why? Had she become intimidated by the pressure surrounding her rape allegation? It was possible. She was already living on the edge and trying to lift herself out of a bad situation, only to end up the victim of a vicious rapist. It was hardly surprising that she would run away from the circumstances that brought her there. The district attorney would no doubt be banking on Rowley to show up again prior to the trial. Otherwise, they would be forced to either proceed without victim testimony or drop the case.

But that wasn't Patterson's concern. She had promised to look into the circumstances surrounding the crime because it was the only way Mark Davis would tell her what he knew about Julie. She was following through on that agreement. How the case played out beyond that was up to Amarillo PD and the prosecutors.

Up ahead, a traffic light turned red. Patterson eased to a stop and sat in a line of traffic waiting for green. She glanced in her rearview mirror. More cars had stopped behind her, including a late-model red pickup truck with a dented front fender that sat a couple of vehicles back. It looked familiar, and then she remembered it had been parked on the opposite side of the street when she left the women's shelter. Most people wouldn't have noticed it, but Patterson constantly took in her surroundings, filing the details away subconsciously only for them to resurface if triggered by circumstance. She had devoted no more than a second to the red pickup back at the woman's shelter and would never have given the vehicle another thought had it not been for the truck's reappearance now. Even then, it was probably coincidence. She wasn't far from the shelter, and it was a main road heavy with early afternoon traffic. More than likely, the truck would turn off at one of the intersections ahead and would almost certainly have deviated from her route by the time she reached the outskirts of town and the motel.

The light switched to green.

The cars ahead of her crept forward through the intersection. A couple turned right. One risked a snappy left turn, cutting across traffic moving in the other direction, and caused a couple of drivers to lean on their horns.

Patterson eased toward the light, picking up speed as the cars ahead of her moved. The next light was green, and she breezed right through. At the intersection after that, she moved into the right-hand lane and turned, heading away from downtown. When she glanced up at her rearview mirror, the truck was still there, now three car lengths back, with only a sedan between them. Nothing to worry about, she told herself. I-27 was up ahead, and the truck was probably on its way there. But when she drove under the interstate and emerged on the other side, the truck followed, maintaining its distance. Patterson's unease turned into concern. While it was still more than likely just another vehicle randomly heading in the same direction, she wasn't willing to make that assumption, even though she could think of no reason anyone would want to tail her.

She had to find out.

This was why, at the next side street, she swung the wheel hard to the right while barely bothering to slow down and turned—her tires biting the asphalt. The back of the car swung out enough that she was forced to turn the wheel the other way to bring the car back under control before her front wheels clipped the curb. Then she realized her mistake. The road was a dead end that terminated in a pair of heavy-duty gates, beyond which she could see squat industrial buildings. There were no other roads on either side—just a couple of driveways and the backs of more industrial units.

She cursed under her breath.

If someone really was following her, she had just provided a perfect spot for them to catch up and do their worst.

Patterson was trapped.

But when she looked in her mirror, the road behind her was empty. She wasted no time in turning the car around and heading back the way she had come, turning back onto the main thoroughfare. And there was the truck again, slipping out of a strip mall parking lot close to the road where she had performed her frantic turn.

More than ever, Patterson felt she was being followed. But whoever was behind the wheel of the truck did not wish her immediate bodily harm. This much she knew because they could easily have cut her off on the dead-end access road. Instead, they had pulled over and waited, knowing that she could go nowhere. Now they were back.

It was time to find out who they were.

There was a discount store up ahead on the right. Part of a national chain called Dollar Down that had sprung up across the country near lower-income neighborhoods. They were like a plague, keeping the larger grocery stores at bay, and often competing head-to-head with other discount chains in the same area, sometimes even on opposite sides of the street. Patterson loathed them and refused to give them her trade, preferring to drive further to a real grocery store if necessary. But now the parking lot looked like a great place to stop and see if her suspicions were genuine or just cops' paranoia.

She slowed and activated her turn signal, acting for all the world like she had no clue about the truck at her rear, then turned into the half-empty parking lot and pulled into a bay. Shutting the engine off, she climbed out and strolled toward the store, watching the road from the corner of her eye, but careful not to turn her head lest she give the game away.

The truck was coming up on the store, slowing as it approached the parking lot entrance. Patterson tensed, ready to turn on her heel and confront the driver as soon as he followed her in. Her hand slipped to the gun snug in its holster under her jacket, ready to draw if the situation demanded. But the vehicle did not turn. Instead, it passed by and kept going. Neither did it pull off into another parking lot to wait her out or turn around and double back. Soon it disappeared from view, lost in the afternoon Amarillo traffic.

Patterson breathed a sigh of relief. Her first instinct had been correct. The truck's movements were nothing but a coincidence. She had let her overactive imagination get the better of her. But just to be sure, she continued into the store and browsed around for a few minutes before stepping back out into the parking lot.

She looked left and right, scanning the road and the businesses that lined it, but saw nothing. The truck was nowhere in sight. Her hand dropped away from her jacket and the Glock service weapon hidden underneath.

Climbing into her car, she pulled out of the parking lot and continued toward the hotel, on high alert now, but didn't see the truck again or any other vehicles that looked like they might be following her. Patterson was alone.

THIRTEEN

AT EIGHT O'CLOCK THAT NIGHT, after eating a sandwich purchased from a neighborhood sub shop down the street from the motel, Patterson called her father, something she had been meaning to do ever since Grant chewed her out two evenings before.

"Hey, Peanut," he said, picking up. "This is a nice surprise. I was beginning to think you'd forgotten my number."

"It hasn't been that long," Patterson said. She was sitting at the table near the hotel room window with Alexandria Rowley's interview transcripts spread out in front of her. She wasn't sure exactly what she hoped to find within the words that she hadn't already seen, but since Rowley had removed herself from the equation by abandoning her job and running from the woman's shelter, her previous interview was all Patterson had. Now she gathered the papers together and slipped them back into the folder and set it aside.

The elder Blake cleared his throat. "I hope you're not becoming too obsessed with this thing, Peanut."

"I'm not."

"Good. Because it was a long time ago, and I'm not sure

what there is to gain by dredging up the past. And believe me, I'm not saying that because I don't want to know what happened to Julie. But I worry about how this is affecting you. I've lost one daughter. I don't want to lose a second."

"You won't, dad." Patterson's throat tightened. "This is what I do for a living. Why shouldn't I apply those skills to finding Julie?"

"I just don't want you to fall down that rabbit hole and never come back," her dad said. "I've seen this before. Your mother couldn't cope with the loss and ended up walking away from us to save her sanity."

"I'm not her," Patterson said. "And I have no intention of leaving you on your own. When this is over, I'll come back and never mention it again if that's what you want."

"When are you coming back?"

"When I get answers I've been looking for."

"I hope you find them soon."

"Me too." Patterson didn't mention Mark Davis. At first, when she visited him in prison, she thought the truth of her sister's disappearance might be close at hand. Now she wasn't so sure. Was it really possible that he could have raped and killed Julie, covered up the crime all these years while possibly committing other offenses, and still been so slapdash as to get caught within hours of the crime he was sitting in jail for? It didn't sit right with her. The more she thought about it, the more she came to believe that Davis was not the person responsible for her sister's disappearance. But that didn't mean he wasn't holding on to information. She would give it another day or two and see if Alexandria Rowley reappeared, check the surveillance tapes from the bar, and follow up on any other leads that presented themselves. After that, she would pay another visit to the prison, her part of the deal done, and ask him what he knew about Julie. In the meantime, there were other issues. Like her boyfriend being up for promotion in New

York and not telling her. Or her father complaining she wasn't keeping in touch. To that end, she said, "I hear you had dinner with Grant the other night."

"He's a keeper, that one. Thinks the world of you." Her father chuckled. "Although I'm not sure he thought much of the pizza. Kind of picked at it."

That sounded like Grant. Patterson couldn't help but smile. "I'm guessing he let you choose the restaurant."

"Yeah. I think he would've been happier going somewhere that had white-pressed tablecloths and a wine menu."

"Park Pizza has a wine menu . . . House white and house red."

Her father laughed. "That's true."

Patterson fell silent for a few seconds. "Did he happen to mention anything about work?"

"Said he's been rushed off his feet recently. He's in charge of some big investigation, apparently."

"He didn't mention anything else?"

"No, why?"

"It doesn't matter." Grant hadn't mentioned his potential promotion to her dad, either. "Forget I asked."

"Is something wrong between you two?"

"Nothing that being in the same city wouldn't fix."

"And who's fault is that?" Her dad gave a little sigh. "Maybe you should take some time out. Come back and see him."

"Did Grant put you up to saying that?" Patterson asked. It was spooky. Like her father had been listening in on their conversation two nights ago.

"Of course not. I just think that working all the time isn't healthy. A break would do you good. While you're here, we could hang out, too. It's only a short flight. You wouldn't have to stay long. Just a few days."

"I'll think about it, okay?"

"I suppose that's the best I'm going to get."

"It is right now. I'm in the middle of something." Patterson sensed that her father didn't believe she would fly back for a visit, and even though she didn't want to admit it, he was probably right. Maybe she was becoming obsessed with finding Julie, but she didn't know how else to be. Until she knew what had happened to her sister and why, it would remain her single driving force. It was all she could think about ever since her father showed her those postcards.

"Do me a favor, okay?"

"Sure. If I can."

"Try to keep some perspective. You may never catch up with the ghost of Julie."

"We've been through this already," Patterson said. "Can we talk about something else?"

"Anything your heart desires, Peanut. I just want you to understand that there are people who are still in your life, and they need you, too."

"Got it. Loud and clear." Patterson heard the fridge open and close, then the clink of a bottle cap being pried off. "Having a cold one?"

"Don't start on me. I work hard, and it's the first tonight."

"I wasn't saying you couldn't have a beer," Patterson said. She went to the mini fridge underneath the TV and opened it. A six-pack of imported Pilsner sat alone on the shelf. She had picked it up before leaving Dallas. Now she pulled one out, found the bottle opener, and pried the cap off. "How about we have a drink together?"

"I'd like that."

"Good." She could imagine her father's smile.

"What are you drinking?"

"You wouldn't like it. Imported from Germany."

"You know, I'm not a complete Philistine."

Patterson almost spat her beer out. "Where did that come from?"

"I don't know. Maybe your boyfriend is right, and I should expand my horizons."

"He told you that?"

"Yeah. Right around the time he was dabbing oil off the pepperoni on his pizza with a paper napkin." Her father took a swig of his beer. "Maybe when you get back, we can try something fancier than our usual hangouts."

"You know, I might just hold you to that," Patterson said with a grin. "And I get to choose."

FOURTEEN

PATTERSON SPOKE to her father for another thirty minutes. After that, she checked her email to see if the surveillance videos from the bar had come through. They had not. If they didn't appear in her inbox by morning, she would follow up with the admin at the FBI office to make sure the request had been put in with Amarillo PD.

Nothing better to do, she dove back into the police reports, but no matter how many times she looked at them, they told her the same thing. Mark Davis must be guilty. Frustrated, she closed the folder and stood up, intending to undress for bed and get an early night. She had barely taken a step when her phone rang.

Thinking it was her father again, or maybe Grant finally calling to tell her about his promotion, she snatched up the phone. But it was neither. The number was not in her contacts. It was also local to Amarillo. She answered, thinking it might be the women's shelter calling to say that Alexandria Rowley had returned. She had left her number with the lady at the front desk earlier that day. But when she said hello, no one responded.

She tried again. "Hello, is anyone there?"

This time, a male voice spoke up. "Miss Blake?"

"Yes?" She didn't recognize the caller.

"My name is Tad Bryant. I wonder if you might have time to answer a couple of questions."

"In relation to what?" Patterson asked, suspicious. The caller had given his name, but not who he worked for, and it certainly wasn't a social call.

"You are Special Agent Patterson Blake, currently assigned to the FBI's New York Field Office and temporarily assigned to Amarillo, correct?"

"Why don't you tell me what this is about and who you work for?" Patterson had no intention of confirming any of that information until she knew more about the mystery caller.

"Of course. How remiss of me. I'm with the Amarillo—" the man on the other end of the line who had introduced himself as Tad Bryant stopped mid-sentence. "I'm sorry. Would you give me a second? I'll be right back."

Before Patterson could answer, she heard Tad Bryant's phone being set down, followed by a muffled conversation too indistinct for her to make out. Thirty seconds later, the phone was picked up again.

"I hope you'll excuse me. Another matter needed my attention."

Patterson was losing patience. "You were about to tell me who you are and why you're calling."

"Absolutely. I'm with the Amarillo Weekly Ledger. We're doing a follow-up story on Mark Davis, and it has come to our attention that the FBI is now involved in the case. I was hoping you could provide some context."

"I'm sorry, but I'm not at liberty to comment." This was precisely what Patterson had been afraid of. Someone taking her discreet inquiries and turning them into a big deal.

"It can be off the record," Bryant said. "We won't mention you by name."

"Not going to happen off the record or otherwise."

"Sure. I understand. Maybe you could at least confirm—"

"Please don't contact me again." Patterson ended the call.

She stared at the phone and the number on her caller list. How had a journalist gotten ahold of her so quickly? She hadn't told the bartender at the Yellow Cactus her name or the fact that she worked for the FBI. She had merely hinted that she was with the police. Moreover, she had not left any contact details, so it hadn't come from there. The only other two locations she had visited were Mark Davis's home and the women's shelter. Carol Davis had refused to even open the door when she thought Patterson was a reporter, and the woman from the front desk at the shelter had made a big deal about privacy. She could not imagine that either of them had provided information to the local press. So that only left two places. The FBI office, which was frankly absurd, and the Amarillo Police Department. That last one was certainly a possibility. Newspapers often had contacts within local law enforcement who were willing to speak on condition of anonymity, but would they really want to raise questions about their own investigation by admitting that the FBI was snooping around what they believed to be an ironclad case?

Patterson didn't have the answer.

Tomorrow, she would pay another visit to the Resident Agency office and Special Agent Ricketts to get his take. She might even drop by the Amarillo Police Department and introduce herself to the detectives running the investigation. It was something she probably should have done already and would give her a better sense of who they were and what they thought of an out-of-town FBI agent sticking her nose into their cooking pot.

Of course, no one there would admit leaking information to

the press, but Patterson was good at reading people, and whoever did it was probably uncomfortable about their actions.

There was one other option. She could call Tad Bryant back and ask him to reveal his source, but that was unlikely to work. Reporters guarded their contacts with ferocious loyalty, especially those willing to speak off the record when others wouldn't comment.

Regardless, there was nothing she could do tonight. Patterson picked up the empty beer bottle and put it in the trash, placed her phone on the nightstand, got into her PJs, then brushed her teeth. She returned to the bed and climbed in, propping pillows up behind her back, before reaching for the remote and turning on the TV. The channel selections were lousy, but she soon found a movie that provided enough distraction to keep her mind occupied and away from Mark Davis, Tad Bryant, and her sister, Julie. The film was already a quarter over, and she had seen it before, which was why an hour later, before the movie had even ended, she switched the TV off, settled down, and was soon asleep.

FIFTEEN

SPECIAL AGENT MARCUS BAUER should have been tired, but he wasn't. Instead, he lay there and watched as the thirty-one-year-old woman he was sharing a bed with slept under a thin cotton sheet. She was facing away from him, slightly curled so that the sheet flowed down around her hips, leaving her bare back exposed to a gentle breeze that wafted through the screen of the half open window.

Bauer would've preferred to close the window and crank the AC up, but Phoebe Cutler, his girlfriend of about a month, and the Dallas Field Office ASAC's administrative assistant, said she liked how the warm Texas air felt on her body as she slept. It was natural, she said. Much more so than a bunch of refrigerant-chilled air circulating around in an endless cycle. There were all sorts of bad things in those air conditioning ducts, she told him the first night she had slept over. Dust mites, pollen, mold spores, and mildew, to name a few. It just wasn't healthy. This was why, whenever she stayed over, he slept with the window open and only a thin sheet on the bed.

His eyes strayed to the Echo Show on the nightstand. It was one in the morning. They had only settled down to sleep thirty minutes ago after coming in from a date that led them first to a Greek joint in downtown Dallas and then a new brewpub with twenty local beers on tap, twelve of which were in-house microbrews. There was no discussion about her staying the night. They had returned to Bauer's place and fell into bed almost immediately, then made love.

He scooted closer to her, slipped an arm around her bare waist, and nuzzled into her through the cascade of hair that fell to the mattress, his lips brushing the nape of her neck. Her body felt warm against his. A faint scent of jasmine on her skin teased his senses.

Phoebe murmured and put her hand over his.

"Go to sleep," she said in a soft and dreamy voice. "It's so late."

Bauer didn't reply.

He closed his eyes and let the memory of their evening play through his mind. Within a few minutes, he was fast asleep.

———

The shrill ring of a phone jolted him awake.

Bauer opened his eyes. It was still dark. Early. He rolled over to answer, but then realized that it wasn't *his* phone. It was Phoebe's, and she was already snatching it up and placing it up to her ear.

He heard the indistinct mumble of a male voice on the other end even as Phoebe was sitting up, the sheet falling away from her pale body.

Bauer couldn't tell who she was talking to, but her answers were curt and laced with concern. After she hung up, he asked, "Everything okay?"

"Yes. No. I mean, I'm not sure." Phoebe was already on her feet and crossing to the chair where she had discarded her clothes earlier, dressing by the silvery light of the moon that slanted in through the open window. "I have to go into the office. There's some sort of crisis."

"At this hour?" Bauer glanced toward the nightstand. "It's four in the morning."

"I know. That was the ASAC. Part of my job is liaising with external agencies, and he needs me. I'm not sure why. He's going to fill me in when I get there."

"Want me to come with you?" Bauer swung his legs off the bed, wincing when he moved his injured shoulder.

"You're on desk duty."

"So?"

"If they wanted you, they would have called. Stay here and sleep. I'll be back when I can."

"Desk duty is really beginning to needle me."

"I know, sweetie. But it won't be for long." Phoebe buttoned her blouse and pulled her hair back into a ponytail. She slipped her shoes on, blew him a kiss, and started for the door.

Bauer watched her go, then settled back down under the sheet. He rolled over and touched the pillow where her head had been minutes before, savoring the lingering yet barely perceptible scent of jasmine that might just have been his imagination.

He drifted back into a fitful sleep only to be reawakened by the sound of another shrill ring only an hour later. This time, it was his phone. He pushed himself up and answered. It was Phoebe. There was a note of stress in her voice when she spoke.

"Marcus, it's me. We have a problem."

SIXTEEN

PATTERSON'S PHONE WAS RINGING.

It was still dark outside. The red glowing numerals of the outdated clock radio on the nightstand read 5:24 in the morning. She reached out with a groan and felt around for the phone, her hand closing over the handset. She pushed herself up in the bed, her chest tightening. No one called in the early hours of the morning unless it was bad news.

The caller ID read Marcus Bauer.

Hell.

Then she noticed something else. He was using his personal phone, not the one issued to him by the FBI. That was weird.

She stabbed at the screen and answered, lifting the handset to her ear. "What's so important that you have to wake me up in the middle of the night?"

"Are you in your hotel room?"

"Where else would I be at this time of the morning?"

"Alright. Don't speak. Don't interrupt. Just listen. There isn't much time. You understand?"

There was a strange tone to Bauer's voice. One she hadn't

heard before. It washed away the last dregs of sleep. "Sure. Talk away."

"There are people on their way to the hotel right now. Special Agent Ricketts, a team from the Dallas Field Office, and detectives from Amarillo PD. They're going to take you into custody. You have to get out of there immediately."

"What are you talking about?"

"I told you to shut up and listen. We don't have time. Grab your go bag, pack whatever you need, and get the hell out. Don't even bother getting dressed. You can do that later. Oh, and don't take your laptop. Leave any electronics in the room except for your phone. I'm going to text you from a California number you won't recognize that can't be traced back to me. The text will look like junk. It will ask if you want to switch car insurance. Write the number down, delete the text, then ditch your phone somewhere it won't be found. Go to the bank as soon as it opens and take out all the cash you can. Go into the lobby. Don't use your credit or debit cards for anything. After that, purchase a burner phone with prepaid minutes, then call me back at the number I texted. Have you got all that?"

"Yes. I think so. Why are people coming to arrest—"

"Dammit, Patterson. I'll explain everything later. Right now, you need to do as I say and do it quickly. I'm putting my ass on the line here. Don't waste it."

"All right. Fine. I'm going." Patterson was already swinging her legs off the bed. She found her shoes and slipped them on.

"Oh. One other thing. Your car. You'll need to ditch that as soon as you can, too. They'll have a BOLO out for it before long."

"It's an old sting vehicle," Patterson said. "There's a GPS tracker."

"In that case, you absolutely have to get rid of it. They won't be tracking it yet because they expect to find you in the hotel room. That will buy you some time, but not much. As soon as you're out of the immediate vicinity, dump the car and get as far away from it as possible. Steal something if you have to."

"I'm not stealing a car."

"Do you trust me, yes or no?"

"Yes. Of course."

"Then do as I say. If they catch you, auto theft will be the least of your problems. Do whatever you need to, and we'll worry about the consequences later."

"It's that bad?"

"It's worse."

A chill ran up Patterson's spine. "I'll pick up a phone as soon as possible and call you."

"Not while I'm at work. They might be watching me to see if you make contact. I'll go to lunch at noon. Call me fifteen minutes later."

"Got it." She was already throwing clothes into her bag.

"Good. I have to go. Keep your head down. Stay safe, and good luck."

The line went dead before Patterson could respond.

She went to the window and peeked through the curtains. The parking lot was quiet. Whoever was coming had not yet arrived.

Her travel bag was mostly packed even before Bauer's call because she had only removed what she needed. She stuffed the last few items inside, including her backup gun and ankle holster, and zipped it up. Then, slipping on her shoulder harness with the Glock service weapon still inside, Patterson grabbed the jacket, picked up her bag, and headed for the door.

On the way past the table near the window, she snatched the folder containing all the police reports on Mark Davis. Her laptop was there, too, but she ignored it. Bauer had told her to leave everything except her cell phone, and with good reason. They could be used to track her. Even the cell phone was a risk, but she needed to keep it long enough to receive the text he was sending her. After that, the phone would be gone, too.

She pulled the hotel room door open and stepped onto the landing, closed it quietly behind her, then hurried to the stairs leading down to the parking lot. She raced to her car and threw the travel bag onto the back seat before climbing behind the wheel. It was weird to be outside dressed in nothing but her PJs and a jacket, but she ignored the sensation. Bauer had been adamant. There was no time to get dressed.

Backing out of the parking space, she headed for the exit, keeping her eyes peeled. So far, so good. There was a bank about a mile from the hotel. She had noticed it a few days before on her way to meet with Special Agent Ricketts at his office. But it wouldn't be open for many hours. She turned in the other direction, figuring any agents on their way to the hotel would come from downtown and the interstate rather than the suburbs and industrial areas to the north.

Her assumption was correct.

As she accelerated away from the hotel, distant headlights appeared in her rearview mirror. Sensing danger, she killed her own lights and pulled off the road onto the forecourt of a closed gas station, where she sat under the canopy next to the pumps with the engine running.

The headlamps grew brighter, and it became apparent there was more than one vehicle. They turned into the hotel parking lot. Three black Dodge Chargers. It didn't take a genius to figure out they were feds. She waited until they were out of sight, then pulled back onto the road and floored it.

There wasn't much time.

After they spoke to the hotel's desk clerk to find out which room she was staying in and discovered it empty, the feds would make use of the car's GPS tracker to locate her.

The clock was ticking.

SEVENTEEN

BAUER'S TEXT came through while Patterson was fleeing the hotel, but she didn't dare look at it until she had put some distance between herself, the three Dodge Chargers, and the federal agents within.

It was getting light, the first rays of sun poking above the eastern horizon and setting the early morning sky ablaze in brilliant shades of red and yellow. She drove north for several miles out of the city until she was surrounded by ochre-colored coarse scrubland dotted here and there with small trees and bushes. There were few cars on the road, mostly heading in the other direction. She passed a sprawling ranch, a truck stop, and several feed stores. Reaching a dusty side road, Patterson turned and pulled over under a billboard advertising tractor repair. She would need to ditch the car soon and find alternate transportation, but first, there was another matter to deal with.

Her cell phone was on the passenger seat. She picked it up and opened Bauer's text message, then found a pen in the glove compartment and wrote the phone number on a slip of paper ripped from the top of one of the police reports in the Mark Davis file. That done, she deleted the text, turned the phone off, and opened the car door, intending to drop it on the ground and crush the device underfoot until it was nothing more than a pile of broken electrical components to make sure the GPS chip inside the handset did not give her location away.

But then she had a better idea. One that would solve the problems of both her phone and car.

Patterson dropped the handset back on the passenger seat and climbed out of the vehicle. She rummaged in her travel bag for a set of clean clothes, then stripped off her PJs, feeling dreadfully exposed until she pulled on a pair of jeans and a navy-blue tee, even though there wasn't a soul around to see her.

Climbing back into the car, she swung onto the road and did a U-turn, backtracking to the main highway and retracing her route. She had passed a gas station and truck stop about a mile back, and she headed there now. But not to fill up. The car still had half a tank. Even if the Corolla was running on fumes, she wouldn't have dared use a credit card at the pump and didn't want to waste what little cash she had on hand.

It was the tractor-trailers filling their tanks that interested her. There had been three trucks when she passed the other way. Now there were only two, both with closed trailers hitched to them. They had probably exited the interstate and headed out onto the high plains with loads meant for the region's agricultural suppliers and cattle ranches. One third the beef consumed in the United States originated within a hundred and fifty miles of Amarillo. If the Great Plains were known as America's breadbasket, then the Texas Panhandle was the country's meat locker.

Patterson pulled into a parking space on the side of the gas station's convenience store and exited the vehicle with her cell phone in hand, turning it back on as she went. Noting the battery's ninety percent charge, she approached the closest truck.

The driver had finished filling the truck's thirsty tanks and was on his way inside the convenience store. He might be in there for a quarter-hour or less than a minute before he climbed back into the truck and headed off deeper into the heartland.

But Patterson only needed a few seconds.

She approached the cab—careful to walk on the far side of the truck to avoid being seen if anyone glanced out the convenience store windows—and used a step on the side of the vehicle to hoist herself up toward the space between the back of the cab and the fifth wheel coupling. There were thick coiled wires running between the cab and the trailer, no doubt connecting the lights and other electronics. An aluminum rack was mounted to the outside rear of the cab, with two chain racks, one on each side of a jail bar window allowing the driver to see through the back of the cab. Heavy tire chains—used during treacherous conditions in winter—hung from the racks and coiled down into a pair of trays beneath.

This was perfect.

Patterson slipped the phone down into one of the trays behind a loop of chain. Since it was summer, the driver would have no reason to look back there for many months.

She hopped down and glanced around, making sure her actions had gone unnoticed, then returned to the car and jumped in. She drove a little way up the road and pulled over onto the shoulder, watching the gas station in her rearview mirror.

A couple of minutes later, the truck turned onto the road and picked up speed. It rumbled past her heading away from Amarillo, carrying her phone and the GPS chip inside along for the ride.

But she wasn't in the clear.

Those agents in the black Dodge Chargers had surely figured out that her hotel room was empty, and she would not be coming back. The first thing they would do was to track her car thanks to the GPS locator the FBI's Chicago field office had installed when the vehicle was being used for undercover work. That locator had saved her life back in Oklahoma City, but now it might land her behind bars—even if she didn't yet know why. Given the requisite amount of knowledge and enough time, she might have been able to rip the tracker out of the car, but she had neither of those things. She could disconnect the Corolla's battery, but there was no guarantee the unit would stop transmitting. It might have its own internal power source. But either way, it didn't matter. Those FBI agents in their black Chargers would just head to her vehicle's last recorded location, and since the car wouldn't operate with the battery disconnected, they would find it in short order. The only question was, would she still be there?

Not if she could help it.

Because Patterson had a plan she hoped would lead her pursuers in entirely the wrong direction. Ditching the cell phone on the tractor-trailer was only the first part. For it to work, she needed another vehicle—fast. And she knew where to get one.

EIGHTEEN

PULLING BACK ONTO THE ROAD, Patterson headed past the gas station where she had gotten rid of her phone and drove in the direction of Amarillo. But she wasn't going all the way back to the city. At least not in the Corolla.

After a mile, she pulled over again, this time into the parking lot of an abandoned building that had once have been a general store. The sign still hung crooked and weather-beaten above boarded up windows. Further down, on the other side of the road was the entrance to a sprawling cattle ranch. She could see a house, several barns, and a grain silo sitting near the horizon across an expanse of flat semi-parched land ringed by a white picket fence. But that wasn't why she had stopped. It was the silver pickup truck parked facing the road at an angle.

A plastic for sale sign—orange lettering on a black background with a white rectangle containing a handwritten phone number—was propped on the dash against the windshield. There was no price, but judging by the state of the pickup, which was an older model with rusted fenders and no tailgate, it couldn't be much. Not that Patterson had any intention of buying the truck. But she was going to borrow it.

Parking the Corolla out of sight behind the dilapidated building, she climbed out and went to the trunk, removing the tools she would need to get the truck's door open. A flat-headed screwdriver she had found in the spare tire compartment and a coat hanger from the dry-cleaners, to which she had taken a couple pairs of pants back in Dallas. She also grabbed a pair of latex evidence gloves from her go bag and slipped them on, just to be safe.

If the truck were a newer vehicle, she would have been in trouble, but it was at least twenty years old and possibly knocking on a quarter-century. It took her less than thirty seconds to get in. Slipping behind the wheel, Patterson did something she never thought she would. Prying the plastic panel away from the steering column, she went to work on the bundles of wires beneath. In short order, the engine was running. She revved a couple of times to make sure it wouldn't stall, then returned to the Corolla, gathered up her belongings, and put them in the truck's cab.

As she did so, her eye caught something behind the driver's seat. A frayed and well-worn baseball cap with an oil company logo on it. She plucked it out and donned it. One more way to look inconspicuous.

Returning to the Corolla, she checked to make sure nothing was left behind, then climbed into the truck, slipped on a pair of dark sunglasses, and peeled out of the parking lot.

At the first opportunity, she turned off the road she had taken out of town and weaved a circuitous route back toward Amarillo. The truck didn't have a GPS, and Patterson's phone was currently on a semi-truck heading in the other direction, so she used her instinct and figured that if she headed in the right general direction, she would eventually get where she needed to be.

On the outskirts of town, she came across what she needed. A branch of her bank, and just as important, a

Walmart superstore one block down on the other side of the road.

It was only seven-thirty. The bank wouldn't open for another hour and a half. Patterson wasn't hungry. In fact, her gut had been in knots ever since Bauer's frantic call a couple of hours earlier. But she knew it was important to eat. It would keep her thinking clearly.

There was a McDonald's next to the Walmart. She drove there and used some of the precious cash she had on hand to pick up a breakfast meal, upsizing the coffee to large, and ate it in the parking lot, keeping an eye on the road for black Dodge chargers. At one point, a Sheriff's vehicle pulled in, and she slipped down in the seat, heart racing. But the cop joined the line at the drive-through, picked up his food, and drove off without giving her or the stolen truck so much as a glance.

And why would he? Right now, her colleagues at the FBI were looking for a lime green Toyota Corolla, which they would find quickly thanks to the tracker. Once they discovered the car abandoned, they would move to their backup plan and track her cell phone. There was no way the pickup truck she was sitting in could have been reported stolen yet. She figured it had been parked in front of the abandoned building with a for sale sign in its window for a while, judging by the weeds that had sprouted through the broken concrete and around the wheels. It might not be missed for hours or maybe even days. But even if it was, her pursuers would follow the cell phone signal north, and who knew how long it would be before they discovered her ruse.

She yawned and settled down in the seat, enveloped by a sudden exhaustion. No one was paying the truck any heed. Patterson closed her eyes, intending to snatch a few moments of rest. When she opened them again, the sun was higher in the sky, and the clock on the truck's dashboard read 9:32 a.m.

She had slept for almost two hours.

Overcome by a moment of panic, Patterson sat up and looked around, half expecting to see federal agents with guns surrounding the truck. She had let her guard down. But all she saw were cars inching through the drive-through and more people going back and forth between the fast-food restaurant and their vehicles, with takeout bags in hand.

She breathed a sigh of relief.

It was time to move. The bank was open, and every second was precious. She needed to get in, make a withdrawal, and get out again before anyone put a trace on her accounts or, worse, froze them. Which was ridiculous, considering Patterson didn't even know what she had done or why her own agency was hunting her. The bank was a risk, but there was no choice. She needed more cash than the twenty-six dollars currently in her wallet. And in all likelihood she would be in and out before anyone even knew she was there. Unlike a debit card transaction using the ATM, there would be no immediate record of her cash withdrawal that could be traced. No electronic ping. By the time anyone knew she had been there, Patterson would be miles away.

NINETEEN

TWENTY MINUTES LATER, Patterson walked out of the bank with two bulging white envelopes in her pocket containing eight thousand dollars split into twenty, fifty, and hundred-dollar bills, which all but cleaned out her meager savings account.

Next, she stopped at the Walmart across the street and purchased a smartphone for fifty bucks and a thirty-day unlimited talk, text, and data phone card to go with it, using the self-checkout with the baseball cap pulled low on her brow. The less people who saw her, the better.

Back in the truck, she activated the phone. Bauer had instructed her not to call until his lunch break. That meant waiting another two and a half hours to find out exactly what her own agency thought she had done. She racked her brain, trying to think of any clue, but came up empty. Everything appeared normal when she visited the resident agency the previous morning. Special Agent Ricketts wasn't even there. After that, she visited the Davis residence and then tried to track down Alexandria Rowley without success. Hardly the kind of activities that would put a person on the run.

The phone, a surprisingly inexpensive touchscreen model, had internet access thanks to the unlimited plan she had activated. She brought up the handset's web browser and opened a private window just to be safe. Even though the phone was not registered to her and there was no way to track it, Patterson figured it couldn't hurt. If the phone somehow fell into the wrong hands, a cursory inspection would not reveal her search history.

She typed in two words—her name—not sure what she was looking for. The results returned by the web browser were underwhelming. Certainly, nothing that would indicate she was being sought for committing a crime. No news articles. No bulletins on either the Amarillo PD or FBI websites. What she did find were several social media profiles for other people with the same last name, a couple of scam websites trying to sell erroneous information about her, and an old article in her hometown newspaper from when she graduated the Academy. Nothing helpful. But there was one way she could find out what was going on without waiting on Bauer.

Her boyfriend and boss back in New York. Jonathan Grant. She started to type his number, almost did, but then stopped. Grant was sure to know what she was accused of, given how dire her old partner in Dallas had made the situation appear. But would he tell her? Maybe. But he might not be on her side. Worse, she would compromise the burner phone within minutes of purchasing it. That was not an option.

Patterson lay the phone down on the passenger seat and sat back against the truck's grubby headrest. She would just have to sit it out until the time came to call Bauer. But what to do until then? She couldn't return to the hotel. That much was obvious. Which raised another question. If the situation was not resolved by the end of the day, which was more than likely, where was she going to sleep? Thanks to her recent withdrawal, Patterson had enough cash to keep her going for a while and could certainly afford to pay for a room at a different hotel, but good luck finding any establishment that would take cash up front without requiring her to provide identification or a credit card for the security deposit. Sure, there were certain hotels that rented by the hour, but they weren't the kind of place Patterson wanted to lay her head, and even if there was such lodging in Amarillo, she wasn't sure how to find it.

Which meant she was looking at an uncomfortable night in the truck. Not an ideal solution, especially since it was stolen and could be reported as such at any time. That was the other problem. The longer she kept her current ride, the more chance some eagle-eyed cop would try to pull her over. Then what would she do? Lead them on a pointless chase in a vehicle that would struggle to top fifty miles an hour downhill with a tailwind or just give up? The solution was obvious. She needed to trade her *borrowed* wheels for something that would not attract attention.

The germ of an idea hovered at the edges of her mind.

Patterson glanced around. The Walmart parking lot was busy. Cars were coming and going. People were hurrying back and forth between the superstore and their vehicles, pushing carts overloaded with groceries and flatscreen TVs, and all manner of other paraphernalia. She considered moving the truck, but what was the point? Anywhere she went would be as much of a risk as anywhere else. At least here she had the cover of anonymity. Out on the road, there was always the risk of running into a cop, or worse, those FBI agents who she knew would not give up looking for her, even if she didn't know why they were doing it.

Patterson checked the time. Almost two hours left until her call to Bauer. In the meantime, she could do some research and find out if her nascent idea was even a possibility. It would certainly solve the problems of both the stolen truck and her accommodation needs.

Picking up the phone again, she opened another private web browser and tapped away. Two hours later, encouraged by what she had found out and relieved to have a possible solution—at least when it came to her immediate situation—she dialed the number Bauer had texted her earlier that morning and waited for him to pick up. Instead, the phone rang four times, then went to voicemail.

TWENTY

PATTERSON DIDN'T LEAVE A MESSAGE. She hung up, waited a couple of minutes, and dialed again. Three rings this time before it clicked over to a generic recorded voice asking her to leave a name and number.

Ending the call, she stared at the phone, overcome by a sudden sense of isolation. Had they gotten to Bauer—whoever *they* were? Was he even now being escorted from the Dallas field office, caught on the receiving end of whatever craziness was currently swirling around her? She hoped his frantic warning hours before had not landed him in hot water. It was a gutsy thing to do, and even though she did not yet know what she was supposed to have done, one thing was obvious. Without Marcus Bauer's timely call, she would not currently be a free woman. Although how long that would last was anyone's guess because it was hard to prove your innocence when you didn't know the nature of your supposed crime.

What to do next?

She could sit there in the parking lot, paralyzed by indecision, or try to stay one step ahead of her colleagues at the FBI until she could figure out why they were pursuing her. One thing was clear. Whatever happened, she needed to get rid of the stolen truck. It was the only way to stay safe. And after spending the last couple of hours on the internet, her previously amorphous plan had solidified. Now all she had to do was put it into action.

Patterson started the truck, touching together the wires she had exposed earlier and bypassing the ignition, then slipped it into gear. She was about to pull out of the parking space when the phone rang.

She snatched it up, noting that it was the same number Bauer had asked her to call him on. But that didn't necessarily mean he was the one making the call. Or maybe he was making it under duress. Regardless, the call could be traced, and her location triangulated within seconds once she answered. Especially if she was sitting still. A moving target was harder, which was why Patterson ignored the call until she was heading for the parking lot exit and about to pull out onto the road. She was relieved to hear Bauer's voice when she finally answered.

"Patterson, what took you so long?"

"I could ask you the same thing. I called twice, but you didn't pick up." She swung down a side road, cutting a zigzag route around the outskirts of the city. If the call was being traced, the erratic movements would make it harder to zero in on her location.

"I got held up in a briefing. Couldn't get away until now." Then, as if reading her mind, he added, "You don't need to worry. I'm not compromised, and the phone I'm using can't be traced back to me. We can talk freely."

"You sure about that?" The delay between the calls she'd placed and Bauer returning them was more than enough time for the FBI's surveillance geeks to do their job. Technically, they would need a warrant to run a trace, which would mean going before a judge, which couldn't have happened yet since she hadn't revealed her new phone number until a few minutes ago, but right now, she did not trust the process. After all, she was currently a fugitive for no good reason.

"You'll have to take my word for it."

Patterson considered this for a moment. She could hang up, ditch the phone, and go to ground. But what would that get her? Bauer was right. She needed to trust him, and she also suspected that if he really had been compromised, he would have found a way to signal as much, either through something he said or neglected to say. "All right. How about you tell me what's going on?"

There was a moment of silence on the other end of the line. Patterson could sense his hesitation. Whatever it was, she thought, it must be bad. She was right.

"You're wanted for murder," Bauer said at length. "Apparently, you blew a guy's brains out last night."

TWENTY-ONE

"WHAT?" Patterson swung the truck to the side of the road and stopped. "That's ridiculous. There must be some mistake."

"Not according to Amarillo PD. They responded to a disturbance call at an apartment complex west of downtown last night. Someone called 911 and said they heard a gunshot in one of the units. When the officers arrived, they found the front door ajar and the victim duct taped to a chair in his kitchen. He'd been shot once in the forehead at close range, execution style."

"And they think I did that?" Patterson's mouth was dry. The world swam out of focus for a moment before snapping back. "Who am I supposed to have killed?"

"Some small-time thug named Leo Galinsky. Has a rap sheet that goes back two decades. Assault. Grand larceny. Even attempted murder. That last charge fell through after the victim refused to testify, and the forensic evidence got contaminated. He's kept a low profile the last few years. Looked like he was on the straight and narrow.

"The bullet in his head would argue otherwise," Patterson said. "But I wasn't the one who put it there."

"Right. Where were you last night between ten and eleven?" Bauer asked.

"Not in some apartment complex putting a bullet through a guy's brain." Patterson wasn't sure if she was angry, scared, or both.

"Hey, easy. I'm not accusing you of anything. I'm just trying to sort out the facts. Answer my question."

"I was in the hotel room."

"Can anyone verify that?"

"No. I was alone, obviously. I spoke to my dad for a while on the phone, but that was earlier in the night."

"And you didn't talk to anyone else, over the phone or otherwise?"

"No. After the call with dad, I looked through the Mark Davis file for a while and then—" a chill ran up Patterson's spine. "Wait. I did receive a call from a local number. I thought it might be the women's shelter calling to say Alexandria Rowley had resurfaced. She's the rape victim. But it was some guy who claimed to be a reporter with the Amarillo Weekly Ledger. He was asking questions about Mark Davis and why I was snooping around. I told him not to call back and hung up."

"What time was this?"

"I don't know exactly. Maybe nine-thirty or a quarter to ten."

"How long were you talking to him?"

"A couple of minutes."

There was more silence. Then Bauer swore. "This is bad."

"It can't be that bad," Patterson said. "I didn't shoot anyone. Unless I didn't get the memo, the FBI needs evidence to arrest a person for murder."

"They have evidence. Lots of it. And every bit points to you."

"That's impossible. What evidence?"

"Well, for a start, there's the text message you sent asking Galinsky to call you."

"I've never even heard of this guy, let alone sent him a text message."

"The data on his phone would beg to differ. And it gets worse. You specifically mention Julie as if he knew something about your sister's disappearance."

"What did it say?" Patterson asked. "What am I supposed to have written?"

Bauer cleared his throat. *"I need to know about Julie. How she died. Let's meet. Tonight. Call me."*

"That wasn't me. The text must have been spoofed."

"Spoofed or not, the guy called your number five minutes after receiving that text."

"That call from a journalist claiming to be with the Ledger. Tad Bryant." Patterson made a mental note to check with the newspaper and see if any such employee existed.

"I bet if we look at your call log, the number will match the phone found at the crime scene. Leo Galinsky's phone."

"That won't be easy. I ditched my cell phone, just like you told me to. Right now, it's taking a ride on a semi. What other evidence do they have?"

"Fingerprints."

"Again, I was never there."

"Well, something you touched was. Your prints are all over a water bottle found discarded outside the apartment. And it gets worse. They discovered a strand of hair caught on the duct tape used to bind Galinsky. How much do you want to bet the DNA comes back as yours?"

"The FBI already has my DNA on file from a comparison we ran in Oklahoma City against the Bracken Island Killer's victims to see if any of them were Julie."

"If that hair is yours, and I'll bet it is, the lab will get a match in no time."

"How the hell did someone plant fingerprints and my hair at the crime scene?" Patterson was baffled. Then something occurred to her. She groaned. "Someone must've broken into my hotel room while I was out yesterday. I had a couple bottles of water in the room fridge. I drank one the night before last while I was talking to Grant. The hair would be easy, too. There's plenty of strands in my hairbrush."

"This doesn't look good, Patterson. Someone is trying to frame you for murder and doing a pretty good job of it. Amarillo PD is theorizing you went to Galinsky's apartment to find out what he knew about Julie, possibly believing he was involved in her disappearance, then got angry and executed him."

"That's ridiculous. I'm an FBI agent, for goodness' sake." If she were going to murder someone, which Patterson could not imagine ever doing, she sure as hell would not leave so much evidence around leading right back to her.

"I agree. You don't strike me as the murdering type, even if you can be tough to deal with sometimes."

"Thanks . . . I think. At least *you* don't believe I killed that guy." Patterson was grateful for Bauer's support. She had a feeling it would be the only way out of this mess.

"If only my opinion mattered," Bauer replied. "But whatever you need, I'm here for you. At least until I get caught for aiding and abetting a fugitive. What have you poked your nose into up there, Patterson, to spook someone enough to set you up for murder?"

"Beats me. I've only been in town for two days. I've barely started. But I intend to find out."

"You'd be better off keeping your head down until some evidence pops up to prove your innocence."

"You know me better than that. Besides, where's this magic evidence going to come from?"

"If the text message was spoofed, the crime lab will figure it out. That's a start."

"Our crime lab or Amarillo PD?"

"PD. They've asked the FBI for help apprehending you, but they're taking the lead on the investigation."

"The same cops who put Mark Davis in jail for rape, even though he claims to be innocent. I won't hold my breath."

"You think there's a connection?"

"Feels a little too coincidental for there not to be, don't you think? The guy didn't even have a parking ticket before this."

"That's somewhere to start, then. But for heaven's sake, Patterson, be careful. I can't help if you're behind bars."

"I'll try to keep the help to a minimum. You've done enough already. You're risking your career for this."

"I know. Don't remind me."

"Worse, you might end up in jail right alongside me."

"Let's try to figure this out and make sure that doesn't happen. What are you going to do next?"

Patterson thought for a moment. "Ditch my current wheels. I'm in a stolen pickup truck right now. After that, I'll regroup and work out my next move."

"If you need a place to hide out, I might be able to find somewhere in Dallas. I know it's a drive, but you might be better off out of the Amarillo area, at least for now."

"I'm going to stop you right there," Patterson said. "There's a line I'm not willing to let you cross. You get caught harboring me . . . let's just say your next job will probably be as a junkyard security guard. Besides, this is where I need to be. Whoever I upset enough to do this must be in Amarillo. I intend to find them and clear my name."

"Figured that was what you'd say. Do you have a plan regarding where you'll sleep tonight?"

"I do. I'm going to take care of that right now. When I'm settled, I'll phone you back."

"Don't call until tonight after I finish work. This is a burner phone, and I don't dare carry it in the office under the circumstances. Besides, that wouldn't be a great place for you to call me for obvious reasons."

"Got it. Why do you have a burner phone, anyway?"

"That story is best left for another time. I need to get back to the office, and you need to offload that stolen vehicle before it gets you caught."

"Right." Patterson was still sitting at the side of the road with the truck's engine running. She hadn't meant to stay in one spot for so long, but at least it proved Bauer wasn't stalling to pinpoint her location. If that were the case, the truck would currently be surrounded by police officers. She put the truck in gear, then said: "Answer me one question. Why did you make that call this morning to warn me? You could have easily stayed out of this and assumed justice would play out."

"Because you're still my partner, even if it's only in spirit since you hightailed it for Amarillo. I've got your back, just like you had mine on that trail in the woods. I could have bled out and died if you hadn't gone after the shooter."

"It wasn't just me in the woods that day. Detective Costa had something to do with it, not to mention Athens PD."

"Yeah, well, I know you didn't kill that lowlife." A moment passed. "Now we just have to prove it."

TWENTY-TWO

AFTER FINISHING the call with Bauer, Patterson drove around until she found an industrial park with rows of units occupied by small businesses. There was a carpentry shop—the roll-up doors open to reveal lathes, huge saws, and other machinery she couldn't identify. A pool chemical company. A place that sold and installed kitchen cabinets. An electrical component supplier. There were also plenty of units with no names above the door to provide a hint of what activity was taking place within. Best of all, there were vans and trucks everywhere. It was the perfect location to park up unnoticed in a quiet corner while she figured out what to do next.

The first order of business was finding somewhere inconspicuous to lay her head. There was also the matter of the pickup truck. She couldn't keep it. Every moment she was in possession of the stolen vehicle increased the odds of her capture, especially since many cities were now using license plate reader cameras that linked to a database of stolen vehicles and alerted local police within seconds of getting a hit.

But she had a plan.

The hours between her trip to Walmart and Bauer's call had given her time to think about what her next move would be. Having dismissed booking into another hotel, which would require a credit card and lead the authorities directly to her, she had remembered the RV parked outside her room a couple of evenings before.

It was a perfect solution.

She would be mobile and out of sight. Even better, she could purchase a vehicle in cash from a private seller, which wouldn't require her to register it on the spot. But when she used the newly acquired burner phone to browse recreational vehicles for sale on the internet, she discovered that even the cheapest camper would use up all the funds she had withdrawn from the bank, and most were too expensive. But there was another option. She had quickly identified several cheaper panel or passenger vans.

One, in particular, caught her eye.

It was an older model Dodge van knocking on a quarter-century with 165,000 miles on the clock. But the transmission had been recently rebuilt, at least according to the current owner, who said that it *ran good*. Someone had attempted to convert it into a camper of sorts. There were two seats in the rear, separated by a center aisle. The rest of the passenger area had been carpeted, padded, and finished with walnut accents. Pull-down blinds hung from the windows. There was even a small AC unit built into the roof, which probably ran off a second battery.

Unlike a real RV, it had no kitchen or bathroom facilities, but it was perfect for her needs. No one would even give it a second glance. Best of all, it was cheap. Twenty-five hundred bucks. She could afford that.

Patterson dialed the number on the listing.

A male voice with a thick Texas accent answered.

Patterson introduced herself, using her paternal grandmother's maiden name—Emily Daniels—and asked if the van was still available. It was. Now came the tricky part. If she went to wherever the owner was keeping the van, she would have to ditch the truck somewhere nearby. While it was still unlikely the stolen pickup would be linked to her, especially since she had worn latex gloves whenever she was in it, she couldn't take the chance that Amarillo PD or the FBI might connect the dots, canvas the area, and discover her purchase. She would need him to bring the van and meet her on neutral ground.

Patterson knew where she wanted that to be.

"Could I look at it this afternoon?" she asked. "The earlier, the better."

"Sure. It's parked out the back of a storage facility right now. I've been keeping it there because it won't fit in my driveway. I can give you the address."

"I'm coming from outside of the city. A little town called Bushland. It's off I-40 to the west. I don't suppose you'd consider meeting me part way," Patterson asked. She had already used Google Earth to find both a suitable location for her fictional home, and a rural yet easily accessible spot to meet the van's seller and leave the pickup truck where it might not be found for a while. At first, she had considered asking him to drive out to the gas station and truck stop where she ditched her phone, but she'd abandoned her Bureau car nearby when she stole the pickup, and it was too risky. "You'd be doing me a huge favor. I can't get a ride all the way into the city."

"I don't know about that." The guy sounded unsure. "I'd have to find someone to give me a ride back."

The van had been online for over a month, and it was still for sale. Patterson guessed he wouldn't want her to slip through his fingers. "I'll make it worth your while. No haggling. As long as it runs just like you said and looks close enough to the pictures, I'll give you full price. Twenty-five hundred cash."

"You'll give me full asking, no fuss?"

"Yep. You bring the van and title. I'll bring the money." She decided to provide some added incentive. "Look. Honestly, I need that van. I'm getting out of a bad relationship. The guy has a heavy hand, if you know what I mean. I want to go back home to New Jersey. I'll be able to pack up all my stuff and get the hell out while he's at work. Better yet, I can sleep in the back to save on motel rooms along the way, then use it until I find a job and get resettled back in Hoboken. Honestly, you'd be saving my life."

The tug of his heartstrings worked. "How can I say no to a story like that. Where do you want to meet?"

"There's a truck stop off the interstate. Place called Lovell's Travel Center. A girlfriend of mine works in the convenience store there. It's a few miles past that row of old cars planted in the ground nose first that all the tourists stop and gawk at. You can't miss it." Patterson was spreading on the lies thick as marmalade on toast now. "Her shift starts at three. I can hitch a ride with her and hang out until you get there."

"And you'll bring the cash?"

"Swear on my life."

"All right. I know the place well enough. I'll ask my neighbor to follow me in his truck. He should be up for it if I throw him a few bucks for gas and a six-pack."

"That's such a relief," Patterson said, and it was mostly true. "I'm more than happy to throw an extra thirty bucks on top to cover your friend's expenses."

"Sounds like you're going to need that money, missy. Let me worry about keeping Elroy happy. Four o'clock work for you?"

"Four o'clock is great."

"I'll text you when I get there. Name's Lucas, by the way."

"Pleased to meet you, Lucas," Patterson said before hanging up. One problem solved. But that was the easy one. Now all she had to do was figure out why someone was framing her for murder.

TWENTY-THREE

TWO HOURS LATER, Patterson pulled off the interstate west of Amarillo and followed a narrow frontage road toward the sprawling and busy truck stop. But she didn't pull in. Instead, she turned right and drove under the highway. There was still forty-five minutes to go until her appointment with Lucas and his van. In the meantime, she wanted to get rid of the pickup truck somewhere it would go unnoticed and knew just where to do it, thanks to Google Earth.

The grassy land on the other side of the interstate ran flat and even all the way to the horizon and a cluster of distant farm buildings. A second frontage road ran parallel to the highway, just like the one on the other side, and a distance beyond that, a rural county road. Residential trailers and assorted outbuildings sat on small plots of land surrounded by chain-link fence. They looked old and poorly maintained, their front yards full of kids' toys, bicycles, and rusting vehicles, some of which looked like they had been parted out, their bare axles sitting on blocks. A few of the dwellings had clotheslines strung across, heavy with garments flapping in the light breeze.

Beyond the trailers stood a couple of metal buildings, one of which was leaning, its panels hanging loose on a rusted and skeletal frame. Patterson couldn't imagine living in a place like this. It must be a bleak, hardscrabble existence with little opportunity and even less money.

Pulling her gaze away, Patterson turned onto the county road and followed it for over a mile, leaving the small community of trailers behind, before veering onto a rutted trail toward a patch of dusty land that had become a graveyard for old vehicles and rusting agricultural machinery. It was not immediately obvious who owned the impromptu junkyard. There were no buildings nearby, and no signage except a single *no-trespassing* notice nailed to a wooden post that leaned at a precarious angle, threatening to give in to gravity. The sign was peppered with small round holes, an indication that someone had used it for target practice at some point in the past.

The cluster of rotting machinery and vehicles looked exactly like when she had explored the area on Google Earth. And it more than suited her purposes. She steered the pickup truck to a secluded spot shielded from view behind what looked like an old combine harvester—its metal frame sporting yet more bullet holes and rims resting on the ground atop flat tires—and climbed out. She would have to make the mile-long trek back to the truck stop on foot and then return here to collect her belongings once the van was in her possession. But there was some business to take care of first.

Screwdriver in hand, Patterson went to the rear of the truck and removed the license plate. She circled to the front and did the same, bent both plates and half, walked over to the combine harvester, and pushed them down inside the rusting machinery where they would not easily be found. This would make the truck harder to identify if it was discovered, which she hoped would not be for a long time.

Next, she went to another vehicle sitting nearby—an old Buick with weeds growing up around it. The license plates were still attached and in fair condition. Perfect to put on the van she was about to purchase rather than drive around without any. The screws were rusted tight, but after a few minutes of exertion and the occasional curse word, Patterson managed to remove them both. There were no registration stickers on either plate, but that was okay. Just like her home state of New York, Texas had dispensed with plate stickers years ago, moving the registration decal to the windshield. The Buick's registration was long expired, but that didn't matter. It would be obvious they were on the wrong vehicle if she got pulled over and the plates were run through the DMV. She would still need to be careful, but at least she wouldn't be driving around in a hot ride.

Patterson returned to the truck and stashed the new plates next to her travel bag sitting in the front passenger seat well. She would come back for everything as soon as the deal was done. She grabbed the burner phone and envelopes of money, counting out twenty-five hundred and leaving it in one envelope while transferring the rest of her cash to the other, then pushed both envelopes into her pocket. Finally, she unclipped her holster and placed the service weapon in her go bag next to the backup Glock and ankle holster Bauer had gotten her back in Dallas. Zipping the bag up, she hid it behind the truck's passenger seat. Leaving her possessions, including both guns, in the stolen vehicle would not have been her first choice, but she could hardly show up at the truck stop packing heat, and the trek back was too far to lug her bags. It wouldn't be for long, anyway, and the chances of anyone stumbling across the truck before she got back were next to zero.

After checking to make sure everything was tucked out of sight in the truck and she wasn't overlooking some small detail,

Patterson adjusted the baseball cap on her head to shield her eyes from the brutal afternoon sun. Then she struck out on foot back toward the truck stop on the other side of the interstate and her appointment with Lucas.

TWENTY-FOUR

LOVELL'S TRAVEL Center was a bustling shrine to the open road and, in particular, the sixteen-wheelers that plied it. There were tractor-trailers everywhere Patterson looked. They sat at the rows of pumps, filling their gargantuan tanks, and idled in a back parking lot designed solely to give these knights of the road a break, at the expense of their wallets, of course. Inside the sprawling travel center, there was a fast-food restaurant, a convenience store that not only sold the usual sugary snacks and drinks but also every conceivable gadget a trucker might need, and a place to freshen up with a hot shower and a shave.

On the other side of the building was another set of pumps devoted to vehicles of the regular four-wheeled variety, although compared to the square footage devoted to trucks, it felt a bit like an afterthought.

Patterson hurried across the frontage road, taking advantage of a break in the traffic to avoid being mowed down by some long hauler in need of fuel or anxious to make up time as they trundled back toward the interstate. She crossed to the far side of the truck stop, sticking to the periphery, and lingered on a grass verge near the road where she could see the van when it arrived. There would be security cameras around the pumps and buildings, which she wanted to avoid. It was unlikely anyone would track her to this location, even if they somehow discovered the abandoned pickup truck, but she couldn't take the chance.

Ten minutes after she got there, the van appeared, exiting the interstate with a red quad cab following behind. The van was easily recognizable from the photo she had seen online, thanks to its age and the distinctive vinyl stripes running along its sides. She raised an arm and waved, then waited until the van came to a stop nearby.

Lucas was a giant of a man with a bald head and scrolling tattoos running up both arms. He jumped from the van's cab and greeted her with an outstretched hand. "You must be Emily."

"And you must be Lucas," Patterson said, her gaze shifting briefly to a second man who had climbed out of the quad cab truck. He was thinner than his friend but no less imposing, with an equal number of tattoos and scraggly blonde hair that fell in Strands to his shoulders. He stood a few feet distant with his arms folded. While she had no reason to believe the pair were anything but what they seemed—a couple of guys trying to sell an old van—she was glad to be in a public place. Even so, she would keep her guard up, especially since her service weapon was currently stashed a mile away in the pickup truck.

"Want to take a look inside?" Lucas asked, tilting his head toward the van.

"Sure." Patterson stepped toward the van's side door and pulled on the handle. The door slid back with a high-pitched squeak. She poked her head inside, ignoring the musty smell that greeted her nose, and studied the interior. It was old and threadbare. Exactly what she would have expected from such a cheap ride. But the van had made it all the way from Amarillo, which meant that it ran, and there was ample space in the rear for her needs. She heaved the door closed again and checked out the cab, then went to the back and opened the rear doors. The tires looked good, too, with enough tread for at least another few thousand miles. Everything checked out.

"I can hop in the passenger seat if you want to take her for a spin," Lucas said after she finished her inspection.

That was the last thing Patterson wanted to do. The longer she was doing business with Lucas, the more chance there was that she would draw attention from someone who might later relay what they saw to the police. She was also eager to get back to the truck, grab her belongings, and put some distance between herself and the stolen vehicle. "I'm good. You wouldn't be here if it didn't run."

"Fair enough." Lucas shrugged. "You got the cash?"

Patterson reached into her pocket and withdrew the envelope containing the van money. She slipped it out and showed him, counting the cash to prove it was all there. "Twenty-five hundred, just as we agreed."

"Looks like we have ourselves a deal," Lucas said, taking the cash and handing Patterson the van's keys. He slipped a piece of folded paper from his back pocket. It was the van's title. "I've already filled out my part. There's half a tank of gas and some invoices in the glove compartment for work I had done on it."

"Great. You're a real lifesaver." Patterson accepted the title and watched as Lucas flicked through the cash one more time, double-checking the amount. Satisfied it was all there, he slipped it back into the envelope, and it disappeared into his pocket.

The guy with the mop of unruly blonde hair was on his knees, removing the back license plate. Once that was done, he went to the front and removed that one, too, then deposited them inside his truck.

Lucas watched with his hands pushed into his pockets, then

tipped his head. "You take care of yourself now, Emily. I hope things work out for you back in New Jersey."

"Me, too," Patterson replied.

She smiled and started toward the van, pulling the driver's door open. When she looked back, Lucas had already hopped into the quad cab beside his friend. The truck's engine roared. As it swung around to leave, he raised a hand to bid her farewell. Patterson returned the gesture, then climbed up into the van and pushed the key into the ignition.

The first time she turned it, the engine sputtered and died, giving her a moment of panic, but on the second turn, it caught, and she was on her way.

TWENTY-FIVE

FIFTEEN MINUTES after she purchased the van, Patterson was back at the dusty boneyard of rusting farm machinery and the stolen pickup. She jumped out and pulled the side door open, then quickly transferred her belongings into the back before attaching the plates taken off the old Buick. Ten minutes after that, she was on the interstate and driving toward Amarillo again.

Lucas had been generous with his assessment of the fuel in the van's tank. The needle hovered a little over a quarter full. She would have to fill up sooner rather than later but hadn't dared to do so at the truck stop. It was too close to where she had abandoned the pickup truck, and she knew that the FBI agents who were hunting for her would check the security tapes of that particular establishment when and if they ever linked the truck to her because that was what Patterson would have done if the tables were turned. And it wasn't a stretch to think they would make a connection with the stolen pickup since her Bureau-issued car had been abandoned close to where the truck's owner had left it for sale. Again, she was drawing on her own instinct to predict what her colleagues would do.

She would look for somewhere less conspicuous to fill up. If all else failed, there was a gas station in front of the Walmart where she had purchased the burner phone, and she was heading back there now. It was far away from both the hotel where she had been staying prior to Bauer's early morning call and the location where she had left her car. There was no way anyone could trace her there, and Patterson needed supplies if she was going to stay one step ahead of the law. Eating every meal at fast-food restaurants was a bad idea. They had cameras, just like everywhere else these days, and Patterson wanted to stay off as many of those as possible.

As she thought about that, her stomach growled, reminding Patterson that she hadn't eaten since breakfast. She was approaching the outskirts of Amarillo. A cluster of hotels beckoned weary travelers off the exit to her left, while in the other direction, she could see a shopping center with big-box stores and one of those discount clubs where members could pay a yearly fee to buy in bulk. There were restaurants, too. Burger King, McDonald's, and a Subway sandwich shop, their signs fighting for domination of her line of sight on tall poles.

She resolved to break her own rule almost as quickly as she had made it. Pulling off the highway, she decided on the sandwich shop and ate it in the van before circling around to the most run-down of the four gas stations clustered around the interstate. The pumps were old, and the convenience store had lost part of its sign, which meant that the cameras, if there were any, were probably in just as bad a state of repair. Going inside, she paid for twelve gallons of gas in cash, figuring it was a safe amount that wouldn't require her to go back inside. As she drove off, the needle hovered between three-quarters and full.

She rejoined the highway and eased into the flow of rush hour traffic moving east through the city. Thirty minutes later, she arrived at the Walmart and parked up, then made her way inside. After taking a cart, Patterson went to the grocery section and filled it with easy-to-eat snacks like chips and cookies. She also grabbed several cans of tuna and chicken, a loaf of sandwich bread, and an assortment of fruits. All stuff that didn't require refrigeration or heating. In the drink aisle, she added two twelve-packs of diet soda, a case of iced coffee, and a tray of bottled water. It wasn't the healthiest shopping trip she had ever been on, but her home on wheels would now be stocked with enough food to keep her going for a few days.

Leaving the grocery section, Patterson headed to electronics and picked up two more burner phones, just in case one or more handsets got compromised, and a pair of thirty-day unlimited prepaid cards to go along with them. She also found an inexpensive laptop that was on sale for a couple of hundred bucks, which would make online research easier whenever she could find an open Wi-Fi signal. And if all else failed, the burner phone included a hotspot she could connect to. Next came a power inverter, which she could plug into the van's 12V outlet when the laptop or phone needed a charge.

She went to the bedding department and found a twin-sized memory foam mattress-in-a-box, two pillows, a sheet set, and a comforter. Last, she visited the outdoors section for a couple of rechargeable LED lanterns with hooks that would allow them to be hung from the van's ceiling, a folding camp chair so she could sit outside if the circumstances allowed, and a small cooler.

Kitted out with everything she would need to live in the van, Patterson wheeled her haul to the self-checkout, which diminished her cash reserves by another eight hundred bucks.

Thirty minutes later, the back of the van looked about as homey as it would ever get. The mattress mostly fit across the space behind the rear seats, lifting at one end because the van's interior wasn't quite wide enough by a few inches, but she made it work. When the sheet set, pillows, and comforter were added, her makeshift bed actually looked comfortable.

With the food stashed in the cooler and the laptop charging through the power inverter, Patterson pulled the van's doors closed and sat back on the mattress with the pillows propped behind her head. The Walmart parking lot was as safe a place as any to linger for a while, and the van was not only inconspicuous in its banal appearance but, more importantly, was not stolen. The only thing that might cause concern was the license plate she had removed from the Buick and transferred, but that would only become an issue if she were stopped by the police, and if that happened, the license plates would be the least of her worries.

She closed her eyes, overcome by sudden exhaustion. To that point, the day had passed in a whirl of frantic activity, but now that she had five minutes to herself, the enormity of the situation crashed down around her. There was no way to sugarcoat it. Patterson was in a world of trouble, and she could see no way out. But that would not stop her from trying. This was why, pushing aside an uncharacteristic moment of hopelessness, she decided to start investigating who was behind the conspiracy to frame her. And the best place to start was with the phone call she had received the previous evening.

TWENTY-SIX

PATTERSON LOOKED up the office number for the Amarillo Weekly Ledger and called it, even though she already suspected what she would discover. And she was right. When the call was answered, she wasted no time in asking to speak with Tad Bryant. Except there was no such person working at the ledger and there never had been. The man on the other end of the line told her that he was the newspaper's only reporter and one of only four employees left at the ailing business, which he speculated would probably be bankrupt by the end of the year thanks to the shift in how people got their news. The internet, he grumbled, was the worst thing that ever happened to his industry.

Patterson sympathized, thanked the guy, and got off the phone as quickly as she could. While not exactly a surprise, she had at least confirmed that the call she received from the man calling himself Tad Bryant was bogus and likely placed by the very person who was setting her up. But who was he? The answer to that would only become apparent when she figured out whose feathers she had ruffled and why.

There was only one reason she could think of for her sudden and illegitimate legal troubles. Her visit to Mark Davis in the Potter County Correctional Facility. When he had claimed to be innocent of the assault on Alexandria Rowley, Patterson had been skeptical. The evidence was overwhelming. But now, in light of her own situation, she couldn't help wondering if Davis really was innocent. After all, the evidence that she had killed small-time hoodlum Leo Galinsky, a man she had never even heard of before that morning, was just as damning. There were hair fibers at the scene, which would almost certainly be a match to her DNA, and her fingerprints were found on a water bottle outside his apartment. Then there was the cherry on the cake. The text message on Galinsky's phone that appeared to have come from her, and the call made to her number from that same phone not long after. Everything had been staged to look like she had tracked Galinsky down after concluding he was involved in the disappearance of her sister, Julie, went over to his apartment, took him hostage, and put a bullet in his head. An execution-style killing that looked for all the world like she was reaping vigilante justice.

Except none of it was true.

Mark Davis was the key to unraveling the mystery of whatever she had accidentally put herself in the middle of. Patterson was sure of it. She would need to take a closer look at Davis and his activities prior to being arrested. Someone, somewhere, must have wanted him out of the picture and they had done it in a devastating way.

It occurred to her that there must be a common denominator between the two of them. Whoever had potentially framed Mark Davis was also behind the murder of Leo Galinsky and the planted evidence that pointed to her. If she could find that link, it would give her an avenue of investigation. None of this would be easy, though. She had left her FBI laptop, which would have given her access to the Bureau's servers and crime databases, behind in the hotel room when she fled. And she could hardly drive over to the resident agency and ask Special Agent Ricketts for help. Once again, she was out in the cold and on her own. Except that this time, she was also on the run.

But there was one person she could count on. Special Agent Bauer. She was loath to drag him any deeper into the situation but could see no other viable option. She still had the hard copies of the Mark Davis file, but that would only get so far, and certainly wouldn't provide any information on the mess she was in.

Bauer had told her to call his burner phone after he finished work. She looked at the time. It was almost eight in the evening. He should be home by now. She dialed the number.

Bauer picked up immediately. There was a note of stress in his voice. "Patterson, I was starting to worry."

"I wanted to make sure you were home before I called," Patterson said. "I was also making sure I had a set of wheels that wouldn't draw attention and somewhere to sleep tonight."

"I take it you achieved both those aims?"

"I did. Both at the same time." Patterson went on to explain about ditching the truck and her new makeshift camper van.

When she finished, Bauer jumped back in. "Nice job. Have you given any thought to who might want you out of the way?"

"I have, and I came up empty. But I still believe it must have something to do with Mark Davis. I don't suppose you could get hold of the file on Leo Galinsky's murder?"

"Way ahead of you, but I have to be careful. I'm still on desk duty and not part of the task force sent up there to find you. If I make it too obvious that I'm digging into this, someone might get suspicious since we were partners and all."

"In that case, maybe you should back off. I'll do what I can from here."

"And just how are you going to do that?"

"I'll figure it out. I always do."

"It won't be so easy this time. You don't have the backing of the FBI, and I don't need to remind you that you're a fugitive."

"Tell me about it." Patterson was still processing the day's turn of events and she didn't like how it made her feel. "Promise me you won't risk your career for this."

"I can't promise anything of the sort. But I'll be careful. I should have that report in the morning."

"How? You just said pulling that report would draw too much attention."

"I'm not the one who's going to do it. SAC Harris was briefed on the situation this morning and already has a copy. So does the ASAC. Phoebe's going to get it for me."

"Absolutely not. I won't draw her into this, too. It's getting out of hand."

"Too late for that, I'm afraid," said a feminine voice. "I owe you for saving my boyfriend's life."

"Phoebe." Patterson groaned inwardly. "I suppose you know everything."

"Who do you think tipped Marcus off about the raid on your hotel room this morning? The ASAC got me out of bed in the early hours to help with the interagency paperwork and act as an administrative liaison."

"This is too much, guys. I don't deserve it." Patterson's throat tightened. Tears welled in her eyes as the day's pent-up emotions came rushing to the surface. She tried not to let it show but failed.

"You okay, there, partner?" Bauer asked.

"Just overwhelmed." Patterson sucked in a long breath. "I'm okay now." She paused, hesitant to ask Bauer and Phoebe to put themselves in yet more peril. "There is one other thing I would like to see."

"Tell me," Bauer said.

"The surveillance tape from that night in the bar where

Mark Davis was supposed to have picked up Alexandria Rowley. I asked Special Agent Ricketts' PA to request it for me from Amarillo PD, but she never got back to me before everything went south."

Bauer swallowed. "I'll see what I can do. Discreetly of course. It might take a day or two."

"Take as long as you need." Patterson was eager to see the footage but realized that she must bide her time and let Bauer do his thing.

"I'll be as quick as I can without raising suspicion. Speaking of files, we need a secure way to transfer information back and forth," said Bauer. "I propose we set up a dead drop email account."

"Wow. Never thought I'd need one of those," Patterson replied. A dead drop email account was a way of communicating without creating an electronic trail of emails. The idea was that both parties would have access to the login information for the account and create draft messages which they would save without sending. Using the shared email account, information could be exchanged by the recipient reading the unsent message in the drafts folder and then replying in the same manner. It was a clumsy answer to secure communications, but it would work and was practically untraceable unless one of the parties exchanging messages betrayed the other.

"I'll create the account in a false name and call you back with the login details," Bauer said. "In the meantime, just sit tight."

I don't have much choice, thought Patterson. Until she got a copy of that report, she couldn't look for a correlation between her situation and Mark Davis. She only hoped there was one. "I appreciate the two of you doing this for me," she said. "Otherwise, I'd be totally alone."

"Don't mention it," Bauer replied. "Have you tried to contact Jonathan Grant?"

"No."

"Good. Don't. At best, you'll put him in an uncomfortable situation, and at worst, he'll turn you in."

She wanted to say that Grant would not do that, but she wasn't so sure given his position at the Bureau and strait-laced attitude. To lighten the mood, she said, "You were going to tell me why you already had a burner phone with an LA number."

"I don't think now's the time," Bauer said quickly.

"I've been wondering that myself," Phoebe said, her voice sounding hollow, like she was standing a few feet distant. "Why don't you tell both of us?"

"All right. Fine." Bauer was obviously uncomfortable. "This is going to sound silly, but I used it back in LA when I was on the dating scene. There are a lot of crazy women out there, and I didn't want to give out my real number until I was sure it was going to go beyond one or two dates. You must think that sounds sleazy."

"Wow. You were a player." Patterson laughed despite herself.

"A total player," said Phoebe with a chuckle. "I might have to rethink this relationship."

"Hey. Take it easy. It wasn't like that." Bauer sounded annoyed.

"Relax," Patterson said. "I'm just teasing. I have girlfriends back in New York who've done the same thing. Some of them have email accounts just for dating, too. It's a dangerous world. You can never be too careful."

"Amen to that," echoed Phoebe. "Just so long as you haven't used it recently, present company excepted."

"Actually, I haven't used it since joining the FBI," Bauer said. "Wasn't interested in dating at first. Too much pressure while I was at Quantico."

"And then you met me," said Phoebe.

"Exactly. I only kept the thing because it still had minutes on it. Now I'm glad I did."

"Me too," said Patterson. "You have no idea."

TWENTY-SEVEN

PATTERSON'S first night in the van passed without incident. She left the Walmart parking lot and drove around looking for somewhere more suitable to spend the overnight hours. After forty-five minutes of searching, she came across a road to the north of the city bounded on one side by scrubland waiting for development and new construction on the other. The houses, sprinkled among rectangular lots that had been cleared but not built on, were not yet complete. They stood as cinderblock shells, with dark and empty holes where the windows would soon go. A few had trusses in place, ready to receive their roofs. It was dark and secluded, yet still within the city. Her van would go unnoticed until morning, when the builders arrived to continue their work. Even then, she doubted anyone would pay the van much heed, but just to be safe, she drove all the way to the end of the street where the lots were still vacant and parked in a roughed-out turnaround waiting to be paved.

With the LED lanterns turned on, the mattress laid out, and the roof-mounted AC running off the second battery installed in the van specifically for that purpose, Patterson's home on wheels was about as comfy as it would ever be. There was no internet she could piggyback off other than her phone's hotspot, but that was fine. It was late, and she didn't want to browse the web, anyway. Tomorrow, Bauer would get back to her with the dead drop mailbox login details, and they would be able to communicate back and forth in relative secrecy.

Hopefully, he would also provide her with digital copies of Amarillo PD's murder investigation reports and witness statements on Leo Galinsky and maybe even the surveillance videos from the convenience store. She hoped something would stand out. Some detail that would provide direction for her own investigation into whoever was framing her. Until then, all she could do was wait.

Patterson wondered how well she would sleep in the van, but she was out within minutes of her head hitting the pillow. The memory foam mattress was less comfortable than her bed back in New York by a mile, but it was adequate, and even after she turned the A/C unit off to save battery power, the van stayed cool enough.

She woke early the next morning with sunlight streaming in through the front windshield. The sound of cars on the interstate a couple of miles distant was a low and steady thrum. The rest of Amarillo was also awake and on the move.

The first thing Patterson did after getting dressed, brushing her teeth, and rinsing with bottled water, was to check the burner phone for any messages from Bauer. There were none.

She swallowed her disappointment at the prospect of another day doing nothing but trying to stay hidden with nothing else to occupy her time than to let the situation stew inside her head—he was doing all that he could without putting his own career and liberty in danger.

Rummaging through the cooler, Patterson came up with the

loaf of sandwich bread and a jar of marmalade. She twisted the cap off the jar and used a plastic knife she had saved from her fast-food meal the day before to spread the marmalade on two slices of bread. She would have preferred the bread toasted, but that wasn't an option. Still, the impromptu breakfast hit the spot when washed down with one of the bottled iced coffees she had bought the day before Walmart, even though it wasn't chilled.

As she was finishing up her phone rang. It was Bauer.

She snatched it up and answered. "Hey."

"Listen, I don't have long. I'm on my way into the office," Bauer said quickly. "I set up that dead drop mailbox last night after we talked. I have the login details."

"Hang on." Patterson found a pen and a scrap of paper. "Shoot."

Bauer relayed the login details of the email account he had set up the previous evening. Afterward, he said, "Phoebe will make copies of everything Amarillo PD has on Leo Galinsky's murder, or at least everything they've sent over to our field office. She'll give it to me, and I'll upload it into the dead drop as soon as I can."

"Don't do it from the office," Patterson said.

"That goes without saying. I have a physiotherapy appointment this morning for my gunshot wound. I can do it then."

"Just be careful." Patterson was worried that Bauer was getting in too deep. This was her problem, not his.

"Always." Bauer cleared his throat. "I do have one piece of information for you although I don't know how useful it will be. The lead detective on your case . . . Sorry, the Galinsky murder."

"You don't need to tiptoe around me. I know how much trouble I'm in," Patterson said. "What's his name?"

"Detective Sergeant Felix Ortega. Thirty-seven years old.

Been with Amarillo PD for fifteen years. Started in uniform and worked his way up."

"Ortega. Why does that name sound familiar?" Patterson reached for the Mark Davis file. She pulled out the report Special Agent Ricketts had given her a couple of days before and skimmed through it until she found what she was looking for. "He was also the first officer to respond when Alexandria Rowley walked into the hospital and said she'd been raped. The report says he was already close by following up on a lead in an unrelated case and took the call. After that, a detective sergeant from the Special Victims Unit took over."

"That's convenient," Bauer said. "He was right there, just by pure coincidence, when the rape victim showed up."

"It could be just that," Patterson replied. "Coincidence."

"It's possible. But it's all we've got right now. I say we tug on that thread and see what unravels. I'll do some discrete digging into his background. See what I can come up with."

"I hate putting all this on you. Please be careful. You and Phoebe both."

"You can count on it." Bauer was silent for a moment. "Look, I'm at the office. I have to get inside. I'm leaving the burner phone in the car so I will be out of contact for a while. I'll let you know when those reports are in the dead drop."

"Sure." Patterson said goodbye and hung up. She would have to move the van soon. The construction crews were already arriving to work on the houses that were going up. She didn't want anyone to pay undue attention to the van that they might remember later. But where to go? She didn't want to drive around aimlessly all day, and neither was she inclined to spend the day in another Walmart parking lot. With nothing better to do, she climbed into the van's front seat and drove toward downtown and the Amarillo Police Department headquarters. She wasn't sure what she expected to find there —it wasn't like she could actually go inside and talk to anyone without getting arrested—but Detective Sergeant Felix Ortega was the only common denominator between the crime she was accused of committing and the one Mark Davis claimed to be innocent of. It might be nothing, or it might be everything. And it gave Patterson something to occupy herself with until Bauer got back in touch.

TWENTY-EIGHT

PHOEBE CUTLER ARRIVED at the FBI's Dallas field office at seven thirty in the morning, half an hour earlier than her shift was due to begin. She made her way through the lobby and the metal detector, flashing her ID badge at the guard seated behind a desk. He glanced up and nodded, recognizing her, even as his eyes fell briefly to the badge and then away again.

She rode the elevator to the fourth floor and went straight to the ASAC's office, passing by a door that read Walter Harris, SAC. The Special Agent in Charge was not there yet, and probably wouldn't be for at least another half an hour. She hoped the same was true of Philip Muir, the Assistant Special Agent in Charge, and her boss. She hoped to use this time to make copies of the Leo Galinsky murder investigation reports that Amarillo PD had sent over when requesting help in apprehending Special Agent Blake.

But when she stepped into the outer office where her desk was located, ASAC Muir was already there, standing in his office doorway with a sheaf of paperwork in his hands.

"Sir?" she said, surprised to see him. "You're in early."

"I could say the same about you, Miss Cutler."

Phoebe glanced toward her desk. "I have a stack of paperwork to finish up. Thought I'd get a head start on it, so I don't have to stay late."

"Wish I could say the same." Muir pressed his lips together. "I have a nine-thirty meeting over at DHS."

Phoebe's hopes soared. DHS stood for the Department of Homeland Security. They had an office not far away on the other side of Trammell Crow Park. "Is there anything you need from me?" she asked. "For the meeting."

"Not unless you can phone me in a couple of hours and make some excuse to get me out of there. I have a feeling it's going to be long and extremely boring."

"If that's what you want," Phoebe said with a grin. "I'm sure we can come up with some suitable crisis."

"Nah." Muir shook his head. He crossed through her office and toward the door. "I'll grin and bear it."

"Don't say I didn't offer."

"This is why you're the best admin I've ever had," Muir said with a smile before stepping out into the corridor.

Phoebe watched him go, then gave it an additional five minutes before hurrying into his office, closing the door, and going straight to the desk. The Amarillo PD murder report had come in a couple of days ago, and she had passed it straight to him. But the desk was piled with paperwork, much of it haphazardly scattered around. Muir was a good leader and a brilliant investigator, but he had zero organizational skills when it came to paperwork. More than once, she had seen him gather everything up in frustration and drop it into a corner of the office, proclaiming that needless paper trails would be the death of him, only for Phoebe to file everything in the correct place later. She sympathized with his irritation. The digital age should have reduced the heaps of paperwork lying around, but for some reason, everything ended up printed out in triplicate and disseminated in hard copy form, anyway.

Now, that lack of clerical organization was amounting to a big problem as she hunted through the piles of reports, laser-printed emails, and memos that took up almost every square inch of real estate on the desk. Then, lifting a particularly weighty report on the crisis at the border and the number of drugs that poured into the United States every year from Central America, she found it.

"Thank the stars," she muttered under her breath, laying the multi-page report out atop an untidy bed of its brethren and taking out her cell phone.

She opened the camera app and clicked an image of the first page, then the second. She continued in this fashion until she had committed the entire document to her phone's storage. Then she saw something else. A call log from Leo Galinsky's cell phone, obtained under warrant from the wireless carrier. It listed every incoming and outgoing call. The call to Patterson's phone on the night of the murder was highlighted. She didn't know if the call log would help, but she decided to photograph it anyway, just in case. There were five pages going back two months. She photographed the first four, but as she reached the last page and snapped one more pic, the office door flew open, and Philip Muir strode back in, a combination of anger and surprise splashed across his face.

TWENTY-NINE

THE AMARILLO POLICE DEPARTMENT occupied an entire block downtown, sharing a building with the municipal courthouse. Further south on Fillmore Street was the Potter County District Court and a slew of bail bonds offices that had sprung up like weeds, eager for the steady flow of business the police and judicial buildings provided.

Patterson circled the block slowly, sunglasses perched on her nose and the old baseball cap from the pickup truck pulled low over her brow. Combined with the van's tinted windows, it was unlikely anyone would recognize her, and even less likely they were looking. After all, most fugitives wanted to stay clear of police stations, not drive straight toward them. But most fugitives were not innocent.

The building that housed the police headquarters rose eight stories, connected to the lower three-story courthouse and an undercover parking lot. To the side of the building was another open parking lot, half full, that contained a mix of regular cars and trucks, police cruisers, and a couple of tactical response vehicles. Surrounded by a five-foot block wall, this was clearly not a public lot, and if there was any doubt, there were strict no-trespassing signs posted at the entrance—unauthorized vehicles will be towed at owners' expense—to dissuade all but the most foolhardy who might think to park there.

As she cruised by, Patterson glanced sideways through the parking lot's entrance. Then she saw it. A red pickup truck. It was no different from any other red pickup truck she might encounter, except that it jogged her memory. Two days ago, before she went on the run, Patterson had noticed a similar pickup truck shadowing her after she left the women's center. It had appeared to follow her for a while, even as she turned onto a side road. Finally, she had pulled into the parking lot of a discount store and watched as the truck continued on its way, seemingly oblivious to her. She had dismissed the encounter as paranoia brought on by a heightened awareness of her surroundings—a skill she had developed in her role as an FBI agent.

Was it the same truck?

Patterson couldn't tell from the road, and she didn't want to drive into the lot with her van. There might be security cameras and an unauthorized vehicle would stand out. Instead, she continued past the entrance and turned at the next block, cruising around until she found public parking a couple of streets away.

She tied her hair back into a bun to hide its length, then slipped the baseball cap and sunglasses on before heading back to the police parking lot on foot. Stopping at the entrance, phone in hand as if she were checking a message, she scanned the lot for cameras. There was one on a high pole near the covered garage entrance and another on the wall of the building. Judging by the angle of their lenses, it would be almost impossible to enter the lot without being caught on video. Patterson was glad she hadn't driven in with the van, but she still wanted to get a look at that red truck.

It was parked two rows over from the entrance, with

smaller vehicles on each side. Pulling the baseball cap lower to hide as much of her face as possible from the electronic eyes guarding the lot, Patterson strolled casually past the no-trespassing signs affixed to the wall on each side of the entrance as if she hadn't seen them. She headed toward the truck and circled around it; head bowed to shield her face. At the front, she stopped and stared at the dented fender. There was no doubt this was the same truck that had tailed her a couple of days before. And she didn't think for one second that it was a coincidence. What were the odds?

The phone was still in Patterson's hand. With her back to the cameras, she took a surreptitious photo of the damage, then one of the front license plate. There was no way to tell who the truck belonged to unless she could convince Bauer to run the plate, but they were inside the Amarillo police headquarters, which meant they must work there since the lot was not open to the public.

"Hey!"

A voice encroached on her thoughts. Patterson glanced around to see a uniformed officer striding toward her from the direction of the building.

"You can't be here. This is a restricted lot," the officer said, drawing closer.

"Sorry. I was looking for my car. I thought I'd parked it here, but I must be in the wrong place," Patterson replied, starting back toward the entrance. She couldn't allow the officer to get a good look at her.

"There's a public parking lot a block south," the cop said, stopping and watching her go. "Maybe you left your car there."

"Probably." Patterson hurried across the lot and stepped back out onto the sidewalk. She crossed the road, aware of the officer's gaze upon her back, and walked away at a brisk pace. Instead of turning at the end of the block to head directly back to the van, she kept going straight out of an abundance of caution before turning at the next block and looping back around.

When she was safely back inside the van, Patterson looked at the photos she had taken on her phone. She logged into the dead drop mailbox that Bauer had set up and attached them to a new message. In the body of the email, she asked him to find out who the truck belonged to, then saved the message in the drafts folder. The next time Bauer went into the mailbox, which she hoped would be soon, he would see the draft message and be able to download the photos, including the one showing the truck's license plate. There were no other messages waiting for her in the drafts folder, which meant that Bauer had not yet been able to send over the police reports on Leo Galinsky's murder. Until he did, she would just have to sit tight.

THIRTY

"SIR? What are you doing back so quickly," Phoebe asked, palming the phone and slipping it into her pocket with a quick and fluid movement.

"Grabbed the wrong report," Muir said, lifting the stack of papers he was carrying under one arm. The same ones he had been flicking through when Phoebe arrived at the office. "Figures. I was already in the car pulling out of the parking lot, when I realized. Had to turn around and come all the way back up." His brow wrinkled. "What are you doing in here, anyway?"

Phoebe thought quickly. "I thought I'd take the opportunity to tidy your desk and file anything that isn't current so that this sort of mix up doesn't happen again."

"Well, it's a shame you couldn't have done it twenty-four hours ago so that I didn't have to slog all the way back here." He dabbed a bead of perspiration from his brow.

"Here, let me see if I can find what you need," Phoebe said, rummaging around and surreptitiously burying the Amarillo PD murder paperwork again in the process. She found the

Homeland Security report and stepped around the desk, holding it out to him. "There you go."

"Thanks." Muir exchanged the papers he was clutching for the report. "I wouldn't bother with all that right now if I were you. It's Thursday. You'll never get it all sorted and filed before the weekend, especially with everything else you have on your plate. You don't have time."

"I know," Phoebe said. "But I can make a dent in it, at least. There's a ton of old paperwork lying around this office, and I can't imagine you've looked at most of it in weeks."

"Months, more like. Which is why it can wait until there's a lull around here. My office has looked like this ever since your last big cleanup back in February, so I'm sure I'll survive a few weeks more. Besides, I know what you're like. You'll still be doing this tomorrow evening and then spend half the night on it even when you should have gone home already. You put a lot of hours in. Enjoy your weekend for once."

"Okay. If you insist." Phoebe slouched with relief. The ASAC hadn't seen her snapping photographs or even noticed the phone. He was in such a dither because of his trek down to the car and back up again that he wasn't paying attention.

"I do. One of us might as well enjoy our weekend. I have to go out of town and visit the in-laws."

"You don't like your wife's family?"

"Oh, it's not that. I like them well enough. But Cindy's mother couldn't cook a decent meal if her life depended on it, and her father is about the same on the grill. I'll have to spend two days at their family cabin eating nothing but burned mac n cheese, undercooked hamburgers, and soggy potato salad."

"Sounds lovely," Phoebe said, forcing a grin.

"You don't know the half of it. I should arrest them both for crimes against my stomach, but then my wife would just be mad at me." Muir tapped a finger against the report cradled in his arms. "Thanks for this. You're a lifesaver, as usual."

"Don't mention it." Phoebe waited for the ASAC to leave, then flopped down into his chair, took a deep breath, and waited for her racing heart to slow. Ten minutes later, composure regained, she hurried from the office to find Marcus Bauer.

THIRTY-ONE

MARCUS BAUER CALLED Patterson at eleven-thirty after leaving the field office for his physiotherapy appointment. When she explained about the license plate and what she wanted him to do, Bauer was less than enthusiastic.

"Absolutely not," he said. "There's no way I can run that plate to see who the truck belongs to without drawing scrutiny, especially since it's likely registered to a police officer or someone else working within the Amarillo PD. I might as well stand up and shout, *hey, I'm helping Patterson Blake evade the authorities.*"

"I need to know who was following me," Patterson said. "Because I'll bet they are also involved in framing me. Someone out there killed Leo Galinsky, and if we don't catch them, I'll end up going to prison while the real murderer walks free."

"I'm aware of the high stakes." Bauer sounded frustrated. "But we have to be careful. I can't get caught helping you."

"I know. I shouldn't have asked."

"It's fine. I'll do whatever I can, but discretion is the name of the game. There is some good news, though. Phoebe came through with the police reports on Galinsky's murder, and they

143

are waiting for you. I also looked into his background, and this is where it gets interesting. Leo Galinsky has stayed out of trouble for the last few years, at least by outward appearances, but before that, he was quite the thug, although not very good at keeping away from jail cells. His rap sheet has everything from auto theft and burglary to assault with a deadly weapon. And get this, he was even accused of raping a woman back in his twenties, but like many such cases, the evidence was shaky, and the DA didn't prosecute. His last arrest was three years ago. He got fingered for a warehouse robbery. A security guard was injured in the process, but apparently got a look at him."

"But he got away with it, I assume," said Patterson.

"The security guard changed his story a month before the trial was scheduled to start. Claimed he hadn't gotten a good look at the perpetrator after all and wasn't sure that it was Galinsky. Then the only other evidence—forensics that placed Galinsky at the scene—was accidentally tainted and couldn't be used in court. He walked, and ever since then, he's either stayed on the straight and narrow or gotten much better at hiding his activities."

"Seems to me that he got just a little too lucky, what with that security guard recounting his testimony and the forensic evidence going south," Patterson said. "How much do you want to bet that someone had a hand in making sure he walked."

"I'd say it's pretty high," Bauer replied. "Especially when you factor in this next bit of information. The lead detective on that case was Felix Ortega. Back then, he was working in the Violent Crimes Unit."

"This guy's name is popping up everywhere we look." Patterson's mind was going a mile a minute. "I wouldn't be surprised if he drives a red pickup with a busted front fender."

"The only way you're going to find that out is to keep an eye on that truck and see who gets in it."

"Hmm. A fugitive FBI agent wanted for murder staking out a police station so she can collect intel on the detective investigating her case. That sounds like a barrel of laughs."

"You'd certainly have to be discreet."

"I don't suppose you have a photo of Ortega?"

"Way ahead of you. I pulled a couple of photos right off the web. I found one right on the Amarillo PD website next to his name in their personnel directory and another on social media. They should be good enough for you to recognize him."

"Thanks. Have you done any digging into Detective Sergeant Ortega's past?"

"Not a whole lot. Haven't had time, and I can't do it in the office, but I did find one thing that might be of interest. There was an excessive force complaint filed against him several years ago, but it never went anywhere. Other than that, he appears to be squeaky clean."

"Or good at covering his tracks," Patterson said with a sigh.

"Yeah. Or that." Bauer hesitated. "You coping okay there, Patterson? I know this must be terribly stressful."

"That's an understatement. I actually had a nightmare last night that I was being chased through dark alleys by shadowy figures I couldn't escape."

"If you need to talk-"

"I'm not going to burden you with my woes. They are what they are, and I'll just have to deal with it. But I'm touched that you're willing to listen."

"Anytime." Bauer sounded distracted now. "Look, I've got to go. I'll catch up with you this evening?"

"Sure."

"Take care, Patterson. We don't know anything about this guy or if he's involved in whatever you've put yourself in the middle of, but if he had a hand in framing you, then he's dangerous. Not only that, but he'll expect you to come after him if you make the connection. Don't do anything rash."

"When have I ever done anything rash?" Patterson asked without a hint of irony.

"The answer to that would take more time than I have right now."

"Ouch."

"Hey, you walked right into that one."

"Guess I did. Don't worry. I'll be careful. Say thanks to Phoebe for getting that information."

Bauer promised he would and ended the call.

Patterson opened the laptop she had purchased the previous day. She checked for an open Wi-Fi connection and found one among the list of nearby signals. A wine bar across the street with three bars of signal. She connected to it and downloaded a virtual private network app with a one-month free trial—no credit card required—installed it, then disconnected and reconnected through the VPN. Now she could browse the web with less fear of being tracked.

Next, she opened the mail account shared with Bauer and found two new messages in the drafts folder. The Leo Galinsky murder files were attached to the first. Phoebe had photographed them with her cell phone at great personal risk. The second message contained the photos of Detective Sergeant Ortega that Bauer had found on the web. The first was a formal headshot. He was wearing a brown suit jacket and looking directly at the camera. In the second, Ortega was wearing a black suit and standing next to an older man with silver hair.

Patterson logged into the mail account on her phone and transferred the two photographs of Detective Sergeant Ortega onto the device. Then she closed the laptop and sat back, pondering how she would keep the red truck under surveillance without getting caught.

THIRTY-TWO

PATTERSON MOVED THE VAN. She drove back toward the lot where the red pickup was parked. There was more public parking across the street. Amarillo appeared to have an abundance of parking. She pulled in and found a space that provided a good line of sight through the driver's side window to the truck on the other side of the street.

Then she settled down to wait.

It was barely noon. Patterson didn't think Detective Sergeant Ortega, or whoever else might own the pickup, would make an appearance anytime soon. She felt exposed in the parking lot, even though no one knew the van was hers. She would have preferred to take off for a few hours and come back later, but she could not take the chance that the red truck would leave while she was gone.

She grabbed the laptop from the back seat and opened it. The Wi-Fi signal she had found earlier was no longer within range, but that didn't matter. She had already downloaded Phoebe's photos to her hard drive. She opened them one by one and studied the pages of the crime scene and forensics reports.

As expected, it was damning. If Patterson hadn't known she was innocent, she might have arrested herself. But other than coming to the conclusion that she was dealing with a sophisticated operative who knew how to rig a crime scene and falsify evidence, there was little else that stood out, at least in so far as finding whoever was framing her and why.

Patterson closed the laptop and sat back in her seat with her gaze fixed on the red truck, glad the van had tinted side windows.

An hour passed, then another.

Police cruisers and several civilian vehicles that probably belonged to staff came and went, but the truck didn't move. The monotony was excruciating. The time dragged by with every minute longer than the last. Patterson had always hated this kind of surveillance. The only thing worse was the hours of paperwork that normally followed hand-in-hand. At least this time, she wouldn't have to fill out any forms or write any reports, so that was something.

Another hour and a half passed by with no sign of the truck moving. It was now almost five in the evening. Patterson's eyelids drooped. She stifled a yawn, struggling against tedium-induced exhaustion. Finally, she slipped from the driver's seat and made her way into the back of the van, opened the cooler, and grabbed a bottle of iced coffee. She twisted the top off and took a long drink before heading back to the front.

When she glanced back over at the parking lot, her heart leaped into her throat.

The truck was gone. The two cars around it were still there, but the middle space was now empty.

"Shit." It figured. She had been in the back for less than two minutes.

Patterson looked left and right, scanning the roads around the police building. And then she saw it. The red truck was sitting in a line of cars at a traffic light two blocks distant. She started the van and turned back out onto the road, pressing the van's accelerator down hard to catch up. The vehicle had about as much pickup as a turtle. By the time she reached the light, it had turned green, and the truck was already cruising through.

Stuck four cars behind, she craned her neck to keep it in sight as the truck made its way through downtown, passing under I-40 without joining the heavy rush-hour flow of interstate traffic and out toward the suburbs. She had no idea who she was following—she had missed getting a look at the occupant before he climbed in, thanks to her decision to grab a coffee from the cooler—but they were probably heading home for the day.

The truck kept going for another thirty minutes, leading Patterson out of the city proper. As the traffic thinned out, she kept her distance, allowing other vehicles into the gap between them and hanging back as far as she could without losing sight of her quarry. This wasn't the first time she had tailed a suspect, and she was sure the driver had not noticed the van, unlike his own less professional surveillance a few days before. Eventually, they ended up in an area with large houses sitting on arid lots of at least an acre in size surrounded by hard landscaping.

When the truck turned onto a narrow residential street and pulled up on a driveway in front of a sprawling prairie-style house with a three-car garage, stone facing, and clay roof tiles, she kept going straight while committing the location to memory. It was still daylight, and even though she was sure the driver of the truck had not noticed the van on his tail, it would be obvious if she turned and drove past the house. Instead, Patterson slowed and watched in her rearview mirror, but when the driver exited the truck, the distance was too great for her to see his features. Only that he was male.

Frustrated, Patterson sped up and quickly left the area, heading back toward the city. She would come back later under cover of darkness to get a closer look at the house and hopefully find out who was behind the wheel of the red truck.

THIRTY-THREE

WHILE PATTERSON WAS WAITING to find out who the red truck belonged to, Marcus Bauer and Phoebe Cutler were at dinner. It was a reservation they had made over a week before, and even though neither was in a romantic mood given the circumstances, they went anyway. After all, they needed to eat.

Conversation was muted during the meal. The restaurant was busy, and they did not want to discuss Patterson in such a crowded location, but now, as they strolled along the sidewalk back to their car, Bauer scratched his chin and finally brought the subject up.

"This Leo Galinsky thing is a hell of a mess," he said. "I'm not sure there's an easy way out of it."

"I hope you didn't say that to Patterson." Phoebe glanced his way and slipped her hand into his as they walked.

"Obviously, I didn't. But it still worries me. She found a truck that was tailing her the day before all this went down. Wanted me to run the plates."

"That would be risky. It would draw attention to us, and that would do no one any good."

"Exactly what I told her. No can do. I think she was expecting me to say as much. But here's the rub. The truck was parked in the Amarillo PD staff lot. It wasn't much of a leap for her to conclude that it belongs to Detective Sergeant Ortega."

"Which would put him square in the crosshairs as our lead suspect in framing her."

"And Mark Davis. Given what we know, this whole thing is starting to look like an elaborate stitch-up job."

"That would take some doing," Phoebe said. "How do you fake DNA evidence in a sexual assault like that?"

"Good question. But all of this began after Patterson visited Davis in jail and started snooping around the case. Someone wants her out of the way."

"I hate to play devil's advocate here, but there is another explanation."

"Patterson didn't execute Leo Galinsky. He wasn't even on her radar. And unless there's something I haven't been told, the man had no ties to Julie or her disappearance. Mark Davis was the reason she went to Amarillo."

"Hey, I'm just making sure we're on the same page here. I don't believe for one second Patterson would ever do such a thing, even if she thought Galinsky was the reason for her sister's disappearance. Vigilante revenge isn't exactly in her makeup. At least, from what I've seen of her."

"I agree," Bauer said. "But proving it is a different matter."

Phoebe was silent for a moment, lost in thought, then she said, "How's she holding up?"

"About as well as can be expected. It's getting her down. She tries not to show it, but I know she's scared, too."

"Who wouldn't be?"

"Right? It isn't stopping her from chasing whoever really killed Leo Galinsky and framed Mark Davis. After I told her I couldn't run the plates, she decided to stake out that parking lot and see who got in that truck."

"That's ballsy. It's a police lot."

"Which is why I'm worried. I hope she doesn't bring more trouble down upon herself."

"She'll be careful," Phoebe said. "It's Patterson Blake we're talking about. Look at everything she's done."

"That's what I keep telling myself. I promised to check in with her this evening."

"You should do that."

"I will. I'm just giving it some time. For all I know, she's decided to tail that truck. She's probably knee-deep in it as we speak."

"That sounds just like Patterson." Phoebe chuckled. They were almost at the car now. She looked up at him, her hazel eyes sparkling in the light from a streetlamp. "You should come back to my place tonight."

"I can't imagine I'd be very good company," Bauer replied. "What with this Patterson thing weighing on me and all."

"There's no need. Being there is enough."

Bauer stopped and turned to her. "In that case, I'd love to come back." He slipped an arm around her waist, pulled her close, and kissed her lightly on the lips.

She returned the kiss, then smiled. "Good. Because I have a crazy idea."

"Want to share?"

"No. Not quite yet." Then Phoebe turned and continued on toward the car, leaving Bauer to wonder what she had in mind.

THIRTY-FOUR

AT A LITTLE BEFORE ten o'clock that night, Patterson returned to the neighborhood where she had followed the red truck. She cruised by the road to make sure the vehicle was still sitting in the driveway. It hadn't moved. She kept going and found a place to park out of sight, then walked back to the road and sauntered casually past the driveway, studying the house from the corner of her eye. There were no streetlamps. The landscape behind the houses fell away into the gloom.

There was a light on at the downstairs front and another at the side behind the three-car garage. She couldn't see any cameras or security lights.

Turning and walking back in the other direction, Patterson veered across a swath of land that separated the red truck's home from the one next to it. She cut diagonally toward the lit window behind the garage, grateful for the cover of darkness. She wore dark pants and a black jacket, under which her Glock service weapon sat snug in its holster. The baseball cap was on her head, but the sunglasses were gone. She would have tripped and fallen flat on her face if she had tried to wear them now, even though she didn't like how exposed her face was.

Reaching the window, Patterson flattened herself against the wall. The blinds were pulled down, but there was a gap of about an inch at the bottom through which she could see a kitchen with a large island in the middle and, beyond that, a dining area with a round table. The room appeared to be empty.

She lingered a while, hoping the truck driver would come into view. When that didn't happen, she decided to circle around the front and try the other lit window. This was more of a risk. She would be exposed and visible if any of the neighbors across the street looked out. But then, just as she was about to move, a figure came into view carrying a mug and entering the kitchen.

Patterson recognized the face immediately from the photographs Bauer had sent earlier. It was Detective Sergeant Felix Ortega. She ducked back out of sight lest he glance toward the window and see her peering in. As she did so, a light snapped on above and to her right.

Patterson took a step back, realizing she was exposed, and glanced up to see a spotlight with a motion sensor mounted under the building's eave. She cursed under her breath, annoyed that she had not noticed the security light earlier.

She heard a door open at the rear of the house. Footsteps crunched on gravel. With nowhere else to go, Patterson sprinted across the slip of land between the detective's house and the one next door, reaching a fenced area at the back that hid a pair of garbage cans from view, and slipping behind it just as Ortega appeared. He stopped and gazed around, a rifle in his hands.

A woman came out behind him wearing what looked like a nightgown with a robe pulled around it. She was slim and attractive with long dark hair.

"What's going on?" she asked, her voice carrying on the warm evening breeze.

"Something tripped the security light," Ortega answered, studying the barren landscape that fell into the darkness behind the house. "Probably that coyote back to route through the garbage again."

"I thought you scared it off."

"I guess it came back." Ortega took another step forward as the light clicked back off. He was dangerously close to the fenced enclosure behind which Patterson was hiding. He turned to his wife. "Jennifer, go back inside. I'll be in momentarily."

The woman in the bathrobe hesitated, then retreated, disappearing from view.

Detective Sergeant Ortega walked toward the front of the house, and the truck parked in the driveway. He gazed in both directions before stepping back between the houses and casting one more glance across the flat and dusty landscape beyond.

Patterson wondered if he really believed the coyote had set off the light or if he suspected her presence. When he moved toward the back door and stepped inside, her shoulders slumped with relief.

She stayed hidden behind the fence a few minutes longer, wondering if the detective was gazing out his kitchen window, looking for movement. Then she crept along the back of the neighbor's house, praying that she wouldn't trip another security light, and turned back toward the road. Sprinting across, she ran between the houses opposite and circled back to her van, which was parked on the next street.

Climbing behind the wheel, Patterson sat for a moment, catching her breath. That had been a close call. If Ortega had wandered into the neighbor's yard, he would have seen her.

Starting the van, she pulled away from the curb and turned around, careful not to drive past the road upon which Ortega's house was situated. She made her way out of the neighborhood and back toward Amarillo, looking for somewhere safe and secluded to spend the night. She pulled in behind a building with boarded-up windows and a lease sign standing out front. Parking up out of sight from the road, she climbed into the back of the van and sat on the mattress with the pillows propped behind her head and the laptop open on her knees.

Using the mobile hotspot on her cell phone, she connected to the dead drop mail account and composed a message for Bauer, letting him know what she had found out, then saved it in the drafts folder. That done, she sat back, deep in thought. Detective Sergeant Felix Ortega had tailed her the afternoon before Leo Galinsky's murder which could only mean one thing. He was involved in the conspiracy to frame her, and maybe even the architect of it. The question was, for what purpose and how did all this tie in with Mark Davis and his missing accuser, Alexandria Rowley?

It also raised another chilling possibility. Given Ortega's prior involvement with Galinsky, he might be the actual murderer. Worse still, he was also the lead detective on the homicide investigation, which would make proving his involvement next to impossible.

THIRTY-FIVE

WHEN THEY GOT BACK to her place, Phoebe poured Bauer a drink—Scotch on the rocks—and told him to take a seat in the living room. She turned toward the back of the apartment and the spare bedroom she used as an office.

"Where are you going?" Bauer asked.

"I want to check on something," she said, glancing back toward him without stopping. "Make sure it's workable before I tell you what I have in mind."

"That sounds ominous. Should I be worried?"

"Just give me a minute, okay?" Phoebe disappeared into the bedroom office.

Bauer sat back on the sofa and asked Phoebe's Echo to play classic jazz. He put his feet up and sipped the whiskey as the melancholy strains of Earle Hagen's Harlem Nocturne filled the room. He closed his eyes and breathed deeply, waiting for Phoebe to come back and wondering what she was up to.

The track ended and another began. Bauer didn't recognize it. By the time a third number started playing, his drink was gone, and Bauer was getting sleepy. He put the glass down and took his phone out—the one with the California number—and tapped out a quick text to Patterson.

'Hey. You still in the land of the living, pardner?'

For a moment, nothing happened, then he saw the three animated dots under his message that meant she was typing back to him.

'Alive, well, and free. Truck belongs to Ortega.'

'Hope you didn't take any unnecessary risks,' Bauer replied, pecking at the small keyboard on his screen with one finger.

'What, me?' This was followed by a round yellow face emoticon graphic, the features scrunched in faux shock.

Bauer snorted and replied. 'Yes, you.'

The three dots appeared again.

'Did you have any luck getting those surveillance tapes from the bar?'

'Not yet,' Bauer typed. 'Called Amarillo RA and spoke to Rickett's PA this afternoon. Told her I was tying up loose ends on the cases you were working on. Asked her to forward them to me.'

'And?'

'She said PD had not sent them to her yet. Promised to prod them. Hopefully, I'll get the footage tomorrow.'

'Want to bet Ortega is stalling?'

'Good luck with that,' Bauer typed. 'It's an official request. Eventually, he will have to cough up.'

'Let's hope,' came the reply. 'Tough day. I'm tired. Going to bed now on my thin and uncomfortably short mattress. Call me in the morning?'

'Sure,' Bauer said. 'Sleep tight and stay safe.'

'You, too.'

Bauer waited a few seconds to see if any more texts would come through. When they didn't, he slipped the phone back into his pocket and stood to get another drink. As he did so, Phoebe returned, looking smug.

"Want to pour me one, too?" she said, eyeing his glass.

"On the rocks?" He asked.

Phoebe nodded.

"Want to tell me what you were up to?" Bauer poured the drinks and handed her one.

Phoebe went to the sofa and sat down, then motioned for Bauer to sit next to her. "I hate the thought of Patterson being all on her own up there and living in the back of a van."

"Me too," Bauer agreed. "But there's not much we can do about it."

"That's where you're wrong. I just booked her a place to stay about ten miles outside of the city. It's a house on two acres of land. Rural and private. She can go there tomorrow after three."

"What?" Bauer was about to take a sip of his drink. He paused, the glass near his lips. "That won't work. It will lead them straight to her."

"Relax. I'm not an idiot. I booked it under a false name . . . Sort of."

"Do I want to know?"

"I have a credit card in my grandmother's name. Use it to pay her bills and buy groceries. It also comes in handy when you want to make a reservation under someone else's name."

"Holy crap, Phoebe. You booked a house in your ninety-eight-year-old grandmother's name and used her money to do it?"

"I didn't use her money. I'm the one who pays the credit card bill every month. And yes, I used her name, which is why no one will track Patterson there."

"Except the owners, who are expecting your grandmother to show up."

"The owners are in Florida. It's an Airbnb. There's no one else at the house or anywhere close by. They have a keypad on the front door. They've already sent the code. The rental is valid for a week."

Bauer didn't know what to say. He just looked at her.

"What? She's living in a crappy van that probably smells like old socks. Where does she even pee?"

"I'm sure the van doesn't smell like old socks," Bauer said. "She's a woman. She probably bought an air freshener. As for the bathroom thing, I don't know, and I'm not asking."

"You're missing the point."

"No, I'm not," Bauer said, smiling. "You did good. I'm sure Patterson will appreciate a real bed and flushing toilet."

"Not just her." Phoebe gave Bauer a strange sideways glance. "It's Friday tomorrow. Since I'm just a lowly admin and you're on desk duty, we both have the weekend off. I figure we can get out of work early and go there to help her. You have the physiotherapy appointment tomorrow afternoon that you can cancel, and I'm sure I can take some vacation time. We might even be able to take a few days off next week. What do you say? The house has two bedrooms."

"You can't be serious."

"Why? She's all alone. After everything she did for my grandmother, not to mention when you got shot, don't we owe her that much?"

"Just stop and consider this for a minute, Phoebe. If we get caught, it's the end of our careers, and we might even get free accommodation for the next five to ten."

"Don't you think it's a bit late to worry about that?" Phoebe took a swig of her drink. "We're already helping her. I photographed confidential documents in my boss's office this morning and almost got caught doing it. You're communicating with a fugitive on a burner phone. Hell, you're the reason she isn't in custody right now, waiting to be arraigned for murder. And let's not forget—"

"Alright, you've made your point." Bauer knew when he was outmaneuvered. "We'll go to Amarillo."

"Yay." Phoebe leaned over and pecked him on the cheek. "I love you. Want to call Patterson and tell her right now?"

"How about we do it in the morning," Bauer said. "I have a feeling she's probably asleep already in her sock-scented van."

THIRTY-SIX

PATTERSON'S second night in the van was less comfortable than her first. The mattress, which hadn't seemed so bad the day before when she was exhausted and stressed, now felt more like she was sleeping directly on the hard floor. Adding to her discomfort was the fact that she could not quite stretch her legs out fully because the van was about a foot narrower than the mattress required. The interior of the van was muggy, too. She had run the regular AC whenever she was driving the previous day and had also let the roof-mounted unit run off the second battery for an hour before bed, but soon the Texas heat invaded her cramped sanctuary, and by morning the sheets were wet and stuck to her.

She rose early, unable to stand lying down anymore, and got dressed, then turned the roof-mounted AC on again for twenty minutes while she ate a peanut butter and jelly sandwich—which only reminded her of Julie—and pushed it down with a bottle of iced coffee. A shower would be nice since she had not washed in two days and felt gross, but it was out of the question. She had briefly entertained driving out to a truck stop on the highway and using the showers they provided for truckers, but the only place she knew of that had such conveniences was the same truck stop where she bought the van, and Patterson hesitated to return there. So instead, she used a lot of deodorant and ignored how uncomfortable she was.

She opened the laptop, connected to the mobile hotspot, and checked the dead drop mailbox. There were no new messages waiting in the drafts folder. But as she was about to climb into the driver's seat and move the van, her phone rang.

It was Bauer.

"Hey, you're calling early," she said, answering.

"I'm on my way into the office," Bauer replied. "How did you sleep last night?"

"How do you think I slept? I have a wicked crick in my back, and I can't stretch my legs out fully on the mattress. Not only that, but I smell like a hobo, and morning hair doesn't even begin to cover it."

"That good, huh?"

"Life on the run is no piece of cake." Patterson figured that if she ever got out of this situation, she would have a new appreciation for the lengths to which people went to evade the law. Not that she was going to stop pursuing them, of course.

Bauer chuckled. "I might have a solution for that."

"I'm not turning myself in, if that's what you're about to suggest."

"Nothing of the sort. Phoebe had an idea last night, and it's actually pretty good. She rented you a house outside of Amarillo. Somewhere safe that can't be tracked back to any of us. Everything is arranged. You can go there after three this afternoon. There's a keypad on the door. I posted the address and the door code in the dead drop."

"Are you serious?" Patterson almost whooped for joy but

managed to restrain herself. "I can actually take a shower and use a real toilet?"

"You can do both of those things and get a good night's sleep to boot."

"Thank heavens. You don't want to know how I took care of business the last few days."

"I absolutely do not, so please don't tell me." Bauer laughed again.

"God bless Phoebe. How did she manage it?"

Bauer filled her in on the details, including how she had booked it in her grandmother's name using the old woman's credit card. "No one will ever know you're there. It sits on two acres of land, which means no one will see you coming and going."

"I can't believe this." Patterson was tearing up. "I still have some of my cash left. When this is all over, I'll pay her back, I promise. Every cent. And please tell her how much I appreciate everything she's done."

"Let's worry about the money when the time comes. We have more important things to take care of. And you can thank her in person this evening. I'm finishing work at noon and then we're heading your way."

"Wait, what?" Patterson could hardly believe what she was hearing. "You mean you're coming to Amarillo?"

"That's exactly what I mean. I was already scheduled for a physiotherapy appointment this afternoon and wasn't going to be at work, anyway. I'll just skip it. Phoebe hasn't taken any time off in a year, so she's sure the ASAC will give her half a day. The house has two bedrooms, so we'll take one and you can take the other."

"You haven't forgotten that I'm wanted for murder, right?" Patterson would love nothing better than to see Bauer and Phoebe right now, but she also worried they were getting in too deep. If you get caught with me, it won't turn out well for either of you."

"Then we'll have to make sure we don't get caught. Any of us. We're coming, and that's all there is to it. You need all the help you can get."

"I'd love to argue," Patterson said. "But I won't because you're right."

"Aren't I always?"

"You really want to go there?" Now it was Patterson's turn to laugh.

"Maybe not." Bauer drew in a long breath. "Look, seriously; we're going to get you out of this."

"I'm not so sure, but thank you." Patterson had seen the evidence, and whoever framed her knew what they were doing. Not that it took much of a leap to figure out who that was. The owner of the red truck. Detective Sergeant Ortega. Even if he wasn't the ringleader, he was in it up to his neck. Of that, she was sure. Who else would be able to plant such damning evidence and make sure it wasn't questioned? After all, he was also the lead detective for the murder she was accused of committing. "Listen, watch your backs when you leave to come here. Who knows if the people that framed me are keeping tabs on you and Phoebe, too."

"I already thought of that," Bauer replied. "I can't imagine we're being physically surveilled twenty-four hours, but I agree that someone might be watching our movements in case you contact either of us. I have a plan to throw any would-be surveillance off our trail."

"Good. I can't wait to see you both." Patterson's mood, although still dark, was lighter than it had been in days. "Send me the details of that house, and I'll be there waiting when you arrive."

"Already done it. Check the dead drop again, and it should be there now."

Patterson breathed a sigh of relief. She thanked Bauer again, then hung up. When she checked the email account, there was a new draft message waiting for her with the address and front door code. Now all she had to do was lie low and occupy herself until she could go there.

THIRTY-SEVEN

BAUER WAS in his office when Phoebe came to find him at noon. She strode in with a determined look on her face. He had already arranged to take the following week off, saying his shoulder was bothering him more than he expected. HR was fine with that, since he had returned to work without taking the two weeks recuperation time the doctor had recommended when he was discharged from the hospital.

"All set. Muir was more than happy to give me the afternoon off and a couple of days next week. I told him I was going out of town for a romantic weekend with my boyfriend."

Bauer stood up and crossed the room. He kissed Phoebe quickly, then pulled back. "It's kind of true. He just doesn't know that I'm your boyfriend."

"If he does, he hasn't mentioned it," Phoebe said. "Not that we're doing anything wrong. I'm allowed to date an agent if I want to."

"I know. Let's keep it on the down low right now, though. Best if we don't draw too much attention to ourselves." Bauer grabbed his jacket and followed Phoebe out into the corridor.

They made their way down to the parking lot without

talking, but then Phoebe grabbed Bauer's arm as he was about to open his car door. "You should park up at home. I'll follow you in my car, and then we can head out together."

"Good idea," Bauer said. He climbed in and waited for Phoebe to reach her own car before pulling out of the parking lot.

Fifteen minutes later, they arrived at his apartment complex. He parked in a covered bay, grabbed the bag he'd packed that morning from his trunk, and joined her, slipping into the passenger seat of her dark blue Civic.

"All set?" Phoebe asked, making her way back toward the exit.

"Sure. You're taking 287, right?" Bauer asked as Phoebe merged onto State Highway 183 and joined the express lane traveling west.

"It's the quickest way."

"Good." Bauer glanced in the passenger side mirror, watching the traffic behind them.

"Worried we're being followed?" Phoebe asked, noticing.

"Just being cautious. I don't think anyone is on to us, but it never hurts to make sure." He scanned the heavy traffic, looking for any vehicles that looked like feds. He didn't see any. When Phoebe changed lanes and moved around a minivan with kid stickers all over the back that had slowed for no reason, then slipped back over in front of it, he noticed no other vehicles repeat the maneuver.

"Why were you asking about our route?"

"What?" Bauer was still watching the traffic at their rear. He tore his eyes away and glanced toward her.

"Is there a reason you want to know which road I'm taking?"

"Actually, there is. We need to go through Wichita Falls. When you get there, take Speedway Avenue."

"Why?"

"I thought it would be prudent to have an alibi, just in case things go south. I booked us four nights at a boutique hotel. Their website said it's great for romantic getaways."

"Sounds lovely and all, but we're supposed to be helping Patterson, remember?"

"We're not actually staying there. I figured we could stop by and check-in. After that, we'll head on up to Amarillo."

"Ah. And what about when we need to check out?"

"Not a problem. I'll go up and leave the keys in the room. That way I can check out through their app. It will look like we were there the entire time."

"Except no one will have seen us."

"Maybe we didn't leave the hotel room all weekend," said Bauer with a mischievous grin. "Probably didn't even get out of bed."

"You wish." Phoebe snorted and turned her attention back to driving. They continued through the city and finally reached 287. After that, they drove for the next hour and a half in near silence, with only a few sporadic bursts of light conversation. Bauer didn't know what consumed Phoebe, but he was already thinking about how to proceed once they reached Patterson in Amarillo.

After a quick detour in Wichita Falls, during which Bauer checked them into the hotel and made a show of going up to the room before coming back down and exiting through a side door to meet Phoebe, their trip Northwest resumed.

As they drove back through the city to rejoin 287, Bauer checked his official FBI email account from his cell phone. If anyone checked the phone and which towers it was pinging off, they would see that he was actually in Wichita Falls. But digital crumbs were not the only reason he had logged on. The admin assistant who worked at the Amarillo Resident Agency had promised to send over the surveillance videos from the bar Mark Davis had visited the night before his arrest. Amarillo PD had been slow-walking the request but had eventually come through. The video files were waiting in his inbox. He didn't dare forward the email to the dead drop account, so he sent the videos to his personal email—there was nothing confidential about them—then turned off the phone.

Switching to the burner phone, he accessed his personal email and downloaded the videos, then attached them to a draft message in the dead drop. This was, he hoped, enough obfuscation to deceive anyone who wished to check up on him. That done, he turned off his personal phone as well and put both phones in Phoebe's glove compartment.

She glanced sideways at him. "Everything okay?"

"Golden," Bauer replied. He was eager to look at the videos, but that would have to wait until they reached Amarillo and the rental house, where they could look at them on the clean laptop that Patterson had purchased. Besides, there was something more immediate on Bauer's mind. They were coming up to a grocery store on the left near the highway. He pointed. "Pull in there. Let's go shopping before we hit the road again. I'm sure there won't be any provisions at the rental house, and I'd rather not shop in Amarillo if I can help it."

Phoebe nodded, put her blinker on, and turned into the grocery store's parking lot. Forty-five minutes later, their trunk now full of enough provisions to last at least a week and probably longer, they pointed the car northwest and left Wichita Falls in their rearview mirror.

THIRTY-EIGHT

PATTERSON ARRIVED at the rental house on the dot of three. It was exactly as Bauer had described, sitting on a large plot of land several miles south of the city and remote enough that no one would notice her coming and going. Even so, she stopped on the road and observed the property for a few moments to make sure nobody was around. Bauer had said the owners lived in Florida, but she didn't want any surprises.

After deciding it was safe, Patterson turned onto the driveway—which was actually just a winding dirt trail bordered by thorny bushes—and drove up to the house. There was a large empty barn at the home's rear standing with its doors open, and she decided to park the van there, where it wouldn't be spotted from the road. She pulled around and stopped, then made her way back around to the front on foot, leaving her possessions behind for now.

The house was a one-story ranch with a wraparound porch. There were four rocking chairs positioned to overlook the parched landscape. It wasn't much to look at now, but she imagined that the view must be stunning come sunset since the porch faced west.

She took out her burner phone and checked the door code, then typed it in. Once inside, she checked out all the rooms. The layout flowed from the front with an eat-in kitchen and living room, complete with a stone hearth, to the bedrooms and bathroom at the rear.

Satisfied that all was in order, Patterson returned to the van and grabbed her belongings, including a bottle of copper-colored hair dye she had stopped and bought at a drugstore on the way there. She hauled everything inside, depositing everything in the smaller of the two bedrooms, which still contained a queen-size bed. More than enough for her needs.

That done, she made a more thorough investigation of the property. The bathroom had a wide walk-in shower clad in natural stone. It looked so inviting that she almost stripped off right there and jumped in. Next to that was the other bedroom with a king-size bed. The living room was tastefully furnished with a leather sofa and two chairs. A woven rug covered the plank floor, its bright Midwest colors adding a pop of contrast to the space. A flat-screen TV was mounted on the wall next to the hearth.

Compared to the hot and cramped van, this was the lap of luxury. She hurried back to the bedroom and undressed then made her way to the shower and stood under the hot water for a good twenty minutes, washing away the grime of two days on the road. She wanted to dye her hair, but it felt like too much work right at that moment, so she decided to do it later.

Afterward, she returned to the bedroom and pulled the covers back, then slipped beneath them without bothering to find her PJs. Phoebe and Bauer wouldn't get there for at least another couple of hours, and she could barely keep her eyes open. The sheets were crisp and cool on her body. Best of all, the mattress was soft, and she could stretch her legs all the way out. Relieved to be safe and comfortable for the first time since her ordeal began, Patterson fell into a deep and dreamless sleep.

———

Patterson woke up two and half hours later to the sound of a car pulling outside the house. She jumped out of bed and dressed quickly, rushing to the front, and peering through the curtains. She recognized the dark blue Honda Civic sitting in front of the house as Phoebe's and breathed a sigh of relief.

When she opened the door, Bauer wrapped his arms around her before even saying a word. Then, sheepishly, he withdrew.

"Sorry about that," he said. "Probably overstepped my bounds a little there."

"You did no such thing," Patterson replied, putting her arms around him in a quick embrace before turning to Phoebe who was standing at his rear. "I'm sorry you got dragged into this."

"Wouldn't have it any other way." Phoebe glanced back toward the car. "You want to help us unload?"

"How much luggage did you bring?" Patterson followed them back down the steps to the car. "I thought you were only staying a few days."

Phoebe opened the trunk to reveal at least ten plastic bags stuffed to the brim. "Not luggage. Groceries."

"We stopped on the way here and bought enough to keep a small army going for a month." Bauer grabbed a couple of bags and started back toward the house. "We figured you haven't had a decent meal since you left Dallas."

"All I've eaten for two days are tuna or PB&J sandwiches. I'll be happy with whatever you have. Believe me." Patterson was overcome with gratitude at the sight of all those bags brimming with food.

Once the groceries were inside and deposited on the kitchen counter, Phoebe busied herself putting stuff away while Bauer made one more trip to the car. He reached in and grabbed a brown paper bag and a tray with three drinks in cardboard cups. He slammed the door with his leg and carried it all into the house.

"Hope you're hungry," he said to Patterson, putting the bag down on the table and pulling silver trays with cardboard tops out.

"I'm starving. Is that what I think it is?" she asked, eyeing the takeout containers.

"That depends if you think it's ribs, mashed potatoes, baked beans, and cornbread." Bauer pulled the top off a container.

A meaty aroma filled the air.

Patterson's mouth watered. "That looks so good. I can't believe you stopped and got all this."

"It's quicker than cooking," Phoebe said, carrying three paper plates and cutlery to the table.

"Don't be shy. Dig in," Bauer said, pulling the drinks from the tray and distributing them.

Patterson didn't need to be told twice. She took a plate, loaded it with food, and sat down at the table. It took all her willpower to wait for the others to fix their own plates and join her, then she chowed down with gusto.

THIRTY-NINE

WITH DINNER over and their stomachs full, they made their way to the living room, where Bauer announced they should talk strategy. The group only had the weekend together before Bauer and Phoebe would depart and head back to Dallas. It was vital they waste no time in figuring out how to clear Patterson's name.

"We're not going to prove Patterson is innocent by focusing on Leo Galinsky's murder," Bauer said. "We need to discover the reason someone wants to frame her and work back from there."

"Mark Davis is the key," Patterson said. "I'm sure of it."

"It makes the most sense," Bauer agreed. "And it all started with Alexandria Rowley. That's where we start."

"How?" Phoebe asked. "Hasn't Rowley dropped off the face of the earth?"

"Which I find suspicious in itself." Bauer sat back on the sofa and folded his arms.

"The woman at the women's shelter said that she's disappeared before and always comes back," Patterson said. "It's entirely possible that she just found the situation overwhelming and walked away. For all we know she will reappear in time for the trial."

"Or whoever framed Mark Davis wanted to make sure that she wouldn't grow a conscience and say the wrong thing. The question is, why would someone want to frame him?"

"I wondered the same thing," Patterson said. "I've looked at this every which way, but I can't find anything in his life that would make him a target of such a complicated plot. He's just an average guy running a small business. He does environmental ground testing, for Pete's sake. His home life is similarly pedestrian. He has a nice little suburban house, a wife who obviously loves him, and a little boy. The wildest he ever gets is stopping by the bar every Friday evening because his wife has a girls' night out. That's it. He's hardly the kind of guy someone would want to get out of the way."

"And yet he either turned from a family man into a vicious rapist pretty much overnight, or that's exactly what someone wanted to do." Bauer rubbed his chin thoughtfully. "If only we could find Alexandria Rowley. I could get her to tell the truth about what happened that night, guaranteed."

"I don't think that's going to happen."

"I agree. She was working the night she disappeared, right?"

"Yes. She pulled the night shift at some convenience store."

"I bet they have the inside of that store covered by cameras. It would be interesting to see what her demeanor was right before she went missing, don't you think?"

"Sure," Patterson agreed. "But we're never going to get those tapes. It's not like we can get a warrant or anything and the police aren't even investigating her disappearance, so I'm sure they haven't pulled the tapes. Everyone seems to think she just went walkabout and will miraculously show up at some point in the future."

"Because she's done so before."

"Yes. But this is different. I can feel it in my gut."

"Which is why we need to see the footage from her last night at work," Bauer said. "And I think I know how to get it."

"How?" Patterson wasn't convinced. When she had asked to search Rowley's room at the women's shelter, the employee she was speaking to had given her an emphatic no. Patterson couldn't imagine the convenience store staff were going to be any more helpful without a piece of paper carrying a judge's signature forcing them to comply.

"The place is open twenty-four seven, correct?"

"Yes." Patterson nodded.

Bauer glanced at his watch. "It's almost eight o'clock. I'll give it a couple of hours, then go over there. It should be pretty quiet that late at night, and I'll bet they'll only have one staff member working and no manager present. I'll just pretend I'm with the local PD following up on Rowley's disappearance and browbeat them into giving me the footage."

"They'll say no and call their manager, who will just back them up," Phoebe said.

"I'm betting that they won't. Did you ever have a dead-end job when you were younger?"

"Sure. Who hasn't?"

"And would you want to phone your manager and get them out of bed at midnight?"

"I don't know. Maybe."

"You wouldn't," Bauer said. "Because I'm going to tell that employee that we already have permission to make a copy of the footage and subtly remind them how annoyed their boss will be if they disturb him so late at night for something they should be able to handle on their own."

"In other words, you're going to bully some poor employee who might end up losing their job."

Bauer shook his head. "They won't lose their job because they probably won't even mention it to their boss. And even if they do, the manager won't want the negative publicity of firing someone for helping a missing persons investigation centered on their own employee. It will work. I'm sure of it."

"Sounds like you've done this kind of thing before," Patterson said.

"When I was a cop in LA, I sometimes had to get creative," Bauer said. "Especially with some of the less salubrious types. Of course, the evidence won't hold up in court because it wasn't legally obtained, but that's not what we're after. We just need to know Alexandria Rowley's state of mind prior to her disappearance and if there's anything suspicious on that footage."

"Let's hope this doesn't backfire on us if we do actually need to use any of this is evidence in court," Patterson said. "My defense might rely on it."

"You won't need a defense because we're going to clear your name without a trial. That's why we're here."

"Great. In that case, have at it because I don't particularly like being on the run."

"That's the plan. Speaking of which, we have one set of footage to review, at least. Amarillo PD finally sent the file from the bar over. It's waiting in the dead drop mailbox as we speak."

"Then why are we sitting here?" Patterson said, jumping up. "Let's go look at it."

FORTY

PATTERSON FETCHED her laptop and opened the dead drop email account. She found the draft message left by Bauer. There were two files attached. One was labeled as the bar interior feed, and the other was for the parking lot. Patterson downloaded both to her hard drive and clicked the interior footage.

The file covered a period spanning noon to midnight. Patterson cued it to a point just before Mark Davis had claimed to enter the bar and hit play.

Bauer and Phoebe leaned in, watching the screen with intense concentration. First, there was no sign of Davis, but then he entered and made his way straight to the bar, climbing up on the stool. He ordered a drink and sat there alone for around twenty minutes. Then a dark-haired woman wearing jeans and a crop top entered and hopped up onto a stool nearby. She looked around, glancing briefly at Davis before turning her attention to the bartender and ordering a drink.

"That must be Alexandria Rowley," Bauer said, narrowing his eyes.

"She looked at Mark Davis the moment she came in," Patterson said.

"I noticed that."

"She might have been checking out her surroundings," Phoebe said. "She is a single gal in a bar, after all."

"Or she might have been looking for her target," Bauer replied. "Assuming she was in on a conspiracy to frame Mark Davis."

"She's getting up." Patterson pointed at the screen.

The woman they assumed was Rowley had slid off her stool and was approaching Davis. She sidled up to him with head slightly cocked, and spoke, her lips moving silently because the feed had no sound.

At first, Davis looked startled, but soon the two had settled into a casual conversation. Another round of drinks appeared, then another. Eventually, Davis slid off his stool and disappeared out of the camera's field of view, heading in the opposite direction to the front door.

"Bathroom break?" Bauer surmised.

"Maybe." Patterson was watching the footage intently now. So far there had been no sign of impropriety, but Rowley was now alone, and the bartender was all the way down the other end of the bar with his back turned. There were only a few other customers, and no one was paying any attention to the young woman in the crop top.

And then it happened.

Rowley glanced around quickly and then slipped her hand into her pocket. She leaned sideways toward the stool Mark Davis had been sitting on. Her hand passed quickly over his drink and then she settled back onto her own stool.

"What was going on there?" Bauer asked, leaning closer to the screen. "Roll it back a few seconds. I want to see that again."

Patterson obliged, pulling the progress slider back to the point right after Mark Davis had left for the restroom.

She hit play.

The footage started up again.

"Can you play at half speed?" Bauer asked.

"I don't think so." Patterson studied the media player but didn't see any way to slow the footage.

Bauer didn't answer. He studied the footage with a frown, then said, "Let me see it again."

"You think she spiked his drink?" Phoebe asked.

"Not sure yet," he replied. But then, on the third pass, he slapped the coffee table with his palm. "Scratch that. She did something there, I'm sure of it."

Patterson tutted with frustration. "The video's too grainy to see exactly what she's up to."

"Let it run, and we'll see what happens next," Bauer said.

Patterson took her finger off the laptop's trackpad and leaned back so that all three had a clear view of the screen again.

Thirty seconds later, Mark Davis stepped back into the frame and sat down next to the woman again. They carried on talking for another fifteen minutes until their drinks were empty. Then she leaned close, her hand falling on his leg, and spoke in his ear. Davis nodded and slid from the stool, then waited for the young woman to join him. He swayed for a moment, shaking his head as if trying to clear it. The young woman reached a hand to steady herself on the bar, then slipped her arm around Davis's waist. Together, they stumbled toward the exit.

"Dang. I can't tell which one of them is holding the other up," Bauer said.

"Alexandria Rowley looked fine when she got off the stool," Patterson replied. She rewound the footage to that point and played it again. "See how she's walking? Much better than

Davis. Then she puts an arm out and steadies herself almost like an afterthought."

"Like she knows the camera is there and suddenly remembers to act inebriated."

"Right." Patterson watched a second time as Davis stumbled toward the door with Rowley's arm around his waist. "I don't think that Davis is faking. He can barely stand."

"On three drinks," Phoebe said. "And he was drinking lite beer. You can see the bartender pour it on the footage."

"Something is off with this." Bauer shook his head. "I bet that Rowley roofied him. That's why he remembers nothing after leaving the bar until the next morning."

"So why didn't Amarillo PD notice that?" Phoebe asked. "They must have reviewed the footage."

"Because they're not looking for it. The Special Victims Unit has all the evidence they need." Patterson paused the footage. "And let's not forget, Detective Sergeant Ortega has his mitts all over it. He was the first responder when Rowley went to the hospital and reported the rape."

"Which is mighty convenient," Bauer added. "He just happened to be right around the corner following up on a lead at almost midnight, even though his shift ended hours earlier. I checked."

"Maybe he just wanted to pull a boatload of overtime."

"Or maybe the whole thing was planned."

"That's what I'm going with," Patterson said, cueing up the second video—the one from the back parking lot—to a time frame that coincided with Davis and Rowley leaving the bar.

They huddled around the laptop, watching the dark and grainy footage.

"It's so murky I can't make out a damn thing," Bauer said as a pair of figures barely distinguishable from the background climbed into Mark Davis's car. Even when the car's dome light came on briefly, they couldn't see anything. It was almost like the camera's lens was obscured by dirt or some other substance. "I don't know which of them is in the driver's seat."

"Given his condition on the way out of the bar, I can't imagine it was Davis," Patterson said, wondering if the camera had been tampered with at some earlier point. "I doubt he could stay awake long enough to start the car."

"Either way, we'll never know from this," Bauer said as the car inched forward and drove slowly out of the camera's field of view.

"That's a shame, but it doesn't alter my opinion. Rowley slipped something into that drink when Davis went to the restroom. I'm sure of it," Bauer said.

"Maybe our digital crime lab in Dallas can enhance the video," Phoebe said. "We might be able to get a better look at the driver."

"I'm not sure they could do anything," Bauer said. "And good luck convincing them to try if Amarillo PD doesn't make a request, which I guarantee they won't."

"I think we need to talk to Davis again," Patterson said, aware of how difficult that would be under the circumstances.

"How?" Bauer asked.

Phoebe drew in a quick breath. "Easy. That prison has a public visitors building off-site from the main facility where you can talk to an inmate via a monitor. I checked it out last night while I was waiting for the reservation to be approved for this place. Figured we might need to see him. All I need to do is make an appointment for tomorrow morning. I'll say I'm his cousin from out of town."

"They'll never believe you," Patterson said.

"Yes they will," Phoebe replied. "They don't do any background checks."

"Absolutely not," Bauer said. "It's too dangerous, as Patterson already found out. And besides, they might not check your background, but I bet they record every second of your conversation."

"Well, we need to speak with him," Phoebe replied. "Have you got a better idea?"

Bauer fell silent.

"That's what I thought." Phoebe gave a satisfied grunt and reached for the laptop. "I'll make the appointment right now, and if you're going to visit that convenience store, you'd better do it."

"Right." Bauer climbed to his feet and made for the door. "Sit tight, you two. I'll be back soon."

Then he scooped up Phoebe's car keys and stepped out into the night.

FORTY-ONE

MACKEY'S DISCOUNT MART was a squat and unattractive one-story building that sat on the edge of Amarillo's downtown. It looked about as welcoming as the name suggested, with paint peeling from the exterior stucco and windows crammed with posters advertising sales on soft drinks, cigarettes, and beer. The lettering on the façade above the entrance was lit except for the D of discount, which flickered in rapid bursts. A parking lot in front of the building had enough spaces for six cars. Five spaces were empty, but Bauer hadn't parked there. He wanted to keep a low profile and had parked a block away on a side street.

It was a little after eleven as he crossed the parking lot and pulled the door open. There were only a couple of customers inside strolling the aisles. He crossed to a row of coolers occupying the far wall and pretended to peruse the wares inside, waiting for them to make their purchases and leave. After ten minutes of studying the various beers on offer behind the cooler's glass doors—mostly bulk standard domestic brands sold in six and twelve-packs—the last of the two customers approached the counter with a couple of family-sized bags of chips and a twelve pack of soda, purchased them, and left.

Bauer waited a minute longer to make sure no other customers would enter, then left the cooler and turned toward the clerk, a waif-thin woman in her late twenties with old acne scars on her face and a name badge attached to her blue uniform waistcoat that read Brittany.

At his approach, she looked up from her phone screen, which she had been tapping away on with long purple painted fingernails filed to points.

"Can I help you?" she asked, not bothering to hide the piece of gum she was chewing.

"I certainly hope so," Bauer replied, pulling his jacket aside and flashing the FBI shield he'd hung on his belt in a movement fast enough that she would not be able to identify the agency.

"You're a cop?" Her eyes widened.

"I'm here about Alexandria Rowley," he said without confirming or denying her statement. "Do you know her?"

"Yeah. I know her. Haven't seen her for a while. She quit or something. Didn't show up for work. Boss was mad. He had to find someone to cover her shift at the last minute."

"She's missing and might be in trouble," Bauer said. He let this sink in before continuing. He glanced up at her camera mounted on the ceiling. "I need to see the security footage for the last night she was working."

"Does this have something to do with what happened to her?"

"What do you think happened?" Bauer asked.

"Wasn't she assaulted outside of some bar?" Brittany removed the chewing gum, pushed it back into its wrapper, and threw it in the trash. "I figured that's why she stopped coming to work. She was, like, traumatized or something. I hadn't heard anything about her going missing."

"Now you have." Bauer leaned on the counter. "The

security footage?"

"You'll have to come back when Denny's here. He's the manager. He'll be able to get it for you. I know nothing about that stuff. Don't have anything to do with it."

"If you can just point me in the direction of the recording system, I can do the rest."

"I don't know. It's in the stockroom and I'm not supposed to let anyone back there, let alone play with the surveillance system."

"I'll only be a few minutes. You can stand there and watch if you feel the need, but I need the surveillance from the last night that Alexandria Rowley was working here." Bauer upped the pressure. "It could be a matter of life or death, and I don't have time to wait."

Brittany bit her bottom lip. "Maybe I should call Denny and ask him."

"You really want to wake your boss this time of night?" Bauer replied. "I can't imagine he'd be thrilled. Especially since we've already filed all the paperwork and gotten approval from the store owner."

"You have?"

"Why do you think I'm here?" Bauer leaned forward. "Look, Brittany, I'm sure you care about what happens to your coworkers, right?"

"Sure. Course I do. I liked Lexie. She'd gone through some hard times, but she was doing her best to get out of a bad situation."

"Then let me help her. It's very important. I need to know what happened last night she was working."

For a moment, Bauer thought Brittany was going to offer more resistance, but then she nodded. "I suppose. But I need to watch you in there, make sure nothing happens."

"That's fine by me." Bauer glanced around. "Where's the stockroom?"

"It's here." Brittany motioned for Bauer to step behind the counter. There was an unmarked door in the back wall, surrounded by shelves containing all manner of items, from cigarettes and vape pens to supplements and bottles of liquor. She opened the door and stepped aside for him to enter.

The room beyond was small with crammed shelves loaded with boxes. There was a desk in one corner upon which sat the surveillance system, which was essentially a server that stored the recorded video connected to a workstation.

Bauer sat in front of it and tapped the keyboard. The screen sprung to life and asked for a username and password, which were handily written on a piece of paper taped to the workstation's tower.

"Some great security you have here," Bauer said, entering the credentials.

"Hey, nothing to do with me." Brittany glanced over her shoulder back toward the store to make sure there were no customers. "Is this going to take long?"

"Hopefully not." Bauer studied the system's software for a moment. It all seemed pretty straightforward. He typed the date he was looking for into a search bar and soon had a list of recordings. They were saved in four-hour increments. Removing a thumb drive from his pocket, he inserted it into a USB port on the front of the workstation, then copied the two surveillance files for the date and time of Alexandria Rowley's last shift—four until midnight—and also added the first file for the early hours of the next morning, just for good measure. He waited a couple of minutes while they transferred, then withdrew the thumb drive.

He stood up. "All done."

Brittany nodded. "What do you think happened to her?"

"I don't know," Bauer said. He pushed the thumb drive into his pocket and stepped back out into the store and around the counter. "That's what I'm hoping to find out."

FORTY-TWO

SPECIAL AGENT MARCUS BAUER arrived back at the rental house around midnight with the thumb drive in his pocket. When he entered, Patterson and Phoebe were still in the living room, perched on the leather couch and hunched over the laptop.

At the sound of the front door closing, Phoebe glanced up. "How did it go?"

"Good." Bauer plucked the thumb drive from his pocket and held it up between finger and thumb.

"In other words, you terrorized some poor minimum-wage employee."

"Terrorized is a little harsh. I prefer to think that I persuaded them." Bauer entered the living room. "What are you two doing?"

"I just made an appointment to see Mark Davis tomorrow," Phoebe replied. "Or, more accurately, to visit the Potter County correctional Facility's visitor center and talk to him via a monitor and telephone handset. He might wonder why he's being visited by his long-lost cousin, Phoebe—who he's never heard of before—but hopefully, he'll be smart enough to go along with it and not ask too many questions."

"It's still a risk," Bauer said. "They might not do a background check, but I bet they'll want to see your ID before they let you in."

"Which is why I had to use my real name. Luckily, I'm a nobody and probably won't raise any red flags with whoever is orchestrating this whole thing."

"I don't like it."

"That's what I said." Patterson glanced up from the computer screen. "But I don't see an alternative. Mark Davis might be able to provide information that will tell us what this is all about, even if he doesn't realize it." Patterson's gaze shifted to the thumb drive. "Want to take a look at that footage?"

"It's late, and there's twelve hours of video on here. We start going through this now, will never go to bed."

"We don't have to watch the whole thing. I'll settle for the last few hours before Rowley left work."

"We also downloaded a new media player that will let us review the file up to 4X speed," said Phoebe. "How about we give it an hour and then hit the sack."

Bauer nodded and took a seat on the couch next to the women. He handed the thumb drive to Patterson, who inserted it into the laptop's USB port and clicked on a file.

"Rowley finished work at midnight, so we'll start with the file covering the last half of her shift from eight to twelve," Patterson said. "After that, we can play the first few minutes of the early morning file, which should show her leaving work." She hit play and then tapped the speed selector all the way up to 4X. "This will move fast, so we'd better pay attention."

"We have three sets of eyes on it, so we should be fine," Bauer replied. "If anyone notices anything unusual, just holler."

Neither woman replied. Their eyes were glued to the laptop

screen. The footage rolled by at a clip, but for the first three hours showed nothing out of the ordinary. Customers wandered in, picked up the usual convenience store fare such as chips, soda, and beer, then left again.

At one point, a man wearing a hoodie pulled over his head wandered into the store, his face shielded from the camera. Patterson stiffened, thinking they might have found what they were looking for, but the guy approached the counter, bought a pack of cigarettes, and left again. But as the hoodie-wearing customer stepped outside, another figure weaved around him and entered the store, glancing briefly up at the camera before quickly dropping his gaze. Patterson's hand flew to the keyboard. She rewound the footage a few seconds and paused the video while the man's face was still slightly upturned and visible under the store's bright neon lights.

"I don't believe it," she said, reaching for the police file on Leo Galinsky's murder. She slipped out a sheet of paper containing a mug shot taken a couple of years before his death and held it up next to the screen. "Look familiar?"

Phoebe drew in a sharp breath. "It's Galinsky."

"This just got a whole lot more interesting." Bauer leaned forward. "Hit play. Normal speed."

Patterson let the footage roll forward again. Galinsky wandered the store for a minute, grabbing a magazine from a rack before approaching the counter. To Patterson, it looked like he was casing the place to make sure they were alone. He also kept his head bent forward to obscure his face from the camera, aware it was there. He dropped the magazine on the counter and spoke to Alexandria Rowley. Her face was not visible because she was standing with her back to the camera, but even so, Patterson could tell she was nervous. The young woman took a step back, her shoulders hunching.

Leo Galinsky placed his hands on the counter, palms down, and leaned forward. His face twisted into a grimace. He said something to Rowley. She shook her head back and forth in denial and raised her hands.

Galinsky spoke again, his lips moving silently on the soundless video.

Rowley took another step away from him. Her back contacted the shelves behind the counter, dislodging a couple of packs of cigarettes, which she ignored.

Bauer narrowed his eyes. "Does it look like he's threatening her?"

"Maybe. Hard to tell without audio," said Patterson. "It's not a pleasant conversation, judging by her reaction."

Galinsky took a step back. He tapped the counter twice with one finger, then raised and pointed it at Rowley as he spoke again. Then he turned on his heel and strode toward the door, yanking it open and stepping out into the night. If there was any doubt before, there wasn't now. Galinsky was either threatening or warning Rowley.

They let the footage play a while longer. Rowley appeared flustered. She paced back and forth behind the counter. At one point she reached for a phone and lifted the receiver, but then set it back down again without calling anyone.

"She's scared," Phoebe said.

"Certainly seems that way," Bauer agreed.

"And then she leaves work and is never seen again."

She sped the tape to 4X speed again, but Galinsky didn't return, and Rowley only served two more customers. Then, just before the file cut out, another girl entered wearing a similar uniform to Rowley, presumably arriving to take the next shift.

The file went dark and ended.

Patterson played the second video from the beginning. It picked up as the new arrival went into a room behind the counter. She emerged a few moments later, minus her coat. Rowley gathered her purse and phone, conversed briefly with her coworker, and then walked to the door. She opened it and stopped, looking around briefly as if checking her surroundings, then stepped outside. The door closed behind her, and she was gone.

Patterson ran the tape for another five minutes to make sure that Rowley did not come back for any reason, then paused it. "If the police had bothered to pull this footage and look at it, they would surely have had questions."

"The woman who Mark Davis is supposed to have raped interacting with the man you're accused of killing," Bauer said. "And it didn't look like that exchange was friendly. A warning to keep her mouth shut, maybe?"

"I wonder how she responded," Patterson said, looking at the frozen image on the screen. "Given that no one has seen her since she stepped through those doors after her shift ended."

"Good question. It will be interesting to see what Mark Davis has to say tomorrow. All of this started because he must have gotten too close to something he shouldn't have."

"Or he inadvertently got in the way of it," Bauer said.

"Then we're all on the same page that Mark Davis is not a rapist?" Patterson asked.

"I think we can safely say he was framed, just like you."

"I agree," said Phoebe. "And since his home life is so squeaky clean, I'll bet it's tied to his company and what he does there."

Bauer yawned. "It's one-thirty in the morning. I'd say it's been a productive day, but I'm wiped out. Let's hit the sack and pick this up tomorrow."

Patterson didn't need any urging. Since Bauer had arrived back from the convenience store, she had been longing for the comfortable bed that waited for her. She closed the laptop and stood up, then followed the others to the back of the house, where they went their separate ways, with Bauer and Phoebe peeling off to the larger bedroom on the left. She entered her own room, closed the door, and stood thinking for a moment.

The man she was supposed to have murdered had been caught on tape threatening the woman Mark Davis was supposed to have assaulted. Immediately afterward, she disappeared. Not only that, but Detective Sergeant Ortega had ties to both of them and was also running the investigation into Galinsky's murder.

But there was still one question.

If Ortega was the puppeteer pulling the strings of this sordid affair—controlling the narrative and sweeping away loose ends—then the question became, who was above him, pulling on his strings? Because Patterson didn't believe for one moment that Ortega was the puppet master. But finding that person, Patterson knew, would not be easy.

FORTY-THREE

AT EIGHT O'CLOCK THE next morning, Phoebe took her car and made the forty-five-minute drive to the Potter County correctional facility on the other side of the city. It was a Saturday, so traffic was light, and by nine a.m., she was showing her driver's license to the guard at the friends and family visitor center, which was, in reality, a building separate from the main prison and outside of the security perimeter. She would have preferred a face-to-face meeting with Mark Davis, like Patterson's visit days before, but that would have required background checks and permission since the in-person interview facility—mostly used by law enforcement and lawyers—was located within the prison proper. This was the best she could hope for.

After checking in, a guard escorted Phoebe down a short corridor to a narrow room with partitioned cubicles lining one wall. There were a few other people sitting in some of the cubicles talking to other inmates. Phoebe was assigned a booth and sat down. In front of her was a monitor upon which Mark Davis would appear, presumably sitting in a similar booth somewhere within the prison complex. There was also a red phone receiver hanging on the side wall. Underneath this was a stern warning that all conversations, video and audio, would be recorded. It was hardly an ideal situation. Phoebe would have to be careful about what she said.

Five minutes after she sat down, the screen lit up, and she found herself staring at a man she recognized from the mug shot in the Mark Davis police file, although now he looked the worse for wear, with bags under his eyes and a three-day stubble darkening his chin. The orange jumpsuit he wore made his skin look even paler than it would have otherwise. His hair had not been brushed.

Mark Davis looked like hell.

She picked up the receiver. As she took a breath to speak, her heart was hammering so loud against her ribs that she felt the guard standing at the door must surely be able to hear it. "Hey there, Cousin Mark. I hope you don't mind the sudden visit, but I'm only in town for a few days. I spoke to that FBI agent who visited you a few days ago, and she said we should talk. The family all believe you're innocent."

Davis observed her for a moment before replying. "The FBI agent, huh?"

"Yes." Phoebe nodded. She wished the conversation wasn't being recorded. It would be so much easier without the subterfuge.

"Why hasn't she come back here herself?"

"I believe she got into some trouble of her own, much like you did," Phoebe replied.

"I understand." Davis glanced around, then turned his face back to the camera. "Want to tell me why you're here?"

Phoebe's shoulders slumped with relief. But now a problem presented itself. She needed to ask Davis some hard questions and could think of no way to do that without just coming right out with it. She glanced up at the warning sign on the wall. Would their conversation be monitored in real-time? She hoped not. She also hoped that whoever was listening would buy the lie that she was just a visiting cousin overcome by concern. "The family believes you're innocent. We think someone is framing you."

"I'm innocent," Davis said, leaning closer to the camera so that his face filled the monitor. "At least, I keep telling myself that. What I don't understand is why someone would want to do this to me."

"We think it might have something to do with your business," Phoebe said quickly. "What were you working on at the time of your arrest?"

"Nothing much. I'm an environmental engineer for goodness' sake. I test soil for heavy metals and pollution. I can't imagine anyone would care about that."

"But you did have active projects, correct?"

"Sure. I was doing some work for a petrochemical company, and the day before my arrest, I was out testing a creek behind a sewage plant to make sure there was no contamination. I'm not sure how any of that relates to me being charged with rape?"

"That's what the family is trying to find out." Phoebe fell silent for a moment, thinking. This wasn't getting her anywhere.

"I'm relieved to hear that," Davis said. "But honestly, I can't think of any reason anyone would want to frame me in such an awful way or even how they could do it." His voice faltered. He closed his eyes momentarily. "Look, I remember nothing about that night after leaving the bar. I want to believe I'm innocent, that I could never commit such a crime, but with all the evidence they have . . . maybe I really did this thing."

"You told the FBI agent that you're innocent. You told me the same thing a few minutes ago."

"I know. But it's hard to be sure when you can't remember."

Phoebe wanted to tell him their theory about the date rape drugs—that Alexandria Rowley had gone to the bar that night specifically to target him—but it would be a mistake since they were being recorded. Instead, Phoebe decided to press on with her original line of questioning. "You keep records of all your jobs and clients?"

"Of course. All businesses do."

"Where do you keep those?"

"On my computer, but the cops took it. My wife said they confiscated all our electronic devices. Phones, laptops, everything, from our home and the office."

"And you don't have any backup copies?"

Davis opened his mouth to speak, then clamped it shut again. There was a moment of silence between them before he shook his head slowly. He glanced up to the left, presumably to a warning sign similar to the one on Phoebe's end about being recorded, then turned back to the camera before saying emphatically, "No. Nothing like that."

"I understand." Phoebe was sure he had been about to tell her where he kept his backup files, but the man was smart. In the nick of time, he realized the danger of doing that. Whoever was framing him might review the recording of the conversation and get there first. Deciding that there was nothing more she could learn, Phoebe engaged in some unrelated small talk, just for the benefit of the recording, then said it was time for her to leave, promising to pass his regards on to the family. She was about to put the handset back on its cradle when Davis stopped her.

"Wait."

Phoebe put the handset back to her ear. "Did you have something else to say?"

"Yes." Davis met Phoebe's gaze through the camera lens. His eyes narrowed. "Go see Cousin Carol. Tell her to share the cloud cake recipe with you. I think you'll like it. It's just what you're looking for."

Cloud cake recipe. That had to be a code for something, but

Phoebe wasn't sure what. She committed his words to memory and said goodbye, then stood up as the monitor went black. She followed the guard back to the front of the building and stepped out into the bright Texas sunshine.

Hurrying to her car, Phoebe climbed in and slammed the door before glancing back toward the facility. The guard was standing there at the door, watching her. And just for a moment, she caught a flash of something in his hand. A phone, maybe? Had he just photographed her? Surely not. Yet . . .

Phoebe was overcome by a sudden sense of danger. She started the car and drove to the exit, turned onto the perimeter road, and continued for a mile before stopping again on a narrow verge. While she was inside, a rush of adrenaline had kept her going even as she lied about her relationship to Davis and risked being recognized and arrested for aiding Patterson —even though the chance of that was relatively small. Now that the adrenaline was abating, her hands would not stop shaking and her chest felt tight. She took several deep breaths and centered herself, waiting for her nerves to calm. Then she pulled back out and continued toward the rental house, carrying the message from Mark Davis inside her head.

FORTY-FOUR

TWO AND A HALF hours after Phoebe left to visit Mark Davis at the correctional facility, Patterson stepped out of the bathroom with a towel wrapped around her and padded into her bedroom to get dressed. She dropped the towel and stood looking at her reflection in a full-length mirror attached to the back of the bedroom door. Her hair, which had been a beautiful warm blonde only forty-five minutes ago, was now a coppery shade of red thanks to the hair dye she had purchased the day before. It was a dramatic change and almost made her look like a different person. She couldn't decide if she liked her new color, but it would make her harder to spot, and that was the point.

Turning away from the mirror, Patterson dressed quickly and stepped back out of the bedroom. She found Bauer sitting at the kitchen table, reviewing the bar room footage again on her laptop.

"Hey," she said, crossing to the coffee maker where half a lukewarm carafe she had brewed earlier waited. She poured a mug and turned back toward him. "Find anything else of interest?"

"Not so far." Bauer looked up from the screen, a flicker of surprise passing across his features. "Wow."

"That's all you have to say?" Patterson asked. "Just wow?"

"Sorry. I just wasn't expecting you to look so different."

"Do you like it?" Patterson flicked her hair back over her shoulder and gave him a twirl.

"I think so. Makes you look badass, not that you need any help in that department."

Patterson was about to respond when the door flew open, and Phoebe came rushing in. She dropped her keys on an end table near the front door and stepped into the kitchen.

"Sorry, I would have called when I left the prison, but I didn't want my phone to ping off any towers here, so I kept it turned off."

"Smart. We should probably get you a burner." Bauer turned toward her. "How did it go?"

"Mark Davis doesn't have any more clue why he's being framed than we do." Phoebe pulled the chair out and sat down. Then her jaw fell open when she saw Patterson's hair. "What did you do to yourself?"

"I dyed my hair," Patterson replied. "Figured it would make me less noticeable."

"You thought that becoming a fiery redhead would make you look less noticeable than a subtle blonde?"

"Okay, wrong choice of words. What I meant to say is it would make me look different."

"You certainly achieved that."

"I assume you don't like it?"

Phoebe hesitated a moment as if choosing her words carefully. "It's different, that's all."

"Isn't it, though?" Bauer added. "I think it makes her look fierce."

"She always looked fierce." Phoebe couldn't take her eyes off the hair.

"Can we get back to Mark Davis?" Patterson asked, uncomfortable with being the center of attention.

"Right. Sorry." Phoebe dragged her eyes away. She told them all about the visit and everything Davis had said, including the cryptic message to visit Cousin Carol about the cloud cake recipe. "I'm not sure what that means," she added at the end.

"I do," Patterson said. "Carol is his wife's name."

"She wants us to visit his wife," Phoebe said. "He could have just said that."

"But there's more to it." Bauer looked thoughtful. "Cloud cake recipe. He's trying to tell us something, and I think I know what."

"The cloud," Patterson exclaimed. "Phoebe asked if there were any backups of his work files, and he said no because the police had taken everything. But there's one thing they couldn't take. His cloud storage. I'll bet he has everything backed up there. That's why he wants us to visit Carol Davis."

"So she can give us access to his cloud account." Phoebe looked sheepish. "I should have got that."

"It was pretty obscure," Bauer said.

"The two of you got it right away." Phoebe looked dismayed. "I guess that's why I'm the lowly admin assistant, and you're the special agents."

"There's nothing lowly about you," Patterson said. "You just walked into a prison facility under false pretenses to interview a man about who might want to frame him. And at great personal risk, I might add. Maybe we should color your hair red, too, then we can both be badass. I still have some dye left."

"That's quite all right." Phoebe's eyes flicked back to Patterson's hair. "I'm not sure I could . . . ahem . . . pull it off the same way you do."

"Thank heavens for that," Bauer said, then glanced quickly at Patterson. "No offense."

"Okay. The votes are in. My hair sucks." Patterson swigged the last of her mostly cold coffee. "How about we circle back to the matter at hand. Mark Davis and that cloud storage."

"Someone will have to visit her," Bauer said.

"I can do it." Phoebe shuffled from one foot to the other, almost looking surprised that she had volunteered for a second mission.

"I think it would be better if I went," said Patterson. "I've already spoken to Carol Davis once. She knows my face. She's more apt to trust me."

"I don't like that idea." Bauer shook his head. "What if Detective Sergeant Ortega or someone else is watching the Davis residence? You'll be walking right into their trap."

"It's a risk," Patterson admitted, "but a small one. Ortega won't have the time to sit outside the place all day long on the off chance that I'll show up there for some reason. He is a working detective, after all."

"True. I can't imagine he'd be able to swing an official surveillance op, especially since the crime you're supposed to have committed has no connection with Davis or his wife. At least, not officially."

"Right. There would be no reason for anyone to think I would go there," Patterson said. "I think it's safe enough."

"There is one thing," Phoebe said, raising her hand to get their attention. "The prison records the audio and video from every visit. I assume that's why Davis was so cryptic about his instructions to visit Carol."

"Ah." Bauer pressed his lips together briefly. "There is a possibility that Ortega or whoever is controlling him has eyes and ears in the prison watching Davis. If they get a copy of that conversation between him and Phoebe, they might come to the same conclusion as us."

"Which is why we need to do this quickly," Patterson said. "I know you think it's a risk, but I'm going to see Carol. If there's a cloud storage account, she's more likely to tell me about it than someone she's never met."

"I'm not going to change your mind, am I?" Bauer asked.

"Nope. But I'll make you a compromise. Phoebe can come with me. We'll go together. She can be my eyes and ears. Keep watch while I'm talking to Carol."

"We could all go," Phoebe suggested.

"No." That was the last thing Patterson wanted. "Someone needs to stay behind just in case this goes south and we get caught. If we're all apprehended together, who's going to figure it out and blow this thing wide open?"

"I'll stay behind," Bauer agreed. "A couple of women visiting Carol Davis will draw less attention, anyway. I look too much like the cop."

"That's settled then. Phoebe and I will go." Patterson stepped toward the door. "And there's no time like the present."

FORTY-FIVE

THE FIRST THING Patterson did after they decided to visit Carol Davis was go to her room and retrieve one of the unopened burner phones. She ripped it from the box and activated it with a thirty-day plan. She added her own and Bauer's phone numbers into the contacts and did the same in reverse to her phone. Then she returned to the kitchen and handed the device to Phoebe.

"Now we'll all be able to keep in touch," she said.

"Thanks." Phoebe took the phone and checked it out, then slipped it into her pocket.

"You just happened to have a spare phone lying around?" Bauer asked, looking amused.

"Two of them, actually. I figured I might need a backup if my phone got compromised."

"Smart." Bauer jotted down Phoebe's new number.

"Ready to go?" Phoebe asked, walking to the door and scooping up her car keys.

"Let's do this," Patterson said and followed Phoebe outside, climbing into the passenger side as Phoebe headed for the driver's seat.

Bauer stood at the door and watched them leave.

As Phoebe turned out of the property onto the road, Patterson glanced back toward the house, but Bauer had retreated inside again, and the door was closed now.

It was early afternoon on a Saturday, so the traffic was light as they headed back into the city. When they arrived at the Davis residence, Patterson instructed Phoebe to park a little way down the street where she could still see the house but wouldn't draw undue attention. It was unlikely the house was under surveillance, but that didn't mean some nosy neighbor wouldn't remember the blue Honda and mention it later if anyone came asking.

Patterson climbed out of the vehicle, then leaned back in before Phoebe had a chance to follow suit. "Stay here and keep your eyes peeled. I'll talk to Carol Davis alone. If you see anything suspicious, call me on the burner phone."

Phoebe nodded and slipped the phone from her pocket.

Patterson closed the car door and started toward the Davis residence. The Ford Mustang she had seen on her previous visit was still parked on the driveway—a good sign that Carol Davis was home. She approached the front door, then knocked three times and waited.

There was no answer.

She was about to knock again when she heard a chain being drawn back, and then the door opened to reveal Mark Davis's wife. She wore faded denim shorts and a pink tee but had no makeup on. Her eyes were red and puffy. Patterson wondered if she had been crying but said nothing.

"The FBI agent," Carol said. "Please tell me it's not more bad news."

"No." Patterson shook her head quickly. She felt exposed on the doorstep. "Can I come in?"

Carol stepped aside and waved for her to enter.

The house was in even more disarray than the first time

Patterson had visited. The piles of clothes had grown larger, and she could see several takeout containers sitting on the coffee table in the living room. She followed Carol to the kitchen, where plates and mugs were piled in the sink. The dishwasher door stood open, but it hadn't been loaded.

A photo album lay open on the kitchen island. Wedding pictures stared up at Patterson. Mark and Carol Davis in happier times.

"I'm sorry, you must think I'm foolish," Carol said, wiping her eyes and closing the album. She rested her hand atop it as if guarding the memories within. "I look at those pictures, and I don't see a vicious rapist. Just a loving man who couldn't wait to marry me. I don't understand how all of this could have happened."

"That's why I'm here," Patterson said, placing her own hand over Carol's and squeezing. "I don't believe for one moment that Mark did what he's accused of doing, and I intend to prove it."

The gratitude in Carol's eyes was overwhelming. After being told so many times over the past few weeks that her husband was a monster, Patterson's words appeared to bolster her. She nodded. "I thought I was the only one who still believed in him."

"You're not." Patterson withdrew her hand. "But to figure out who would want your husband out of the way, I need some information from you."

"Anything."

"An associate of mine spoke to your husband this morning. He mentioned you could give us access to his work files."

"No. I already told you; the police took our computers from here and the office."

"I know that. But he mentioned a cloud server account."

"Of course. The backups. Mark had a bunch of data wiped

out one time, and it set him back weeks. Now he's paranoid about making copies of everything. He stores everything in the cloud." Carol was heading toward the living room. "I bought a new laptop last week since it doesn't look like I'm ever going to get my old one back. I can get the files for you right now."

"That would be a tremendous help." Patterson followed Carol to the living room. There was a new laptop sitting closed on the couch.

Carol picked it up and swept the fast food containers from the coffee table. "Sorry about the mess. I haven't exactly been in the frame of mind to clean."

"I've seen worse," Patterson said. She sat on the couch next to Carol and watched as the woman opened the laptop and brought up her cloud account.

She scrolled through folders for a minute, becoming increasingly frantic, then frowned. "Something isn't right. The business folders aren't here, none of them, which is impossible. Mark would never have deleted those."

"I don't think it was Mark who deleted them." Patterson cursed under her breath. She should have anticipated this. The police took all the computers. Whoever was framing Mark Davis could have easily accessed the cloud server from one of those confiscated machines and deleted the files. But all was not lost. "Check the deleted files folder. Most cloud services have a recovery period of at least ninety days in case something gets wiped by accident."

Carol clicked on the deleted files folder and opened it, but other than a few unrelated items that Carol herself must have deleted, it was empty. "It's all gone."

Patterson stared at the laptop screen. Whoever removed the files also had the forethought to go one step further and permanently purge them from the deleted files folder. There was no way the backup copies could be recovered. They were gone for good, and with them went any hope Patterson had of figuring out who Mark Davis had inadvertently crossed and why they wanted him out of the way. It also meant she was no closer to clearing her own name.

FORTY-SIX

PATTERSON STARED at the laptop screen for a moment longer, then stood up. There was no point hanging around any longer and risking discovery. "Sorry that I wasted your time. I should go."

"You didn't waste my time." Carol closed the laptop. "Just the opposite. You gave me hope. It feels so good, knowing that I'm not the only one who thinks my husband didn't do this thing."

"We still have to prove it," Patterson cautioned. "And without those files, it just got a lot harder."

"You really think this is to do with his work?" Carol asked, standing. "He's an environmental engineer. Checks sites for chemical contamination."

"It's the only thing that makes sense." Patterson started toward the front door. "Somehow, he must have gotten in someone's way."

"It would have to be someone pretty powerful to do this to him." Carol followed Patterson to the door and stood with her hand resting on the knob. "And they would have to be ruthless to ruin his life and tear a family apart in such a horrendous fashion."

"There are a lot of ruthless people out there."

"What made you change your mind?" Carol asked.

"I'm sorry?" Patterson shook her head.

"You weren't so confident about Mark's innocence the last time you were here. You didn't say as much, but I could tell. Now you seem sure of it. What changed?"

"It's a long story, and there isn't the time." Patterson wasn't about to tell this woman that she was accused of murder and a fugitive on the run from her own agency and the Amarillo PD. "Maybe I'll tell you about it when we get Mark out of that place and clear his name."

"I'd be interested to hear it." Carol's gaze lifted to Patterson's hair. "I like the new color. It makes you look . . ."

"Fierce?" Patterson said, remembering Bauer's description.

"I was going to say confident," Carol said. "But fierce works just as well." She opened the door for Patterson to leave, then closed it again. "Wait. I just remembered something. There may be another backup."

"Where?" Patterson backed up.

"His office. Before we had the cloud account, he used an external hard drive. Updated his files every evening before he left work. He might still copy it. He doesn't totally trust the cloud. Says one glitch and everything will be gone."

"I thought you said the police had taken all the electronics?"

"They wouldn't have taken this because I doubt they found it. He used to keep the hard drive stored in a fire safe mounted in the wall behind this really ugly picture he picked up years ago before we were married. I couldn't stand the thing in the house, so he hung it at work to cover up the safe."

"Do you still have access to the office?"

"Yes. I suppose if the worst comes to the worst, I'll have to clear it out and close the business, but right now I'm still clinging to the hope that Mark will come home, so I'm still paying the rent. If you give me your number, I'll text you the address. You can go there right away."

"I'll need a key to get in and the combination for the safe."

"The front door and the safe both have electronic codes. I'll text those to you as well."

"My phone isn't getting great reception in Amarillo," Patterson lied. "Perhaps you could write everything down on a piece of paper?"

"Sure." Carol turned and went into the kitchen. She came back a minute later with a sheet of paper that she offered to Patterson. There was an address and two codes written on it. "This should be all you need."

Patterson took the sheet of paper. "And I'll know which picture the safe is behind?"

"You'll know. It's an oil painting of a reclining nude. At least, that's what he says it is, but all I see are splotches of color. He bought it at some art fair years ago. I've told him more than once he should get rid of it and get something more appropriate, but he loves the damn thing."

"Got it." Patterson moved back toward the door and opened it. Then she turned back to Carol. "Would you do me a favor?"

"Sure. Name it."

"If anyone comes around, like the police or other FBI agents, don't tell them I was here. I'd like to keep my visit a secret for now. It may be vital to clearing your husband's name."

Carol's face twisted with concern. "You think a police officer might have something to do with this?"

"I don't know, but maybe," Patterson told her, hoping the woman would believe her. Apart from the fact that it was probably true, she didn't want Detective Sergeant Ortega or Special Agent Ricketts to know she was still investigating. It would not only put Patterson in danger of being found, but it might put Carol in danger, too, if they thought she knew something.

Carol observed her for a second as if weighing this request. She dipped her head. "I'll keep quiet. You can count on that. Just bring Mark back to me."

"I'll do my best," Patterson said. Then she stepped outside and hurried back to the car, where Phoebe was waiting.

FORTY-SEVEN

LATER THAT NIGHT, under cover of darkness, Phoebe and Patterson drove to the address Carol Davis had given them. The office Mark's company rented was in a business park surrounded by other small companies. Patterson would have preferred to go there that afternoon, but after a discussion back at the rental house, they had decided it would be safer when there was less chance of being observed.

Once again, Bauer stayed behind. As an active FBI agent, he worried that his presence might be construed as an illegal search even though Carol Davis had given them permission to be there. She was not listed as a company owner and therefore had no authority over the premises. The one person who could officially give them permission was sitting in jail. It was a technicality, but one which Bauer knew could be used by a lawyer to have any evidence found at the premises excluded during a trial if he was present when and if they found the hard drive.

The office that housed Davis Environmental Solutions was toward the back of the business park. After driving around for a few minutes, hunting for the correct address, Phoebe pulled up in front and parked. Patterson climbed out and went to the door, typing in the code Carol Davis had given her before stepping inside. She waited for Phoebe to enter, then locked the door behind them before finding the light switch.

The unit was small, comprising a lobby area with one desk and two ten-by-ten work spaces off a short corridor behind. A restroom at the back completed the floor plan. The office on the right contained an oblong table with enough seating for six. An overhead projector at one end was aimed toward a white-painted wall. This was obviously a meeting room where Davis connected with clients. The other office contained a desk and two chairs. Bookshelves full of volumes on subjects like geology and chemistry covered the back wall. There was also a baseball in a clear plastic box on a shelf and framed photos of Davis's family.

Three paintings hung in the office—two on one wall and one on the other. The single painting was crudely done and appeared to show the vague outline of a reclining woman, although it looked more like random paint splotches in garish colors than anything else.

This must be the picture to which Carol Davis referred.

Patterson went straight to it and lifted the painting from the wall, placing it on the floor. She was rewarded with the sight of a safe recessed into the wall. When she touched the keypad and typed the code in, it lit up. There were two beeps, followed by the sound of bolts retracting. The safe door popped open.

Inside was a portable USB hard drive sitting on the top shelf. The only other thing in the safe was a check that had not yet been deposited in the bank.

Patterson grabbed the hard drive and turned to Phoebe. "This is what we came for. Hopefully, he was still copying files to it every night."

"Great, let's get out of here." Phoebe turned to leave.

Patterson turned back to the safe and was about to close it

again when she heard three sharp knocks coming from the direction of the small lobby.

Patterson froze. "There shouldn't be anyone around at this time of night."

"Well, there is." Phoebe was at the office door. She peeked out, then pulled her head back quickly. "Crap. There's some guy in a uniform out there. A security guard." She looked at Patterson with wide eyes. "I think he saw me."

FORTY-EIGHT

THE FRONT DOOR RATTLED. "Whoever's in there, open up. Now."

"What are we going to do?" Phoebe hissed. There was panic in her voice. "He's not going to go away. He knows we're in here."

"It's fine. I'll handle it," Patterson said. She closed the safe quickly and locked it again, then lifted the painting from the floor and hung it back up. Slipping the hard drive into her pocket, she started toward the front of the office suite.

The security guard was standing with his arms folded. He peered in through the glass door at the front of the unit, a scowl plastered on his face. The guy was older, with gray hair and a paunch. Behind him, parked sideways blocking their own car, was a rent-a-cop vehicle painted to look like a police cruiser, except that the words Gideon Security were splashed down the side instead of the police department name. The light bar on top was Amber—another giveaway that this was not an official law enforcement visit.

Patterson unlocked the door and opened it.

"Can I help you, officer?" she said, playing to the guy's ego with that last word. She had come across more than one security guard who had washed out of police training and wanted a uniform so badly that they went to the next best thing.

"What's going on here?" The security guard asked, peering past Patterson to get a look inside the office unit. His gaze alighted on Phoebe, who was standing in the corridor watching the exchange. "Who are you people?"

"We're friends of Mark Davis," Patterson said in an even voice. "He owns the company that rents this unit."

"It's ten o'clock at night. Bit late to be snooping around his office, isn't it?"

"I can assure you we are not snooping. Mark is currently incapacitated, and we're fetching some of his work files."

"Yeah. I know exactly where the guy who rents this unit is cooling his heels right now," said the rent-a-cop with a sneer. "I'm surprised that a pair of attractive young women like yourselves want anything to do with him."

"We're just trying to help his wife out," Patterson said. It figured the security guard would know about the allegations against Mark Davis. He looked like the type who spent his free time sitting in a corner of his garage listening to a police scanner. Normally, she would have whipped out her credentials and put the guy in his place, but under the circumstances, that would be a bad idea. "If you don't mind, we'd really like to get back to it. It's getting late, and we don't want to be here all night."

"Mind if I come inside and take a look around?" The security guard's hand fell to a baton on his belt.

Patterson noticed that he wasn't armed. That meant he hadn't completed the required training to carry a firearm on the job and wasn't licensed to do so. She decided to go on the offensive. "I don't think that would be advisable. We're two young women on our own. We don't know who you are or what your intentions are toward us. No offense."

The guard looked mildly put out. "Miss, I'm wearing the uniform. You can trust me."

"No," Patterson contradicted him. "You're wearing *a uniform.* That doesn't make you any more trustworthy than the next man." Patterson made sure to keep her body blocking the doorway. The only way he would be able to enter was by making bodily contact, and she guessed he wouldn't dare to do that. She slipped the burner phone out of her pocket. "If you really want to come in, we can call the police and wait for them to arrive, and then you can wander around as you see fit."

"There's no need to do that." The guard took a step back, his hand falling away from the baton. He looked at the door, studying it for a moment, then shrugged. "Doesn't look like there's any sign of forced entry, and the two of you look pretty harmless. Maybe I don't need to take a look around inside after all."

"My thoughts exactly," Patterson said. She had a feeling the security guard wouldn't want the embarrassment of having the real police show up to what he probably already felt was a non-event. He was just throwing his weight around to feel better about himself, and she had called his bluff. She made one more play on his ego. "Thank you for stopping and checking on us, officer. We appreciate it."

"You're welcome," the security guard said in a tone that implied he didn't really mean it. His ego was dented. "Don't stay too long, now, you hear? I'll be swinging back around here in another hour, and if you aren't gone by then, I'm coming in to look around. No ifs or butts."

"We're almost done," Patterson replied in the sweetest voice she could muster.

"Well, all right then." The guard turned on his heel and stomped back to the car. He climbed in and started the engine, then flicked his amber light bar on like some petulant child, proving he had a better toy. Then he turned the roof mounted lights off again and swung the car around, disappearing back toward the front of the business park.

Patterson closed the door and turned back to Phoebe. "If I wasn't a wanted woman right now, I would've put that guy well and truly in his place. The jerk."

"I have no doubt that you would," Phoebe replied. "Even without your FBI credentials, you proved what Marcus said about your hair earlier and then some. You don't just look fierce. *You are fierce.*"

"I'll take that as a compliment." Patterson grinned.

"For a second there, I thought you were gonna make that poor guy cry."

"Now, that would have been satisfying." Patterson checked her pocket. The portable hard drive was still there. "Want to get out of here before he decides to come back?"

"Hell, yes." Phoebe stepped toward the door. "I've had enough excitement for one day."

FORTY-NINE

BAUER WAS WAITING for them when Phoebe and Patterson arrived back at the rental house. He was pacing the living room and casting quick glances out of the window. When their car pulled up, he met them at the door.

"What took you guys so long?" he asked. "I was starting to think you'd gotten yourselves caught."

"We had a run-in with an overzealous security guard who wanted to know what we were doing there so late at night," Patterson replied.

"But he was no match for Patterson," Phoebe said. "She put him in his place so hard that he ran with his proverbial tail between his legs."

"That's a bit of an exaggeration." Patterson smirked. "But I admit, it was satisfying."

"Did you find the hard drive with the backup files on it?"

"We have the hard drive." Patterson pulled the slim drive from her pocket and held it up. "I have no idea what's on it, but it was the only one there."

"Well, don't keep me in suspense." Bauer glanced across the

entryway toward the kitchen table, where Patterson's laptop was still sitting open. "Fire it up and let's see what we have."

Patterson led the way into the kitchen and plugged the drive into one of the laptop's USB ports. She waited for the machine to recognize the hard drive, then opened it. There were hundreds of file folders organized by date. The newest was dated the day before Mark Davis was arrested. She opened it to find several files. There was a report detailing high levels of arsenic in a stream near an elementary school, several photographs of the stream in question, and a bunch of Word documents that appeared to be unrelated business correspondence.

"Looks like he was still backing up to the hard drive," she said, clicking on a couple of earlier dated folders and seeing more of the same. "Guess he really didn't trust the cloud."

"And with good reason." Bauer leaned over Patterson's shoulder and watched her troll through the files. "All his business documents ended up wiped out, although I'm sure he couldn't have imagined it would be a deliberate act by someone with a grudge against him."

"It's going to take us days, or maybe even weeks, to go through all this stuff," Phoebe said. "There must be tens of thousands of documents going back years. It's a needle in a haystack. How are we ever going to determine which, if any, of these files are related to him being framed?"

"I think we can discount most of the older folders," Bauer said. "If Mark Davis ran afoul of someone because of something on this hard drive, it will probably be more recent. We should start there." He yawned and glanced toward the bedroom. "But not tonight. I'm absolutely frazzled. Let's sleep on it and pick this up in the morning."

"Sounds good to me." Phoebe started toward the bedroom.

Patterson hadn't responded. She was engrossed in the

contents of the hard drive, clicking on files and opening then closing them again when she realized they were not relevant.

Bauer nudged her. "Did you hear what I said?"

"Yeah. I'll go to bed in a moment. I just want to look through a few of these first." Patterson could feel the exhaustion creeping around the edges of her consciousness, but this was the closest she had been to figuring out what was happening and why since fleeing the hotel in the early hours of the morning.

Bauer stood there for a moment longer, watching her work through all the files in the newest dated folder. Then he gave a small sigh. "Please don't stay up too late. That hard drive isn't going anywhere. It will still be here tomorrow."

"I won't," Patterson said absently. She barely registered Bauer stepping away and joining Phoebe in the larger of the two bedrooms. For the next ten minutes, they went back and forth between the bedroom and the bathroom. She heard water running. A couple of flushes. Then the bedroom door clicked softly closed for the last time she was surrounded by silence.

Her world collapsed down to nothing but the hard drive and the file folders it contained. She worked back through each date, checking every document and skimming them for clues, but found nothing that leaped out. By the time her eyelids began to droop, she had gone all the way back to three months before Mark Davis was arrested and was beginning to think they were wrong about his business dealings precipitating the entire chain of events. Everything was so . . . boring and bland.

She stifled a yawn, surprised to see that it was one-thirty in the morning already. Soft snores were coming from the bedroom Phoebe and Bauer occupied. The refrigerator hummed softly on the other side of the room, occasionally emitting a low gurgling noise. The house around her fell away into darkness except for one light fixture that burned in the small hallway between the two bedrooms and the bathroom, and a dim hood light over the stove.

Unplugging the hard drive, she closed the laptop and headed for her bedroom, taking the drive with her and placing it on the nightstand for safekeeping. It wasn't until she climbed into bed and her head hit the pillow that Patterson realized just how wiped out she really was because the next thing she knew, it was morning.

FIFTY

WHEN PATTERSON CAME out of her room the next morning, she found Bauer sitting in the living room with his feet up and a mug of coffee in his hands. The TV was playing. Local news. She headed into the kitchen and poured herself a mug, then went to the living room and sat down next to Bauer.

"Where's Phoebe," she asked, looking around.

"Still in the bedroom, making herself pretty or some such thing. She'll be out in a minute." Bauer's eyes flicked back to the TV, where a presenter was standing in front of a patch of barren land on the side of the city. A large for sale sign at the edge of the property had been covered with another smaller sign announcing that the land had been sold. Next to the presenter was a lean man in his mid-fifties wearing blue jeans, a button-down shirt, and a wide-brimmed hat. On the other side of her stood another, younger, man in a suit and tie. A banner scrolling across the bottom of the screen identified the man in the hat as Senator Bill Newport and the other man as Bob Iverson, CEO of a company called Jericho Leisure Investments, LLC.

"What's the deal with these guys?" Patterson asked, noticing Bauer's intense interest.

"They're going to build a huge sports complex outside of town on some old industrial site that's been sitting vacant for years," Bauer said. "And not just sports. There are plans to have music festivals there, concerts, all sorts of things. The investment company had narrowed it down to either Amarillo or Flagstaff, but thanks to that senator, they're putting it here. He gave them a bunch of tax and other incentives worth tens of millions to bring it to Texas. Claims it will revitalize the economy, increase tourism, and create hundreds of jobs."

"And why is this of interest?" A vague feeling lingered at the back of Patterson's mind. The senator looked familiar, but she couldn't think how.

"Because they're building a baseball stadium, too. Going to use it as a spring training facility. And guess who's going to be coming here."

"You'd better not be talking about baseball again." Phoebe had come out of the bedroom and now stood in the doorway with her arms folded. She was wearing a robe and her hair was tied back. "That game is so boring."

"Only because you haven't given it a chance," Bauer retorted. "But you're in luck because once this stadium is built, my hometown team will be here every spring. The LA Thunder."

"Never heard of them," Patterson said.

"They're a minor league team. I used to watch them when I was a cop in LA. Haven't been to a baseball game since applying for the Academy, so this is awesome."

"And a five-hour drive each way," Phoebe said. "You can count me out."

"Really? We could take weekends and come up here, find a cozy little bed-and-breakfast. It will be romantic."

"It will be an entire weekend of you doing nothing but talking about baseball." Phoebe shook her head. "No thanks."

"But—"

"If you want to take me on a romantic weekend, you can do that anytime. We don't need the excuse of a bunch of sweaty guys hitting balls with bats."

"I'm with her," Patterson said. "Sorry, Marcus. We girls just don't find sports romantic."

Bauer shrugged. "Your loss. I'll go on my own."

Phoebe glanced toward the screen where the senator was still giving an interview. "Doesn't look like they've even built the thing yet."

"They haven't. Only sealed the deal last week. The sports complex won't be open for another two years, minimum."

"Great." Phoebe grinned. "That means I don't have to worry about it anytime soon."

"You have no soul. Either of you." Bauer turned the tv off, then stood and went to the kitchen, where he poured himself another coffee. His eyes fell to the laptop still sitting on the kitchen table before looking at Patterson. "I hope you didn't stay up too late going through those files last night."

"I didn't," Patterson said without mentioning what time she went to bed. "I just browsed through the most recent folders to see if anything jumped out."

"And did it?"

"Not so much." Patterson joined Bauer and Phoebe in the kitchen. "Unless I'm missing something, I can't see any reason for someone to frame Mark Davis over the contents of that hard drive. It's nothing but boring land-use reports, chemical analysis results, and recommendations for cleaning up old brownfield sites. It's hardly the stuff of thrillers. I almost fell asleep at the table just reading it."

"Well, it's all we've got," Bauer said. "Unless either of you can think of another reason someone would want Mark Davis out of the way."

Patterson and Phoebe both shook their heads.

"That's what I thought." Bauer finished his coffee and put the mug in the sink. He started toward the back of the house. "I'm going to take a shower."

"And I'll dive back into that hard drive and keep going through the files," Patterson said, pulling out a chair and sitting at the table in front of the laptop. "Wish me luck."

"You want some help?" Phoebe asked.

"I'm not sure it's really a two-person job." Patterson glanced toward the coffeemaker and the now empty carafe. "But you can put another pot of coffee on. I have a feeling I'm going to need it."

"Sure." Phoebe busied herself with the coffee.

Patterson went back to her bedroom, retrieved the hard drive, and plugged it in. She started where she had left off the previous night and was soon feeling hopeless as file after file turned out to be nothing. But then, when she opened the backup folder for the month of March, her eyes grew wide.

She jumped up with a cry of satisfaction. "Guys. I think I've found something."

FIFTY-ONE

BAUER WAS STILL in the bedroom when Patterson shouted out. He came running, buttoning up his shirt.

"What did you find?" He asked.

Phoebe turned away from the coffeemaker and stepped toward the table. "Please let it be something good because I don't know where we'll go from here otherwise."

"It's good," Patterson said. "I just don't know how good, yet."

She sat back down and clicked on the file she had found. It was a contamination report on a brownfield site outside of the city that had once housed a fertilizer manufacturing company. She pointed at the screen. "Look at the name on that file."

Bauer leaned over her shoulder. "Jericho Leisure Investments Site Contamination Report." He paused a moment. "Wait. That's the company building the leisure complex and stadium. The one from the TV."

"Exactly." Patterson opened the report and scrolled through it. "I don't know much about brownfield redevelopment, a lot of the technical stuff in here is way over my head, but it looks like that site is hopelessly contaminated. They manufactured fertilizer there for decades until the company closed down. The ground is full of nasty chemicals like phosphate, nitric acid, and ammonia. That's just the ones I can pronounce. There's a bunch of other chemicals listed here, too." She skimmed through the report to the last page, which was a recommendation for cleanup. "It says the entire site will have to be decontaminated. The soil needs to be treated by a process called bioremediation. The worst of it will still have to be removed and disposed of. The entire top layer of earth to at least a depth of five feet."

"That can't be cheap to do," Bauer said.

"Apparently not. It could run into the tens of millions and take upwards of two years, according to this report."

"What's the address of that site?" Phoebe asked.

Patterson flicked back through the report and told her.

Phoebe typed into her phone's web browser and then looked back up. "I guess they must have fast-tracked the cleanup process because that's where they're building the stadium."

"That report is only from four months ago." Bauer didn't look convinced. "There's no way they could have cleaned it up in such a short amount of time. It's impossible. I think we've found the reason why Mark Davis is sitting in prison. Someone wanted to bury that report so that it wouldn't get in the way of their billion-dollar development project."

"That's why the backup files on the cloud were deleted," Phoebe said.

"And why I'm being framed for murder," Patterson said. "When I went to see Davis about my sister, it must have spooked whoever is behind this. An FBI agent talking to the man they just unjustly put in jail for a crime he didn't commit."

"That doesn't make sense." Phoebe looked at Patterson. "If whoever is behind all of this thought the FBI was investigating them, taking one agent out of the picture wouldn't put a stop to that."

"They didn't think I was investigating them. I suspect there's a mighty powerful person behind this project, given what they have achieved so far. They probably knew I was looking for my sister, but when Mark Davis said he was innocent and asked me to investigate the circumstances of his arrest, they got nervous."

"They thought you would stumble onto something," Bauer said.

"Exactly. They decided to be proactive and get rid of me before my investigation became a problem for them."

"But there's one thing we're forgetting," Phoebe said. "Given the history of the land, that company wouldn't be able to build without a clean site report."

"Which they obviously skirted somehow," Bauer said. "I suspect they hired Mark Davis to provide that report because his company is small, and they could contain the situation if the worst came to the worst."

"Which it apparently did," Patterson said. "The developers knew if they built on that site so quickly, it would raise a red flag. Especially if Mark Davis heard about it, which he was sure to do. His report would contradict their own claim that the land was fit for use. If his findings went public, they would lose hundreds of millions and possibly face criminal charges."

"That extends to the senator, too." Bauer frowned. "At the very least, it puts him in political jeopardy instead of being the hero of the day and bringing jobs to the state."

"The question is, how much did he know if anything?" Patterson said.

"And where do Detective Sergeant Ortega, Alexandria Rowley, and Leo Galinsky fit into all this?" Phoebe asked.

"That's what we need to find out." Bauer sat down next to Patterson. "I think it's time we do some digging on that investment company and the good senator."

"Agreed." Patterson closed the report and copied it to her hard drive. "And the sooner, the better."

"I can do that," Phoebe said. "I worked as an admin assistant with the Bureau's Forensic Accounting Unit before I was transferred to the ASAC. I learned a few things about following paper trails and how companies hide their dirty little secrets. All I need is a few hours with that laptop, and I'll know everything about Jericho Leisure Investments."

"Perfect." Bauer kissed her on the cheek. "I knew there was a reason we're dating."

"Ouch." Patterson winced.

"Yeah." Phoebe smirked. "He might be sleeping on the couch tonight."

FIFTY-TWO

FOUR HOURS LATER, Patterson was climbing the walls. Phoebe was still sitting at the kitchen table hunched over the laptop, going between stretches of silent reading and furious typing. She had only moved once to grab a soda from the fridge, then went right back to it.

Bauer was sprawled on the sofa, watching a football game and occasionally voicing his dissatisfaction with the way it was going. Between plays, he paced to the kitchen and looked over Phoebe's shoulder, which earned him a stern glare and an admonishment to go away and let her work in peace.

Patterson dragged him back to the living room. "We aren't going to get anywhere by hurrying her."

"I know. I'm not used to this. Having nothing to do."

"What do you normally do on your days off?" Patterson asked.

"This isn't a day off." Bauer sank down onto the sofa. He clenched a fist and unclenched it again. "We should be out there hunting down the people responsible for all of this."

"And we will, just as soon as Phoebe gets us the information we need."

"Hey," came a voice from the kitchen. "I might have sone intel on that score."

"About time." Bauer jumped back up and strode to the kitchen.

"You really are earning yourself a place on that couch tonight." Phoebe swatted at him. "I was going as fast as I could."

"And we appreciate it," said Patterson. "What did you find?"

"Lots." Phoebe took a deep breath. "Back when it was a fertilizer manufacturer, the land in question, and the business that operated there, were owned by a business called HRN Corporation. The initials stood for the three founding partners. Namely, Thomas Herrington, William Russell, and Oliver Newport. They made various forms of fertilizer there from 1946 until 1998 when the company went out of business."

"Newport," Patterson said. "Like the senator on TV?"

"Exactly like him. Oliver was his great uncle. He died in 1986 and passed his share of the company on to his son, who bought out the other partners, all of whom were of advanced age at that point. The son was not the businessman his father had been, and the company went bankrupt. When the son died childless, what remained, namely the land and buildings, passed to William Newport and his sister, Linda."

"Newport and his siter owned that land sold to Jericho Leisure Investments?"

"Not so fast. He bought out his sister's share and demolished the buildings in the early two thousands to develop the land for housing, but he never got that far. My guess is he suspected that it might be too contaminated from the fertilizer manufacturing. It lay empty for years until he sold it last year to a company called Texland LLC., who in turn recently sold all four hundred acres of the parcel to Jericho Leisure Investments for nine million in cash and a twenty percent minority stake in the leisure complex."

"Wow."

"It gets better. Texland is owned by a shell company registered in Texas called Northstar Holdings Corporation. That company, in turn is owned by a Delaware corporation—Windsong Ventures. Here's where it gets interesting. Windsong is held in a trust by another shell company, and the list goes on. Twelve corporations in all, some of which own other companies, too. All nested inside each other like Russian dolls. Which leads us to Newport Ventures Corp, a company registered in the Bahamas."

"Newport. There's that name again."

"Exactly. Guess who owns Newport Ventures Corporation."

"William Newport." Patterson replied.

"Exactly. He distanced himself from the land by selling it to a company controlled through a string of shell companies and a trust, just for good measure. To the casual observer, he has nothing to do with that land anymore."

"Except you were able to follow his trail," Patterson said.

"That's because I'm good and know what to look for."

"To sum up what we've found," Bauer said. "Bill Newport still owned that toxic land where his family ran a fertilizer company, transferring it through a list of shell companies to hide his ownership. That company then sold the land for cash and equity to the people building the leisure complex."

"And Texland stands to make millions every year from its twenty percent stake," Patterson said.

"All of which, including the nine million purchase price, will flow back through to the senator through his Bahamian corporation and shell companies."

"Not to mention that he unloads that tainted land," Bauer said.

"That's why he wanted to bring the project here," Patterson

said. "And he used his position to make sure it happened by lobbying for the project and giving all sorts of tax breaks."

"Which has to be illegal," Phoebe said.

"And provides a very good motive to get Mark Davis out of the way and bury his report on the land."

"Right." Patterson watched Phoebe save everything she had found to a folder on the laptop's hard drive. "Now we just need to find a link between the senator and the detective."

"There's one more thing we need to do," Phoebe said. "Go and see Mark Davis again."

"What? No way." Bauer shook his head. "It's too risky."

"I agree with Phoebe," Patterson said. "He's the only one who can confirm our theory that he was framed to bury the report on that land he produced for Texland LLC."

"I don't like it," Bauer grumbled.

"You don't have to." Phoebe was already on the prison's website. She tapped away for a minute, then looked up. "I've made an appointment to see him tomorrow morning. Now all we can to do is wait."

FIFTY-THREE

AT SIX P.M. THAT EVENING, Mark Davis walked into the rec yard of the Potter County Correctional Facility. He would have preferred to stay in his cell, far away from the prison's general population, but the facility required at least one hour of exercise every day. Davis had found that by early evening, right before the yard closed at dusk, most prisoners had retreated back inside.

Today, there were about thirty other men in the yard, mostly sitting around on bleachers talking or strolling the perimeter. A few lifted weights on exercise benches set up in the center of the space. A cliché that Davis had thought only occurred in movies and TV shows until he found himself here.

He glanced up past the concrete walls surrounding the yard and the razor wire that topped it toward a sniper tower occupying one corner, within which he could see the vague silhouette of an armed guard. If any of the prisoners below him somehow scaled one of those walls, they would be cut down in an instant.

Davis shuddered and dropped his gaze, wondering, not for the first time, how his life had taken such a tragic turn when he had done nothing wrong. Not only was he being accused of a crime he had not committed, but the judge had decided at his arraignment that he was too dangerous to release, given the accusation levied against him. So now, Davis sat in pretrial detention. His only consolation was the FBI agent who had promised to look into the circumstances of his case, but she had not returned since. Instead, he received a visit from a woman claiming to be his cousin, which, of course, was untrue. He had never seen her before—ever. It soon became apparent she was there at the request of the FBI woman, although he didn't know why Special Agent Patterson Blake had not shown up in person.

Something was going on. He knew this not just because of the strange and cryptic visit from his *cousin* but also because, later that evening, he had received a second visit, this time from a detective sergeant in the Amarillo PD. The man had quizzed him about the woman he spoke to earlier in the day, asking what she wanted. It was obvious he had already reviewed the interview recording because he inquired about the coded message—the cloud cake recipe. He also pressed Davis on the exact familial relationship between himself and the visitor. Davis clammed up and said he would speak only in the presence of his lawyer, after which the detective reluctantly backed off. Davis wondered how the cop even knew about the visit but figured a guard must have passed the information on. And he thought he knew which guard was responsible. Officer Monahan. A towering brute of a man with broad shoulders and bulging biceps. He was a bully who took a little too much pleasure in his work. He had also taken an interest in Davis, always seeming to be in the vicinity during mealtimes or out in the yard. The man had even whispered a few veiled threats for Davis to watch his back, although never within earshot of another guard or inmate.

The exercise yard was in the shape of a rectangle with a

hard concrete floor. Davis followed the routine he had settled into over the past few weeks, following the perimeter of the yard and walking in circles as quickly as possible while avoiding eye contact with the other inmates. When he got to the end, he turned, stepping over the faded outline of the basketball court sprayed onto the concrete. The hoops had long since vanished, and all that now remained were a couple of round holes in the floor with the stubs of filed-down metal posts embedded in them. Apparently, team sports were not something the prison administration thought to be important.

He followed the lines of the court to the other side, then turned back in the other direction, heading back toward the prison building.

And then he saw the two men. Officer Monahan and an inmate of equal size he hadn't seen before.

They were standing shoulder to shoulder near the rec yard exit and looking directly at him. Davis slowed his pace, sensing he was in trouble.

The inmate glanced sideways and said something to Monahan. The guard tilted his head down in a slow nod. Then the inmate stepped into the yard and started across it.

Davis glanced around quickly. There were no other guards visible. A gaggle of inmates looked on from the bleachers near the side wall. More inmates, those walking the yard or pumping weights on the benches, retreated to the side, leaving the center of the concrete space empty except for Davis, as if they sensed something was about to go down and didn't want to get caught in the middle of it. After all, it wasn't their fight. That was one of the unwritten rules of prison life. Don't get involved in crap that doesn't concern you. So instead, they watched with rising interest as their fellow inmate closed in on him.

Davis turned back in the other direction, aware he had nowhere to go but hoping someone would intervene before it was too late. He looked over his shoulder. Saw the burly inmate closing on him, fists clenched.

Further back, officer Monahan hadn't moved from the rec yard entrance. He stood with his arms folded, watching the scene play out. There would be no help from that quarter.

Davis summed up his situation and concluded that retreating further toward the back wall would only trap him, yet there was nowhere else to go. His pursuer's intentions were clear and obviously violent. And if he needed any convincing of that, the object now clutched in the man's hand was proof. A slim piece of metal honed to a point at one end, probably in the prison machine shop. A shank. Whether the inmate had made it himself or the guard furnished it to him was of little importance. It amounted to the same thing. Davis was in trouble. Real big trouble.

FIFTY-FOUR

BAUER HAD FOUND a propane grill at the back of the house and decided he would cook dinner that evening. To that end, he grabbed frozen hamburgers, lettuce, tomatoes, slices of cheese, and buns that he and Phoebe had purchased on the way to Amarillo. He fired up the grill and threw four hamburgers on. One for each of the women and two for him. He stood there with the spatula, turning the burgers with a beer bottle in his other hand.

When Patterson stepped outside, he looked up from his task. "Come to check on my cooking skills?"

"I'm sure your burger cooking skills are up there with the best of them. You look like the outdoor grilling type," Patterson said. "I wanted to talk to you about something else."

"What's on your mind?" Bauer sipped his beer and stared out across the darkening landscape.

"I think the two of you should go back to Dallas tomorrow after Phoebe visits Mark Davis," Patterson said. "I don't want to jeopardize your careers any more than necessary."

Bauer shook his head. "Forget it. Phoebe took time off, and

I'm owed sick leave. We have a couple of days before we need to make that decision. We're not going anywhere right now."

"Look, I appreciate what you're trying to do, but—"

"We're seeing this through, and that's all there is to it." Bauer transferred four sliced buns to the heating rack above the grill. "We're almost at the finish line with this. I can feel it. Soon we'll have enough evidence of a conspiracy to prove you innocent."

"We don't have anywhere near enough proof. There's still no link between the senator and that police detective. We also don't know how DNA from Mark Davis ended up inside Alexandria Rowley when he swears they didn't have sex. And let's not forget, someone killed Leo Galinsky, and it wasn't me."

"I'm aware of all that, but I still think we're close." Bauer dropped the slices of cheese onto the hamburgers and watched while they melted, then transferred the burgers to their buns and topped them with lettuce and tomato. He put the burgers on a plate and turned the grill off, then stepped toward the door. "Come on, let's eat. We can figure this out later."

Patterson followed him inside.

Phoebe had set the table with ketchup, mustard, and a family-size bag of chips.

They settled down and ate in silence. All the while, everything they had discovered rolled through Patterson's mind. She felt like most of the pieces were there, but gaps remained, and it drove her mad. Worse, she still had a nagging sense that she had seen the senator somewhere before, but she couldn't reel it in.

After the food was finished, they cleared the plates away, and Patterson suggested they get an early night. It was nine-thirty already, and they had spent the entire day following the senator's paper trail of companies and the shady land deal that stood to net him millions in profits at the expense of his constituents. Even though she wanted to keep on investigating, she was wiped out.

They moved to the living room and sat there for an hour watching TV and getting some much-needed downtime, then went their separate ways, with Bauer and Phoebe going to one bedroom and Patterson heading toward the other.

By eleven o'clock, Patterson was in bed and reading a book she had purchased while she was still in Dallas, mostly to take her mind off the swirl of events surrounding her. But she could barely keep her eyes open and soon put it down. Ten minutes later, she was drifting off to sleep. And then it clicked.

She knew why Senator Newport looked so familiar.

FIFTY-FIVE

PATTERSON JUMPED out of bed and pulled on her robe, then left the bedroom and went to the laptop, which was still on the kitchen table. She opened it and accessed the dead drop mailbox and the draft message Bauer had saved but not sent days before. The message with photos of Detective Sergeant Ortega.

The first one was a headshot, and she ignored this. The second one was a picture of Ortega standing next to another gentleman. She opened it and stared in disbelief. This was why the senator had looked so familiar.

"Hey, what are you doing?" a voice said from behind her. "It's so late."

Patterson looked up to see Bauer standing there with Phoebe hovering behind him. They looked bleary-eyed.

"I just figured out the connection to Senator Newport," she said, moving aside so they could see the screen. "I couldn't shake the feeling that he looked familiar. Now I know why."

"The social media photo I sent you," Bauer said. "That's Newport, all right."

"There's no doubt about it." Phoebe stepped closer to the

computer. "But we still don't know the relationship between them."

"That's easy enough to find out. We just have to go back to where I found that photo." Bauer pulled out a seat and sat down.

"Can you remember where you found it?" Patterson asked.

"Not exactly. It's probably in the browser history of my laptop, but I left that back home because I didn't want to leave a digital footprint here." Bauer reached toward the laptop. "May I?"

"Knock yourself out." Patterson pushed the laptop toward him and watched as Bauer opened a browser window.

"I remember the search term I used." Bauer typed away, entering a phrase into the search engine. He was rewarded with a list of hits. He clicked over to the image tab and scrolled down through the results. "Just give me a minute."

They waited while he studied the results.

Phoebe covered her mouth to stifle a yawn. "I wish you'd remembered this earlier."

"So do I," Patterson replied, watching Bauer.

After a few moments more, he clicked on a link. "Got it."

Patterson shuffled her chair closer to him as Phoebe leaned over his shoulder.

They all looked at the screen.

The photo of Senator Bill Newport and Detective Sergeant Felix Ortega—captioned *one proud Detective Sergeant*—was on the page of someone called Jennifer Ortega. It was dated five years before.

"Detective Ortega's wife?" Bauer said.

Patterson recognized the name from her visit to the Ortega residence a couple of nights before when she had almost gotten caught snooping. "That's his wife. Ortega said her name when they came outside."

"Do I want to know?" asked Bauer.

"I tripped a security light when I was checking on the red truck. It's fine. They didn't see me." Patterson turned her attention back to the screen. "Does it say anything about how the senator and Ortega know each other?"

"Hang on." Bauer clicked on the comments next to the photograph. There were eight of them in total. Most were vague compliments. *Looking good. What a pair of handsome guys.* And such like. But the fourth comment down was different.

The senator wrote it himself.

Me and my new nephew-in-law.

Bauer clicked to the next photo. This one showed Ortega and his wife, Jennifer. He was in the same black suit as in the previous picture. She was wearing a wedding dress. It was posted on the same day as the photo of Ortega and Newport.

Patterson stared at the screen, hardly able to believe her eyes. "Senator Newport has a sister. We know that because of the research Phoebe conducted into the land deal. Her name is Linda. Her daughter must be Jennifer."

"And guess who she's married to," Bauer said.

"Detective Sergeant Felix Ortega," Patterson replied.

"Right." Bauer clicked back to the original photo and the comments. Linda Newport had posted her thoughts, too.

A son-in-law to be proud of.

"I guess we have our connection," Phoebe said.

"It looks that way." Patterson studied the photo of the two men, looking so comfortable with each other. "Detective Sergeant Ortega is using his position to do the senator's dirty work."

"Makes you wonder who killed Leo Galinsky, doesn't it?" Bauer said.

"I think the most obvious suspect is right in front of us on that screen," Patterson said. "Ortega himself."

FIFTY-SIX

THE NEXT DAY Phoebe left early to visit Mark Davis for the second time. It was Monday morning. Unlike her previous visit two days before, traffic was heavy. It took almost an hour and a half to reach the Potter County Correctional Facility. She went to the same building as before, parking in the visitor's lot, but when she got inside, the guard gave her some unsettling news.

"I'm sorry, miss, but you won't be able to see Mark Davis today."

"What? Why not?" Phoebe wondered if there had been some glitch with the appointment she had made to visit him. "I booked this yesterday online."

"I'm aware of that, but there's been an incident. Mr. Davis isn't in any shape to receive visitors."

"What kind of incident?" Phoebe's gut tightened.

"Another inmate stabbed him in the rec yard."

Phoebe could hardly believe what she was hearing. "Are you trying to tell me Mark Davis is dead?"

"No. He's alive and currently in the infirmary, but it was touch-and-go for a while. He's stable, but critical right now."

"How could you let something like this happen?" Phoebe

asked, indignant. "He hasn't even been to trial yet. Why did you even put him in the general population with people that would do something like this to him?"

"That isn't my decision to make. I'm merely passing on the message. Once he's stabilized and feeling better, you might be able to visit him in the infirmary, but not now."

"I see." Phoebe tried to contain her frustration and anger. "Is there anything else you can tell me?"

"Only that he's lucky to still be alive. Beyond that, you'll have to put your inquiry through regular channels. There's a contact form on the prison's website."

"Really? You want me to fill out a contact form?"

The guard shrugged. "I've told you everything I know."

"And you couldn't have called to tell me this before I drove all the way here?"

"You should have received a call to inform you of the situation first thing this morning. If you didn't, then I'm sorry."

"I guess it's too late now." Phoebe turned and stomped from the lobby. She crossed the parking lot back to her car, keys in hand. As she went, her mind turned to the guard who watched her leave after visiting Davis two days before. He had photographed her. She was sure of it. She hoped Mark Davis had not been silenced at the end of a homemade knife simply because she wanted to visit him again. That would be too much to contemplate. But there was nothing she could do about it now.

She climbed into her car, pushed the key into the ignition, then drove to the exit. As she pulled out onto the road and drove back toward the rental house on the other side of town, another vehicle slipped out behind her and followed at a distance.

A prickle ran up her spine.

A red truck with a dented front fender.

She reached for her cell phone, the burner Patterson had

given her, but then cursed her own stupidity. When she arrived at the visitation center, she had put her purse and the phone within, inside the trunk because she wasn't allowed to bring them inside with her. She was so frustrated when she left the facility that she forgot to retrieve it. Now it was out of reach, which meant she was on her own.

Phoebe wasn't a special agent. She was just an administrative assistant, which meant she didn't have the training Bauer and Patterson possessed. They would surely know how to handle this situation, but she was not so fortunate. She knew one thing. She couldn't lead that red truck back to the rental house and also couldn't let it catch her. Somehow, she had to lose it, and fast.

Phoebe pressed down on her accelerator, pushing the car up to ten miles over the speed limit. The truck hung back but kept pace. She knew who would be behind the wheel. Detective Sergeant Ortega. That was why no one had called to tell her about Davis being stabbed. He wanted her to show up so she could lead him back to Patterson. And it should have worked. Phoebe would never have given the red truck a second glance under normal circumstances. But Ortega had miscalculated. He didn't know Patterson had already identified him and the truck and therefore didn't account for it.

Phoebe was heading back toward the city. Normally she would have driven straight through, but at the first opportunity, she turned, unsure where she was going, and sped up again to put as much distance between herself and the truck as possible.

When she glanced in her rearview mirror, it was still behind her but further back. And then a horrible thought occurred to her. Ortega was a police detective. All he had to do was call in a description of her car, and every cop in Amarillo would be looking for her. And she was sure he would know her license plate because he must have been waiting for her to show up in the parking lot. That posed another problem. If he ran that plate, he would quickly figure out who she was, and it wouldn't be much of a leap to assume that Special Agent Marcus Bauer was with her, especially when he found out that they had both taken time off. That meant there were targets on all their backs. Her only consolation was that Ortega might not involve the police department. He was probably at the correctional facility on Senator Newport's orders and would not want them asking questions he couldn't answer.

There was another side road up ahead, leading into an industrial park. Phoebe pushed her luck and sped up even more, then slowed at the last moment and swung the car into a hard left turn. Her tires screeched. She felt the back fishtail but wrestled it under control.

The red truck hadn't made it to the turn yet.

She needed to get out of sight. And quickly.

There were industrial units on both sides of the road with large roll-up metal doors, most of which were closed. But she saw one unit with the door up and cavernous space beyond. She made a snap decision and turned into the industrial park, then made a beeline for the unit, praying she hadn't just made a tactical error. If Ortega realized where she had gone, there would be no way out, and it would all be over.

FIFTY-SEVEN

AFTER PHOEBE LEFT for the prison, and with nothing else to do, Patterson sat at the kitchen table and continued her quest to put the pieces together while Bauer retreated into the living room to browse the web on his phone. She returned to the social media page displaying the photo of Ortega and the senator, but there was nothing beyond what they had discovered the night before.

Next, her thoughts turned to Alexandria Rowley. She wondered if the woman had reappeared, but an anonymous call to the women's shelter confirmed that Rowley was still unaccounted for. Patterson was fearing the worst. She suspected that Detective Sergeant Ortega had used Rowley to get Mark Davis out of the way, convincing her to say he raped her. Yet there was still that one nagging question. The DNA evidence in the form of sperm upon Rowley's person when she went to the hospital, along with signs of trauma. It was damning and conclusive. How had they done it?

Frustrated, Patterson typed the name Mark Davis into her search bar. There wasn't much. Mostly business-related stuff, such as his corporate registration and name attached to some old projects. Then she took a different tack, typing in the band's name—*Sunrise*—alongside his name. That was when she found it. An old article about Davis had appeared in a now-defunct online magazine called Texas Business Today. They had interviewed him about his fledgling company many years before, probably as part of what was called an advertorial package in the magazine industry. An advertiser can pay the magazine to include an article about their business next to a regular panel ad. For all intents and purposes, it would look like a regular editorial and thus provide the business with an air of credibility that advertising alone cannot achieve.

She almost skipped the article until she caught sight of something that piqued her interest. Davis was talking about his college days and his time with the band. She sucked in a quick breath.

"Marcus, come look at this."

Bauer sauntered in from the living room. "Did you find something?"

"And then some. It's a long shot, but it might be how they framed Mark Davis."

Bauer furrowed his brow. "An old article in some business magazine?"

"Yes but listen to this." Patterson took a deep breath and read him the relevant paragraph as told by Mark Davis himself. *"Back then, in college, we were so broke. The band hardly made any money because, honestly, we weren't very good and mostly played small joints that barely had any entertainment budget. Even the one festival we played didn't pay us. TexFest. It turned out to be the last gig we ever did. Instead, I got creative to make money. I guess you could say I was an entrepreneur even back then. The blood bank paid for donations. It wasn't much, but it bought groceries. I could give blood several times a month.*

"But it wasn't just that. There was a sperm bank in Flagstaff where I attended college, and I went there pretty regularly, too. I

won't go into detail, but you can guess why, and it was more fun than giving blood. They paid better as well. I got seventy-five dollars each time. I don't think I've ever told that to anyone before and probably shouldn't have mentioned it now, but you asked about my entrepreneurial spirit, and I think that sums it up as well as anything. When you need money, you find a way." Patterson stopped reading. "There's a lot more to the article, but that's pretty much the important bit."

Bauer rubbed his chin thoughtfully. "I don't know, Patterson. It's a leap."

"Where else would they get what they needed to frame him?" Patterson asked.

"You're seriously suggesting that Detective Sergeant Ortega came across this article, tracked down that sperm bank, and then somehow got hold of the deposit Mark Davis made, then used it to plant DNA evidence on Alexandria Rowley?"

"Why not?"

"Because it's ridiculous. That sperm bank might not even be in business anymore."

"How about we find out?" Patterson went back on the web and did a search. It only took a few moments to find what she needed. "I've got it. GRT Fertility Solutions. They're the only sperm bank in that area and they have been in business since 1996."

"That still doesn't prove anything."

Patterson was still scrolling through search results. She clicked over to the news tab and let out a triumphant cry, pointing at an article from several weeks before. "How about this, then?"

Bauer leaned in to look at what she'd found. "GRT Fertility Solutions was broken into last month."

"Right." Patterson clicked on the link. "It says here that the place was trashed, but nothing was taken. The office was vandalized, though. Spray-painted with slogans saying that artificial insemination is against nature. The storage facility at the rear of the building was untouched."

"Which is why they put it down to activists."

"It's a great way to cover up the real reason they were there. Except the activist story doesn't really make sense. Think about it, if you were an activist who didn't agree with artificial insemination, why would you leave the storage facility intact? Wouldn't that be the first thing you would vandalize?"

"I don't know because I'm not an activist," Bauer replied. "But I still think it's a longshot and circumstantial at best. It's all so bizarre."

"Which is exactly what makes it perfect. Who would ever think to connect the evidence from a rape in Amarillo to a sperm bank in Flagstaff?"

"We're going to need more evidence than some loose connection. Now, if you could tie Detective Sergeant Ortega to Flagstaff at the same time as the break-in, that would be different."

"There's no way Ortega would have gone there himself." Patterson thought for a moment. "But we know Leo Galinsky had his mitts all over this because he visited Alexandria Rowley at work the night she went missing. It seems pretty clear that Ortega used Galinsky when he didn't want to get his own hands dirty. We need to prove Galinsky went to Flagstaff."

FIFTY-EIGHT

PHOEBE SPED toward the industrial unit, and safety of the open bay door. When she looked in her rearview mirror, there was still no sign of the red truck, although it couldn't be far behind.

She was almost there. From the road, the space within had appeared empty enough for her to drive into and hide out of view, but if she got there and was mistaken, then she would be forced to keep going and try to lose Ortega among the rows of industrial units while attempting to double back around to the road. Something she did not wish to do. Her plan also hinged on Ortega not seeing where she had gone, which meant there wasn't much time.

She reached the unit and was relieved to find the bay beyond the door empty. She swung the wheel and pulled inside with another screech of tires, narrowly missing a concrete post to the left of the door. She screeched to a halt, the nose of her car mere feet from the back wall, and sat there, breathing hard. Hopefully, Ortega would keep going, unaware that she had swerved into this particular industrial park.

"Hey, what the hell do you think you're doing," came an angry shout.

Phoebe turned her head to see a guy dressed in dirty blue overalls stalking toward her from the next bay over, which held a pickup truck on Axel stands with the hood open.

He carried a large wrench in one hand.

Another man appeared from the other side of the truck and started toward the car.

Phoebe pulled on her door handle and jumped out of the car, deciding there wasn't time for long explanations. "You have to help me. Some guy in a truck has been following my car. He tried to force me off the road back there. I didn't know where else to go."

The man with the wrench stopped short. He turned to his companion. "Sean, get the door. Pull it down. Quick."

The other man veered left and went to a looped chain next to the door that ran up to the top of the opening. He pulled on it, and the metal door descended with a rattling clack.

Once it was closed, both men turned toward Phoebe.

The one with the wrench lifted it. "If anyone tries to follow you in here, they'll get the business end of this around their head."

"Thank you so much," Phoebe said. "I was so scared. I didn't know what to do."

"Come on," the man said, turning back in the other direction and motioning for Phoebe to follow him to an office at the end of the workshop. "Let's see if anyone is out there."

Phoebe picked her way through the workshop and around the truck with the open hood, following Sean and Wrench Guy into the office.

There was a small window.

As she stepped inside, she caught a flash of red pass by outside. A truck.

Wrench Guy was already at the window. "Is that him?"

"I think so." Phoebe realized she was shaking. Ortega was right outside. Had he seen her pull in here, or was he just driving around looking for her? Phoebe lingered near the doorway, her eyes fixed on the window. After a while, she gathered her courage and stepped further into the room, staying back far enough that she wouldn't be in view if Ortega drove past again.

The two mechanics exchanged a look, and then Sean made his way back to the office door.

"I'll take a drive around to make sure he's left," he said. "You stay here."

Phoebe had no intention of going anywhere until she was sure Detective Sergeant Ortega was long gone. She nodded mutely.

Sean disappeared into the workshop. Seconds later, she heard the door open and then close, followed by an engine starting up. She gathered her nerves and stepped to the window in time to see a blue truck, smaller than Ortega's, drive past. The windows were tinted, but the sun was slanting in enough that she could see Sean behind the wheel. He reached the end of the row and turned.

"You want anything to drink?" Wrench Guy asked. "Coffee or soda?"

"No, thank you." Butterflies swarmed in Phoebe's stomach. She hadn't even considered the possibility that her previous visit to the prison had attracted unwanted attention, let alone that someone would be lying in wait for her. If she hadn't spotted that red truck, she would have led Ortega right back to Patterson. Who knew what would have happened then? The least dangerous outcome would be they ended up under arrest. Patterson would go to prison, convicted of murder, while she and Bauer would probably end up out of a job and charged with aiding and abetting a fugitive. The worst-case scenario was that they ended up dead, shot by Ortega, who would claim they became violent, and he was forced to take lethal action.

"You okay, there?" Wrench Guy was observing her through narrowed eyes.

"Just a little shaken, that's all." Phoebe retreated from the window just as Sean's truck returned.

The truck door slammed. Another door opened and closed. Sean stepped back into the office. "All clear. No sign of a red truck. He's gone."

Phoebe slumped with relief. "I can't thank you enough for this. I don't know what I would have done if the two of you weren't here."

"Our pleasure." Wrench Guy walked with Phoebe back to her car while Sean lifted the roll-up metal bay door again. He poked his head outside quickly and looked in both directions, then gave her a thumbs up.

She inched forward and pulled back out, waving with gratitude to her saviors, then made her way back to the road and left the industrial park behind. As she rejoined her original route, she couldn't help but wonder if Ortega had parked up somewhere, hoping she would drive back past him. Sean was right. The red truck was gone, at least for now.

FIFTY-NINE

"I HAVE an idea how we can link Leo Galinsky to Flagstaff," said Bauer. "But I warn you. It's a long shot."

"Tell me," Patterson said.

"How about I show you?" Bauer jumped up and hurried toward the bedroom he shared with Phoebe. He went inside and returned a minute later, clutching a thumb drive just like the one he had used to copy the surveillance videos at the convenience store, except this one was a different color. "I copied all the photos Phoebe took in the ASAC's office onto this because I only put what I thought was relevant in the dead drop."

"What else is on there?" Patterson watched Bauer plug the thumb drive into a USB port on the laptop.

"A call log. Leo Galinsky's call log, to be precise. Amarillo PD obtained a copy of it to check the veracity of the call he placed to you."

"They did that, but they didn't take a closer look at the spoofed text message I was supposed to have sent?"

"Detective Sergeant Ortega knew what he would find on the

phone log because the outgoing call to you was genuine, but he wasn't so confident the text message would fool the Amarillo PD media lab. My guess is he never even asked them to look at it. But that doesn't matter. Once we gather enough evidence of this conspiracy, we'll let the FBI crime lab inspect the message. In the meantime, I'm looking for something else."

"Want to share?" Patterson asked.

"As soon as I find what I'm looking for." Bauer had all five pages of the call log open on the laptop screen. On the third page, he stopped and slapped his palm on the table. "Got him. Look at this."

Patterson leaned over Bauer's shoulder. At first, she didn't understand what he was so excited about, but then she saw it. A call from a few weeks back and a few days before Mark Davis got arrested. A call placed to a number with a 928 area code. It stood out because apart from the call to her, all the other calls were to local Amarillo numbers. "Is that the area code for Flagstaff?" she asked, not daring to hope.

"Sure is." Bauer was already searching the web for the number in question. Getting his answer, he looked up at her. "It's for a takeout pizza place called Pie Perfection in downtown Flagstaff. And look at the date."

"The same day the fertility clinic was broken into." Patterson could hardly believe their luck. "That's the proof we need."

"Damned right it is. This puts Leo Galinsky in the right place at the right time. That can't be a coincidence. He must've ordered a takeout pizza while he was waiting to ransack the fertility clinic later that night and steal one of the deposits Mark Davis made back when he was in college."

"He slipped up and used his own phone instead of a burner."

"Right. One tiny mistake that gave him away."

"Not that he'll care either way," Patterson said. "He's dead."

"And this gets us one step closer to proving you weren't the one who killed him."

Patterson's mind turned to the confrontation at the convenience store between Alexandria Rowley and Leo Galinsky. "She's dead, isn't she?"

Bauer picked up on her train of thought. "Rowley?"

Patterson nodded.

"It's a fair bet. Galinsky probably killed her the same night he visited the convenience store. That's why no one has seen her since."

"And then they killed Galinsky to make sure he wouldn't talk and used his murder to frame me," Patterson said.

"They were cleaning up loose ends."

"Which would have worked if it hadn't been for your warning to get out of the hotel room before Ortega, Ricketts, and that FBI team arrived to arrest me." A terrible thought occurred to Patterson. "You don't think he's in on it, too?"

"Who, Special Agent Ricketts?" Bauer shook his head. "Unlikely. He arranged for you to visit Mark Davis in prison, and his PA got Amarillo PD to send over the surveillance footage from the bar and then passed it on to me. He's clueless about Ortega and Senator Newport's shady dealings and efforts to conceal them."

"Now all we have to do is gather the evidence and convince someone to listen to our theory." Patterson wasn't sure how easy that would be.

"I can think of the perfect person," Bauer said. "You're dating him."

"Jonathan?"

Bauer was about to reply when the front door flew open, and Phoebe rushed in. She slammed it behind her, a look of panic on her face. "Mark Davis won't be talking to anyone. He got stabbed in the prison yard last night."

"What?" Patterson jumped up, her seat almost tipping over.

"And it gets worse. Ortega was waiting when I arrived at the prison. He followed me."

SIXTY

PATTERSON RAN to the window and looked out. "You led him back here?"

Phoebe shook her head. "No, I lost him in an industrial park, thanks mostly to a couple of helpful mechanics who hid me in their shop. I told them some creep was following me. That he tried to run me off the road. But it was a close call."

"You shouldn't have gone back there," Bauer said. "I knew it was a mistake."

Patterson stepped away from the window. "Tell me about Mark Davis. What happened?"

"When I arrived at the prison, they turned me away. Said I wouldn't be able to visit. Davis was stabbed yesterday evening."

"Is he still alive?" Bauer looked shocked.

Phoebe nodded. "He's in the infirmary. Critical but stable. Another inmate with a shiv got to him in the rec yard. He's lucky to be alive. That's all they would tell me."

An icy dread enveloped Patterson. "I guess we're not getting any more information out of Davis anytime soon." She looked at Bauer. "It's our fault Mark Davis almost died. The senator must have wanted him silenced before Phoebe had a chance to visit again. They obviously have someone inside the prison. A guard, maybe. It wouldn't take much to convince another inmate to do Davis in. Even a few packs of cigarettes would probably do the trick."

"Especially if it was a lifer with no hope of parole," Bauer said. "Someone like that would jump at the chance to have a friendly guard in their corner in exchange for a bit of dirty work."

Patterson swore and kicked the chair she had just vacated, sending it skittering across the floor. "Worse than that. They used him as bait. They knew Phoebe would show up and be turned away, then drive right back here and reveal our location."

Phoebe looked at Patterson. "If you hadn't noticed Ortega tailing you, the ruse would have worked. I only recognized the red truck with the dented fender because of your description."

"This is bad," Patterson said, pacing the kitchen. "Ortega will have Phoebe's license plate. He'll know who she is by now." She looked at Bauer. "It won't take much to make the connection with you, and then this whole thing crumbles like a house of cards. We'll all end up the subject of a manhunt."

"Or dead just like everyone else," Bauer replied grimly.

"We can't stay here anymore. It's not safe." Patterson scowled. "Now Phoebe's been discovered, they'll trace this rental back to her grandmother. I don't know how long that will take, but once they do, we'll have a whole yard full of cops and FBI agents pointing guns at us."

"Maybe even a SWAT team." Now it was Bauer's turn to scowl. "I bet Ortega would like nothing better than a siege-style shootout that takes care of us for good. This whole thing went south in a hurry."

"We have to make that call to Jonathan." Calling Grant was the last thing Patterson wanted to do under the circumstances.

She had no idea if he would help her and was also loath to drag him into this mess. That was the very reason she hadn't contacted him before. But there was no choice.

"What call?" Phoebe asked, looking between the two of them.

"I think we've gone about as far as we can on our own," Bauer replied. "It's time that we put trust in our colleagues to believe us and do the right thing."

"And if it backfires?"

"Then at least we're still alive." Bauer put his arm around Phoebe. "You took a risk that put you in harm's way this morning and I let you do it. Ortega is dangerous. We don't have any proof yet, but we think he killed Leo Galinsky. He wouldn't hesitate to kill the three of us and claim we were the ones who shot first. Hell, all he'd have to do is say we were armed when he got here, and we refused to surrender."

"He'd get away with it, too," Patterson said.

"I don't like this." Phoebe looked up at Bauer. "If we let Patterson turn herself in, if we go along with her, and they still think she's a killer, we might all end up in jail. That's no protection. Look at what happened to Mark Davis."

Patterson stepped close to Phoebe and put an arm on her shoulder. "I don't think we have a choice. There's nothing more we can do on our own, and the rental house isn't safe anymore."

"Unless you're suggesting we all live in that van of Patterson's. You know. The one you said probably smells like old socks," Bauer said with a grin.

Phoebe looked at Patterson. "I didn't say it like that."

"Hey, you're not wrong. Now that I think about it, there is a bit of a sock odor in the thing, despite the air freshener I bought," Patterson said. "And I think it might be a bit cramped with the three of us living in it while we make for the border."

"So we turn ourselves in and hope it all works out," Phoebe said.

"How about we speak to Jonathan, see what he has to say, and take it from there," Patterson said. "And then we need to get the hell out of here before Ortega connects the dots and comes looking for us."

SIXTY-ONE

PATTERSON FELT BETTER NOW they had a plan, even if it was risky. She took out her phone and turned to the others. "Are we in agreement on this? Because once I make this call, the rental house won't be safe anymore."

"We don't have a choice," Bauer said. "This house stopped being safe the moment Ortega got a glimpse of Phoebe's license plate number. He's probably running it as we speak. We should have left the car parked at the decoy hotel and driven here in a rental."

"That wouldn't have helped," Phoebe said. "He would've just pulled the rental company records and traced it back to us, anyway."

"Which would require a warrant, buying us more time."

"Guys." Patterson clapped her hands. "We don't have time to debate how poor your evasion skills are. Are we doing this, or not?"

Phoebe and Bauer exchanged a glance, then he said, "Do it."

Patterson dialed Jonathan Grant's number. She hesitated, her finger hovering over the call button. "The two of you should gather your stuff. Pack everything up and put it in the van. Regardless of what happens on this call, we need to get out of here."

"We can take my car," Phoebe said.

"No." Bauer shook his head. "The car will have to stay here. Ortega might have issued a BOLO on it. Patterson's right. The van is safer."

"I want be out of here in an hour or less," Patterson said. "The longer we stay, the greater risk we incur."

"Come on. I guess the romantic weekend is over." Bauer led Phoebe back to the bedroom to gather their belongings.

Patterson watched them go. She took a deep breath, then placed the call.

Grant answered on the first ring, almost as if he'd been sitting at his phone waiting. But of course, he didn't recognize the number, so had no idea it was Patterson.

"It's me," she said. "Before you say anything, please know that I didn't kill that man."

"Never thought you did," Grant said, the relief in his voice clear. "You might be a lot of things, but a murderer isn't one of them. I've been worried sick. Why did it take you so long to call?"

"Because I didn't know if we were still on the same team, and I didn't want to put you in an impossible position." There was so much she wanted to say to Grant, but now was not the time. "I need your help. I'm being framed for the murder of a small-time crook named Leo Galinsky, and we have proof of why."

"We. You're not alone?"

"Not exactly." Patterson didn't want to say anything more, but it wouldn't matter soon, anyway. The walls were closing in around them. "I'm with Special Agent Marcus Bauer from the Dallas Field Office and Phoebe Cutler, the ASAC's admin."

"The rookie agent SAC Harris saddled you with and an administrative assistant?"

"It's a long story which I don't have the time to tell you," Patterson said. "Do you want to listen to what I have to say, or not?"

"Yes. Absolutely I do. But I'm not the person you need to tell."

"You won't help me?"

"I can't. Not directly."

Patterson swallowed her rising anger. "Because you don't want a stain on your precious career."

"That isn't it. We're in a relationship. I'll be perceived as biased. Whatever evidence you have, and I hope it's good, you need to convince someone who doesn't have a personal stake in your future."

"Do you have any suggestions? I'm blowing in the wind here, and the people who framed me are closing in."

"Actually, I do. Call Walter Harris. Tell him what you told me and show him your proof. I've been in communication with him since this whole affair began. He'll lend you a sympathetic ear or at least listen to what you have to say. But you'll need to trust him."

"I'm finding it hard to trust anyone at the moment," Patterson said.

"Apart from your old partner and his girlfriend," Grant retorted.

"I didn't want them involved. And what makes you think they're dating?"

"Come on, Patterson. Harris told me. They weren't fooling anyone. And it's fine so long as it doesn't interfere with their work."

"You mean like having a girlfriend on the run accused of murder is interfering with yours?"

"I never said that."

"Just like you never said anything about your impending promotion," Patterson replied, unable to stop herself even though she knew it wasn't the right time or place for that particular conversation.

Grant ignored the comment. Instead, he gave her a cell phone number which he told her would go straight through to the Dallas SAC and said nothing while she wrote it down. Then he said, "Call Walter Harris, Patterson. Don't wait. Do it now."

Patterson did as she was told, a subtle loneliness descending upon her as Grant disconnected and empty silence rushed in to fill the void. She lowered the phone from her ear, dialed the number Grant had relayed to her, and waited for Walter Harris to answer.

SIXTY-TWO

"YOU NEED to come into the office right now. Today." Harris said after Patterson told him she possessed proof of a conspiracy involving the lead detective on the Leo Galinsky murder investigation and a high-ranking politician, which had gotten both herself and Mark Davis framed for crimes they did not commit. She didn't go into details and avoided mentioning the senator by name, preferring to hold that information back until they met face-to-face. She also kept quiet about Marcus Bauer and Phoebe Cutler being with her, even though she knew he would find out eventually since she had already admitted as much to Jonathan Grant.

Finally, she said, "I'll meet you on neutral ground. Not at the office. And you can't inform Amarillo PD or Special Agent Ricketts that I'm coming in."

"You aren't in much of a position to bargain," Harris said. "Where are you at this moment?"

"Still in Amarillo," Patterson replied. "It's noon. I can be back in Dallas by seven."

"All right. Meet me in Pacific Plaza Park under the pavilion at nine. We'll talk, and if I think your claims have merit, we can go from there."

"And if you don't?"

"Then I take you into custody."

"You'll come alone?"

"Don't be so naïve, Special Agent Blake."

Patterson considered this in silence. Meeting Walter Harris was a huge risk—even on neutral ground he would be in control—but it was the only way to clear her name.

"Do we have a deal?" Harris asked when she didn't answer.

"You promise to hear me out?"

"That much I can guarantee."

"Then we have a deal. Nine o'clock at Pacific Plaza Park."

"I'll see you there." The line went dead.

Patterson slipped the phone into her pocket and turned toward the back of the house and her bedroom, even as Bauer came the other way carrying a large duffel bag.

He stopped when he saw her. "Is it done?"

Patterson gave a slight tilt of her head. "I'm meeting Walter Harris tonight."

Bauer considered this a moment, then continued on his way to the front door without comment.

Patterson headed in the other direction and quickly packed her bags. Soon they would be on the road and heading back to Dallas, where she would find either salvation or a set of handcuffs waiting for her. But either way, she wouldn't be running anymore, and that much was a relief.

SIXTY-THREE

THE TRIP back to Dallas was a tense affair. Patterson was in the driver's seat, once more wearing sunglasses and the baseball cap she had found in the old truck. Bauer and Phoebe occupied the rear seats, leaving the front passenger seat open. Behind them, in the spacious cargo area that Patterson had turned into a makeshift bedroom on wheels, were all their bags and the groceries they had purchased. At least the ones that wouldn't spoil. The rest they left in the rental house to be collected later, along with Phoebe's car.

Assuming they didn't all end up under arrest before then.

After an hour on the road, they pulled into a gas station and filled the van's tank, then parked up on the far side of the forecourt and made sandwiches from the bread, deli meat, and cheese they had packed into the cooler. They washed it down with sodas—not Patterson's first choice but convenient—and then continued their journey.

The trio rolled into Dallas against the backdrop of a fiery red sunset sky stitched with ribbons of cloud that caught the light and dispersed it in dazzling shades of gold.

Patterson weaved through the streets and found a public

parking lot two blocks north of Pacific Plaza Park where the van could remain out of sight and ready should the situation go awry, and a quick exit became necessary. She would have preferred to stop closer but was sure Walter Harris would have agents watching the roads next to the park.

They were almost an hour early.

Patterson took the time to go over what she was going to say in her head, collecting her thoughts and calming her nerves. At twenty minutes to nine, she decided it was time. She would go alone. They had agreed on this during a brief but heated conversation on the road. Bauer thought it was a bad idea, but Patterson insisted. If the meeting went south, there was at least some chance they could escape the mess without ruining their careers, small as that was considering Phoebe had been seen at the jail by Detective Sergeant Ortega, and Jonathan Grant knew of their involvement.

Gathering up the laptop which held all of their evidence, Patterson stepped out of the van at a quarter to nine and started toward the meeting without looking back. The burner phone was in her pocket. The baseball cap was gone. There was no point in hiding her identity any longer.

She saw the pavilion as soon as the park came into view. It sat like a hollowed-out flying saucer hovering above a knoll of grass and supported by columns at intervals. Outdoor furniture was placed on the pavement, circling the grass. Red metal tables and chairs—perfect for sitting and eating lunch or watching the world go by. Strategically placed spotlights ringed the structure so that it seemed to glow against the surrounding buildings and the dark night sky beyond.

Hours before, the park would have been filled with office workers and tourists taking advantage of the recently constructed free-form oasis of greenery that had once been a bland and featureless parking lot. Now, it was mostly empty save for a clutch of city dwellers walking their dogs or strolling arm in arm as they took in the cool evening breeze.

But these were not the park's only occupants. She spotted four men wearing black suits and white shirts. They stood at intervals a short distance from the pavilion, and she knew instantly from their stance and demeanor who they were. She suspected there would be more federal agents further afield. If the SAC didn't believe her, the options for retreat would be minimal.

She approached from the opposite end of the park and approached the pavilion, passing the FBI agents without acknowledging their presence.

And then she saw him.

Walter Harris crested the grassy rise in the middle of the pavilion moments before she reached the imposing circular structure. He stood above her, arms at his sides, and waited while she climbed toward him.

"Special Agent Blake, how lovely to see you again," he said with no hint of sarcasm as she closed the distance between them.

"A shame it isn't under better circumstances," Patterson replied.

Harris shrugged. "I must say, I was surprised to hear about your predicament."

"Not half as surprised as me."

"I can imagine. You must find it ironic that Special Agent Bauer saved your hide after the fuss you put up about being paired with him."

"I don't know what you're talking about," Patterson replied.

"Come now, Special Agent Blake. We both know he tipped you off the morning of the raid on your hotel room. He's not as smart as he thinks he is. Like right now, he'd have us believe he and Phoebe Cutler are enjoying a romantic long weekend in Wichita Falls."

Patterson dropped her gaze to the ground. "I didn't want to involve either of them in this. I told Special Agent Bauer to stay away."

"Which was never going to happen. He's loyal to a fault, and that fault might cost him his job and liberty."

Patterson looked up again. "If you knew what he was doing all this time, why didn't you stop him?"

"We didn't know . . . at first. But it didn't take long to figure out. And don't worry, your boyfriend in New York wasn't the one who told us about him."

"That doesn't answer my question. If you knew Special Agent Bauer was in contact with me, why didn't you stop him?"

"Because it served our purposes."

"Would you care to explain?"

"Not just yet." Harris nodded toward one of the table and chair sets. "How about we go sit down, and you can show me what you have."

He started down the slope without waiting for a reply.

Patterson lingered a moment, casting her gaze out across the park toward the waiting FBI agents standing like statues at a distance, then she followed behind.

They sat down. Patterson opened the laptop, typed in her password, and brought up the documents detailing Senator Newport's web of holding companies and shell corporations. She also cued up the surveillance video they had obtained from the convenience store and the bar footage from the night Alexandria Rowley approached Mark Davis. She explained everything, going through all that she, Phoebe, and Bauer had discovered and their theory of how it all tied together.

SAC Harris listened without interrupting, nodding his head occasionally or making a small tutting sound. When she was done, he reached out and closed the laptop screen, then met her gaze over the top of it. "This is all very interesting, but mostly circumstantial. You don't have any hard evidence that Leo Galinsky killed Alexandria Rowley after convincing her to set up Mark Davis or that Detective Sergeant Ortega killed Leo Galinsky, in turn, to silence him and frame you. The work Phoebe Cutler did in uncovering Senator Newport's shady and possibly illegal backroom dealings is compelling, but not enough to get you off the hook. I'm sorry, Special Agent Blake. I know that's not what you wanted to hear."

Then he raised a hand and beckoned to the closest agents, who started toward them with determined looks upon their faces.

SIXTY-FOUR

PATTERSON SHIFTED in her seat as the agents closed in upon them. She looked around. Gauged her chances of escape. Decided they were nil. "We had a deal."

"That's right, we did. And I said you would need to convince me of your innocence." Harris waited for the two agents to reach them before looking up at them. "Special Agent Bauer and Phoebe Cutler are in a ratty old van two blocks from here in a public parking lot on Elm Street. Take a couple of the agents stationed around the perimeter and go get them. Bring them both back here."

"Yes, sir." The taller of the two agents nodded, then they turned and started back across the park in the direction of the van, moving at a trot. One of the pair spoke into a mic pinned to his lapel, no doubt directing other agents in the area to close in on the van. Patterson weighed up the odds of whipping out her cell phone and warning Bauer and Phoebe but concluded she wouldn't even have time to dial before Harris took it from her. She glared at him from across the table. "How did you know?"

"Because I'm very good at what I do," Harris said. "The city installed hundreds of surveillance cameras a couple of years ago that transmit in real-time to a monitoring facility at police headquarters. Some of those cameras cover the roads around this park. We identified your vehicle the minute you stepped out of it."

Patterson swore under her breath. She should have expected that.

"Don't feel bad. You couldn't have known." Harris sat back in his chair and looked around. "It's a nice night, don't you think? Not too oppressive, with a pleasant breeze."

"I'm about to be arrested for a crime I didn't commit, and you want to chat about the weather?" Patterson could hardly believe her ears.

"Who said anything about arresting you?"

"But I thought—"

"You thought wrong. I said the evidence you've gathered so far is not sufficient, but I don't believe you killed Leo Galinsky in cold blood. I think you're correct in hypothesizing that Detective Sergeant Ortega is responsible for that. But thinking a thing and proving it are two different matters. I also agree with you that Alexandria Rowley is probably dead. An unfortunate consequence of her own involvement in this sordid affair."

"You're not taking me into custody?" Patterson wasn't sure if she was relieved or angry that Harris had let her go on believing she was a fugitive when he obviously knew more than he was letting on. Maybe it was both.

"I am not. Now, how about we sit here and enjoy this lovely evening while we wait for your co-conspirators to show up?"

Patterson opened her mouth to respond in a manner befitting her mood, then thought better of it and settled back in her seat.

Harris folded his arms and let his gaze wander across the plaza. They sat in silence for ten minutes before Patterson saw a pair of familiar figures crossing the grassy expanse toward them, flanked by the two agents Harris had previously dispatched while another pair brought up the rear.

Phoebe looked despondent. Bauer's shoulders were hunched in coiled agitation. Patterson hoped he hadn't put up a fight when his colleagues arrived at the van, but she didn't see any bloodied noses or black eyes on his stewards, which was a good sign.

As they drew close, Harris unfolded his arms and stood to greet them. "Ah. Special Agent Bauer and Miss Cutler. So good of you to join us."

"It's not like we had much choice," Bauer said through gritted teeth.

Harris motioned to a pair of empty chairs. "Please, won't you both sit down?"

Bauer pulled a chair out for Phoebe, then walked around the table and took the other one. His jaw was clenched. A vein in his temple throbbed.

"Wonderful." Harris dismissed the agents, who retreated to a distance. He looked around the table. "Now the gang's all here, we can get down to business."

SIXTY-FIVE

"ARE WE UNDER ARREST?" Bauer asked, barking the words.

"Not at this moment." Harris shook his head. "We've been running an investigation into Senator Newport for the past six months. We know about the shell companies, but so far, he's managed to stay within a legal and political gray area." Harris turned his attention to Patterson. "Then you paid a visit to Mark Davis in prison and apparently spooked the senator, at least if the evidence you presented to me is correct."

"You didn't know about the report Mark Davis prepared on the brownfield site."

"No. We suspected the senator was dirty. We just didn't know how dirty. He's been using Detective Sergeant Ortega as his personal bulldog for years, but they're careful."

"And cunning," said Bauer.

"Precisely." Harris directed his attention to Patterson again. "If Special Agent Bauer had not told you to flee that hotel room, things might have turned out very differently. You would be sitting in jail on murder charges right now, and Mark Davis would have no hope of clearing his name despite his protestations of innocence. There is, however, a problem. The evidence you gathered in an effort to clear your name is compelling but not airtight. I don't believe for one moment you put a bullet in Leo Galinsky's head, but I'm not the one who gets to make that decision. The senator and his lackey detective have done a good job of setting you up."

"It helps that the detective investigating the murder is the same person who committed the crime," Bauer said.

"That goes without saying. He controls the narrative and the evidence." Harris leaned forward, resting his elbows on the table. "And therein lies my problem."

"Patterson is still a wanted individual," Bauer said.

"Yes. Officially, I'm duty-bound to take her into custody right now and let the courts decide her fate, but in this instance, there is sufficient reason to believe that would not ultimately serve the course of justice."

"So where does that leave us?" Bauer asked.

"Between a rock and a hard place," Harris replied. "If I do my sworn duty, I risk committing two innocent people to prison, possibly for the rest of their lives. If I take the other route, I jeopardize my career and that of every agent who has become involved in this. I also can't ignore the fact that one of my own agents, along with the ASAC's admin, took it upon themselves to aid a fugitive. I should place both of you on suspension while your actions are investigated."

"Or you could give us access to the Bureau's resources and the time to snare Newport and Ortega," Bauer said. "Reveal them as the murderers they are."

"My thoughts exactly," Harris replied. "Which is why I spoke with Marilyn Kahn and the deputy director this afternoon and convinced them to let me assess the evidence before committing to a course of action. Furthermore, they agreed to allow a special covert operation should I deem that evidence to be compelling. Which is why none of you are under arrest at this moment. But we don't have much time. By necessity, Amarillo PD cannot be read into this. Not even Special Agent Ricketts will be appraised of the situation." Harris turned to Patterson. "We have to maintain the illusion that the FBI is still actively hunting for you, which means you are still at considerable risk."

"I understand." As they drove back to Dallas, Patterson had considered the possibility she would be placed under arrest the moment she walked into the plaza and decided the odds of that occurring were about seventy percent, despite the evidence they had gathered. She believed Walter Harris to be a fair man, but also a stickler for the rules. It was a relief to know she wouldn't be behind bars, at least for now.

"It also means you cannot go anywhere near the Dallas Field Office. We need to keep a lid on this. The agents who accompanied me to the plaza have been vetted to ensure they have no links to either the senator or Detective Sergeant Ortega. They have also been briefed on the potential special operation and included in the task force that will run it. As such, they are sworn to secrecy and can be trusted."

"How are we going to proceed?" Bauer asked.

"Right now, you all need to get some rest. It's late, and there's nothing more we can do tonight. We'll pick this up in the morning. I've arranged for a secure facility from which to run the operation."

"Where?"

"Tomorrow, Special Agent Bauer."

"What about me?" Phoebe asked.

"You're included in the operation, of course. We could use someone with your administrative skills, although you've proven yourself to be adept at so much more." Harris straightened up and settled back into the chair. He looked between Bauer and Phoebe. "Since Ortega is almost certainly aware of your involvement with Special Agent Blake, you won't be able to return to your homes. It's too dangerous. Apart from the obvious legal peril you placed yourselves in, we know what these people are capable of. All three of you will be taken to a safe house."

"Fair enough," Bauer said.

"There's one more thing. I had to make certain concessions in order to convince the deputy director. While Special Agent Blake is not currently under arrest, she must be supervised at all times when not directly involved in the operation."

"That sure sounds like being under arrest." Patterson scowled.

"It's better than the alternative, I can assure you."

There wasn't much Patterson could say to that. "Who's going to be doing this supervising?"

"A person you trust and who has your best interests at heart," replied Harris.

Patterson was about to say that his answer wasn't exactly helpful when she heard footsteps approaching from her rear.

A shadow fell across the table.

A familiar voice spoke over her shoulder. "I know this isn't exactly what you had in mind when you said we should get away, but I'm hoping you'll make the most of it."

SIXTY-SIX

"WHAT ARE YOU DOING HERE?" Patterson jumped up and swiveled toward Jonathan Grant. She threw her arms around him and planted a kiss on his lips. They held each other tight for almost a full minute. Becoming aware of several sets of eyes on her back, she drew back and looked at the others, feeling sheepish that she had displayed such an outburst of emotion in front of her colleagues. "I thought you couldn't get involved."

"I couldn't until Marilyn Kahn called me into her office and briefed me on this little operation. She was under the impression you would listen to me. Goodness knows where she got that idea."

"Glad I'm not the only one," Bauer mumbled under his breath.

Patterson shot him a withering glare. "Hey, I listen when it's necessary. And I don't need the pair of you ganging up on me."

"Relax. No one is ganging up on you." Grant took a step toward her. "Would you rather I wasn't here?"

"No." Patterson grinned. "I guess if I must have a jailer, I'd glad it's you."

"First off, I'm not your jailer. The deputy director is just covering himself in case it turns out you really had gone rogue and taken vengeance on Leo Galinsky."

"You know that's not true."

"Everyone here knows you wouldn't do something like that. Sometimes you have to play the game."

"Hey, I'm not complaining about spending time with you." Patterson pushed her hands into her pockets. "Where is the safe house, anyway?"

"I have a car waiting to take you there," said Harris, standing up.

"I'd rather take the van."

"Not going to happen. I'll have an agent follow behind in it. Once you're at the safe house, the three of you can grab whatever you need from inside the van, but the keys stay with us. I can't risk you getting some crazy idea in your head and taking off again. From now on, we do this my way."

"Guess I don't have much choice."

"Not if you want to spend the night in a comfortable bed instead of a jail cell." Harris motioned for everyone to follow him, then started across the grass. "Come along. Your chariot awaits."

A black Escalade was waiting at the curb when they reached the edge of the plaza. One of the agents Patterson had seen earlier was sitting behind the wheel. He kept his eyes fixed firmly forward even when Grant opened the back door and stepped aside to let Patterson and the others climb in.

Bauer and Phoebe took the rearmost of the three rows of seats. Patterson settled in the second row behind the driver before Grant climbed in next to her. As they were clipping their seatbelts, Harris leaned in.

He held out a hand. "Keys to the van?"

Bauer dug into his pocket and produced the keys, then handed them to the SAC.

"Thank you." Harris pocketed the keys. He glanced toward the man in the front seat. "Special Agent Musgrove will drive you straight to the safe house. He'll come back for you at eight a.m. sharp. Be ready."

"Will he bring Starbucks?" Bauer asked with a mischievous grin. "I'll take a Mocha Latte."

"Don't push it, Special Agent Bauer." Harris narrowed his eyes. "And I expect you all to behave yourselves. Just because I'm not posting agents inside the safe house doesn't mean you're not being surveilled."

"That's disturbing." Bauer glanced at Phoebe. "Should we check the air conditioning vents for hidden cameras?"

"The only camera in the safe house is trained on the front door and it was already there. An agent will be outside at all times. It's as much for your safety as anything else."

"And we appreciate it," said Phoebe quickly, before Bauer could open his mouth again.

"Sweet dreams, kids," Harris said. He slammed the car door and banged his palm twice on the roof of the vehicle. Then they were speeding away from the plaza through the quiet city streets toward the safe house.

SIXTY-SEVEN

THE FBI safe house was a two-story Spanish colonial residence sitting on a gated one-acre plot behind high walls on the north side of the city in an affluent suburb. It was hardly the epitome of what a person would think of when a safe house came to mind. This was no grungy apartment or run-down block building in a seedy area of town. It looked more like the sort of place a corporate CEO might inhabit. And in a way, that was true. Except that the CEO in question had run a drug and human trafficking operation that landed him thirty years in prison when his activities finally caught up with him. The house had been confiscated and now served its own sentence protecting people instead of harboring those who would do harm. At least, that was what Special Agent Musgrove claimed because he was, apparently, on the task force that took the drug lord down.

The Escalade, shiny and black, would not raise a single eyebrow in this swanky community, but the van trailing it was not so easy to overlook. Patterson almost laughed at the sight of her aging wheels following the Escalade up the driveway as the gates closed behind them.

They stopped in front of the house next to a black Cadillac that was already waiting with an agent Patterson didn't recognize behind the wheel. This man would be their guard for at least the first part of the night. Musgrove and the special agent who followed in the van helped them inside with their belongings. The man in the Cadillac stayed where he was, observing their activity with faint disinterest.

"If you're hungry, there's pizza and garlic knots in the kitchen. Soda too," Musgrove said, nodding toward the door at the back of the house beyond the marble-tiled entrance hall. "Special Agent Hunter picked it up for y'all on his way over here. The SAC figured you might be hungry."

"That's the guy in the car outside," Bauer said by way of explanation. "He's alright. We've sank a few beers on occasion."

"We appreciate the pizza," Patterson said to Musgrove. "I don't know about anyone else, but I could use something to eat. Would the two of you care to join us?"

Musgrove smiled and declined politely. "We have other places to be."

Then the two special agents stepped back outside and jumped into the Escalade. The engine roared to life before the vehicle swung around on the wide driveway and headed back toward the gates which opened automatically to let them through then slid closed again.

"So, pizza?" Bauer asked, already on his way to the kitchen.

"If a way to a man's heart is through his stomach," Phoebe said with a laugh, "then I think I have competition from Special Agent Hunter out there."

"There's no food he likes more," Patterson agreed, following Bauer to the kitchen.

Two pizza boxes sat on the island, along with a smaller box and paper plates. They dug in and ate their fill, sitting at a breakfast nook that overlooked a brick patio at the back of the house and the grounds beyond. When they were done, Phoebe collected up what was left of the pizza and put it in the fridge.

"I don't know about you guys," she said. "But I'm beat. Want to check out the bedrooms and pick where we're going to sleep?"

"Sounds like a plan." Patterson reached across the table and squeezed Grant's hand. "What do you think?"

He didn't have to say anything. The look in his eyes told Patterson that he wanted to be alone with her. She smiled and slipped from the booth, then headed back toward the front of the house as the others followed behind. She went to a narrow vertical window beside the front door and looked out. The Cadillac was still there, the faint glow of a cell phone screen visible through the windshield, dimly illuminating Special Agent Hunter's face. Satisfied, she turned back to the others and headed for the stairs. There were five bedrooms on the second floor, including two ensuites. They each took one.

Alone at last with Grant, Patterson closed the bedroom door and turned to him. She was pleased he was there, but she had to know why he was holding back. "Before we go any further . . . Why didn't you tell me about your promotion?"

"That's the first thing you want to say to me after everything that's been going on?" Grant raised an eyebrow. "Seriously?"

"It is if you want us to spend the night in the same bed."

"I wasn't keeping anything from you. I just didn't know . . ." Grant expelled a long breath. He took a step toward Patterson. "I was worried you might not take it well. It complicates things."

"That's not the point. I get to decide that, not you."

"And that's why I didn't tell you. I was trying to pick the right time. I didn't want you to freak out and do something rash like end our relationship. I won't be your immediate boss anymore. You'll answer to a new ASAC. He will answer to me. Like I said—"

"I know. It complicates matters." Patterson was drained. She didn't want to argue with Grant. "Do you think we can still make it work?"

"I believe we can." Grant moved even closer. "We'll just need some new ground rules. We'll have to set boundaries."

"Like what?"

"Well, first start, when you don't agree with the ASAC, you can't just do an end-around to me."

"You really think I'd do that?"

Grant raised an eyebrow.

"Okay, fine." Patterson couldn't help laughing. "I probably would do that. Maybe we should make a pact to keep work and play separate."

"I think that's a fine idea," Grant said. "Besides, if I do get promoted to special agent in charge—and it's not guaranteed—we won't see as much of each other in the office."

"That's true." A weight fell from Patterson's shoulders. "You really weren't keeping it a secret because you thought me a liability to your career?"

"Of course not. And I'm sorry, I should've told you immediately when the opportunity was presented to me."

"Yes, you should have." Patterson glanced toward the bed. "I know it's late, but we haven't seen each other in weeks, and I've missed you lying next to me. How about we take this conversation to bed."

"I can think of better things to do than talk. Besides, I've never dated a redhead before. This is an unexpected bonus." A grin broke across Grant's face.

"Redhead, huh?" Patterson rolled her eyes. "Just don't keep me up too long. I suspect we have a big day tomorrow."

SIXTY-EIGHT

THE ESCALADE RETURNED for Patterson and the others
first thing the next morning. They drove across town to a
nondescript office plaza and climbed to an anonymous second-
floor unit. Special Agent Musgrove led them inside and
through an empty lobby to a back room furnished with a dark
wood conference table and chairs. An air conditioner hummed
overhead. A cheap print hung on the wall. Some sort of beach
scene with palm trees and a teal-blue ocean. The only other
item in the room was a fifty-inch monitor attached to the wall at
the far end of the room, and a small media cart beneath it. The
monitor's screen was black and dark.

Walter Harris was seated at the head of the table with the
monitor to his rear. Two of the agents from the Plaza the
previous day were sitting one on each side of him. All three had
paper cups of coffee in front of them. Four more coffees were
waiting in the middle of the table, along with a pile of creamers
and sugar sachets.

Harris stood and dismissed Musgrove. "Right on time."

"Nice place you have here," Bauer said, looking around at

the mostly unfurnished office space. "I didn't know we had a secret meeting facility."

"There's a lot you don't know, Special Agent Bauer."

"Apparently."

Harris looked at Patterson. "Are you ready to clear your name?"

"Hell, yes."

"Good. Sit down, all of you." Harris sank back into his chair and waited for everyone else to settle at the table and take their drinks. Then he cleared his throat. "First, some news. I put in a request for Amarillo PD's media lab to let us look at Leo Galinsky's cell phone, or rather, a digital forensic clone of it. They were hesitant, possibly because of interference from a certain detective sergeant, but ultimately could not think of a reason to deny our request. They sent it over to us about an hour ago, and I put one of our best digital forensics guys on the job—specifically to look at the text message Galinsky was supposed to have received from Special Agent Blake. The one where she asks him to call her. I expedited the process, so we should get something back on that soon."

"That's good news," Bauer said, glancing at Patterson.

"But still might not be enough to get me off the hook." Patterson pulled the plastic lid off her coffee and stared down into the black liquid before ripping the top off a creamer and dumping it in.

"I agree." Harris sipped his coffee. "Which is why we're taking the fight to Senator Newport."

"And how do you propose to do that?" Grant asked. "This isn't some low-level drug dealer or minor mob boss. This is a United States senator we're talking about. We'll never break through his layers of protection."

"We don't need to." Harris smiled thinly. "We have an ace in the hole. Neither Ortega nor the senator know that Special Agent Blake is back in the fold. As far as he's concerned, she is a fugitive on the run. They are also not aware the senator is under investigation. We've done a good job of keeping that under wraps for obvious reasons."

"I still don't see how that helps us," Grant said.

"Senator Newport is having a campaign fundraiser at his house outside the city on Friday evening. I propose we put a wire on Special Agent Blake and send her in."

"I'm sorry. What?" Grant looked incredulous. "Just how do you propose we do that?"

"Senator Newport will be in Dallas?" Patterson asked.

"Yes. His main residence is here." Harris shifted his gaze to Grant. "And to answer your question, Senator Newport won't suspect that Patterson is working with us. She will gain entry to the grounds and find the senator, tell him that she knows all about his dirty dealings and that if he doesn't make her predicament go away, she will reveal everything she knows to the press and the authorities. The shady land deal. Framing Mark Davis. Using his pet detective to commit murder. The works. He'll think that she's a desperate woman looking for a way out of her situation."

"That isn't going to work," Bauer said. "Newport is a dangerous man. Patterson might just be making her situation worse."

"I agree," said Phoebe. "We already know he doesn't mind having people killed. Why wouldn't he just do the same to Patterson?"

"Because she's also going to tell him that she attached the proof to an email scheduled to be sent in twenty-four hours. The only person who can stop that delivery is her."

"An insurance policy."

"Yes. Although there won't really be an email, of course, since we already have all the information."

"And what are we expecting the senator to do, exactly?" Bauer asked. "He's clearly a smart man and didn't get as far as he has by opening his mouth when he shouldn't. Whether or not he suspects a wire, Newport is going to be cagey."

"I agree. But it's our best shot of getting Newport to incriminate himself and also Detective Sergeant Ortega."

"I don't like it," Bauer said.

"Me either," Grant agreed, but then he sighed. "Sac Harris is right, though. This is an opportunity we can't squander, and it's our quickest way of clearing Special Agent Blake's name. We have the element of surprise on our side. Newport will think Patterson is still on the run. He will also be caught off guard. He probably doesn't expect her to know why she was framed or even that he was involved."

"Newport thinks he's free and clear," Phoebe said. "As far as he's concerned, Patterson is alone and scared, wanted for murder. Mark Davis, the only person who could dispute the suitability of the senator's land for building on is sitting in jail on rape charges. The victim, Alexandria Rowley, is MIA and presumably dead. Killed at the hands of Leo Galinsky."

"Who is also dead," Patterson said. "The only two people left who know the truth are Newport and Ortega."

"And whoever approved that brownfield land for use," Bauer added. "The senator must have received a clean report from the Texas EPA or the deal wouldn't be going through."

"Yes," Harris said. "And we are looking into that." He glanced around the table. "So, are we all in agreement that Special Agent Blake will go undercover and infiltrate the senator's fundraiser to smoke him out?"

"I didn't know this was a democracy," Bauer said.

"It's not." Harris leaned forward. "But everyone at this table has a vested interest in making sure Special Agent Blake does not fall victim to this man. She's one of us. More than that, she's our friend. If we were in the same situation, she would go to the ends of the earth to help us, and we all know it. This isn't just another FBI operation. This one is personal."

Grant nodded. "Well said."

Harris pushed his chair back and stood up. He leaned on the table, palms down, and looked around the room. "So, I'll ask again. Are we all in agreement?"

One by one, everyone nodded.

Harris looked to Patterson, sitting at the other end of the table. "And you?"

"What do you think?" Patterson stood up and met the SAC's gaze. "I'm in. Let's bring this bastard down."

SIXTY-NINE

THE MEETING WAS AT AN END. Patterson made her way to the door with Grant, Bauer, and Phoebe right behind. But before she could step into the unit's empty reception area, the SAC's phone rang.

"Hey, hold up a moment," he said before answering. After a brief conversation, he hung up. "That was the digital forensics lab. They've had a chance to look at the phone data and, specifically, the text message sent to Leo Galinsky's phone, purportedly from Special Agent Blake. I won't go into the technical details because, quite frankly, I don't understand half of what I'm told when they resort to geek speak like data packets and control channels, but the preliminary findings point to the message being faked. It's not conclusive, at least not yet, but all indications are that it's a sophisticated spoof generated by a dark web app."

"Well, that's good news, anyway," Bauer said, glancing at Patterson.

"We still have to expose Senator Newport and Detective Sergeant Ortega," Patterson said, although she was relieved that a damning piece of evidence had been discredited.

Harris noted. "Elliott says hi, by the way."

For a moment, Patterson was blank. Then she remembered. Elliott was the technician who had worked on Claire Wright's phone and extracted the text messages when Patterson was searching for the missing woman weeks before. She wondered how Elliott knew she was there. "I thought we were keeping this operation secret."

"We are," Harris replied. "But he put two and two together, given the nature of his assignment. Don't worry. He can be trusted."

"I'm sure he can," Patterson said. "Say hi from me when you see him."

"You got it." Harris was standing flanked by the two agents from the Plaza. Neither had said a word throughout the meeting, and they weren't getting any chattier now. "Your ride is waiting. Go back to the safe house. If the situation changes or anything comes up, I'll let you know. And stay out of sight. We don't want to blow this before Friday."

"Suits me." Patterson had been in a couple of safe houses back in New York guarding witnesses. They were small and dingy. This one was anything but. A better description would be swanky. Even better, she didn't have to look over her shoulder anymore. It was only Tuesday. A couple of days sitting around and resting sounded like heaven. Especially as Grant would be there with her. But there was one more thing she wanted to clarify before she left. "What's going to happen when all this is over?"

"If we do our jobs, the good senator will be sitting behind bars along with Ortega."

"No. I didn't mean that." Patterson had every intention of sending Newport to jail. "What's going to happen with Special Agent Bauer and Phoebe?"

"I haven't decided yet," Harris said. "But when I do, y'all will be the first to know."

"I'd rather know now." Patterson was standing in the doorway. "They risked their careers to help me."

"And they broke protocol, not to mention aiding a fugitive." Harris folded his arms. "Even if that fugitive turns out to be innocent, the ends don't justify the means."

"That's not fair. If they end up—"

"Patterson, it's fine," Bauer said, stepping in front of her. "Let's go."

"Not until I get—"

"Leave things be—it's fine. I knew what I was doing when I warned you they were coming. I knew it when I set up a dead drop and fed you information. And when we drove to Amarillo to help you beat his thing."

"Me, too," said Phoebe. "I helped because I wanted to. I knew the risks."

"We both did. Whatever happens, we'll take our medicine."

"I don't like this. It's not fair." Patterson turned and stomped from the room.

"Hey." Bauer chased after her and caught Patterson at the unit's front door. "SAC Harris hasn't even said what our punishment will be. Let's wait until he does before getting indignant, okay?"

"He's right," Grant said, coming up behind Bauer. "We have bigger fish to fry."

"I still don't like it."

"You don't have to." Grant held the door open. "Let's go."

Patterson stepped out onto the walkway. She looked over the railing. The black Escalade was waiting for them, the engine idling.

Bauer and Phoebe were already heading toward the steps. Grant hesitated, then did the same.

Patterson glanced back inside the unit toward the rear room, but there was no sign of Harris or his agents. Maybe he was waiting until they were gone. She took a deep breath, pushed aside her frustration, and followed along behind.

Ten minutes later, they were on their way back to the safe house.

SEVENTY

PATTERSON COULDN'T SLEEP. They had returned from the meeting with Walter Harris in the office plaza many hours before. Later toward evening, Special Agent Musgrove had returned in the Escalade and brought with him buckets of fried chicken and biscuits which they all ate out on a patio area behind the house. It was now two in the morning and the house was still and silent. A pale shaft of silvery moonlight slanted in through the window and splashed across the dark oak floor of the bedroom. Beside her, Grant snored and rolled over so that he was facing away from her.

Frustrated, she slipped out from under the covers and crossed to a pair of french doors on the opposite side of the bedroom. She looked out. Beyond them was a wide balcony that overlooked the grounds. She unlatched them and stepped outside, then went to the railing and looked off toward the distant glow of downtown Dallas.

A cool breeze tugged at her nightshirt and raised goose bumps on her exposed flesh. If everything went to plan, a few days from now, all this would be over. Her name would be cleared, and Mark Davis would hopefully be out of jail and recovering from his injuries. Then, she could finally ask him about Julie. Patterson hadn't intended to spend much time in Amarillo because she doubted her sister had stayed long all those years ago. Even though Julie had been gone for over a decade and a half, and her trail wasn't getting any colder, Patterson didn't want to lose any more time than necessary. Because experience had taught her that fate had a way of throwing a wrench in the works. She was lucky Mark Davis hadn't died in that prison rec yard and taken whatever knowledge of Julie he possessed with him to the grave. Then the trail would not just have been cold, it would have been arctic. Impossible to follow. Patterson's quest would have been over.

"Hey, what are you doing out here?" said a voice to her rear.

It was Grant. He stood in the doorway wearing a pair of black boxers.

"I was awake and wanted some fresh air," Patterson said, glancing over her shoulder toward him.

"Are you sure that's all it is?" Grant asked, stepping onto the balcony, and slipping his arm around Patterson's waist. "Maybe you're thinking about Friday night, and how much danger you'll be putting yourself in?"

"It's not that, although the risk of confronting the senator has not eluded me. He's a dangerous man in more ways than one and quite capable of destroying his enemies. If this backfires, it could have dire consequences for all of us."

"Then what is it?"

"Nothing. Or maybe everything. I've been thinking about Julie. Until my dad gave me those postcards—the ones he kept from me all this time—I'd put my sister in a little mental box and consigned her to the past . . . At least, mostly. My life was separated into the time she was with us, and after she was gone. Then everything changed with those postcards. The line feels blurred now. Julie is still missing, and I've accepted she's probably long since dead, but I'm straddling both worlds. I have one foot in the past where Julie is still alive, and another in the present where she isn't. It's like the years we've been without her have just melted away and everything has gotten mixed up."

"I must admit, I was worried when you took off on the search for your sister." Grant held Patterson close. "I was afraid you would get sucked down a proverbial rabbit hole and never find your way out. Your unresolved emotions about Julie are what started all this. I thought you might only make the situation worse by chasing her ghost across the country."

"Maybe I have."

"No. You haven't. You've proved to be just as effective an FBI agent during your quest to find Julie as you were before. Perhaps even more so. Look at what you've done."

"You mean like getting framed for murder?" Patterson laughed despite herself.

"Okay. Maybe not that one so much." Grant moved his arm from around her waist and took her hand. "Come on, let's go back inside to bed."

Patterson nodded. She gazed out one more time toward the distant skyline of Dallas, then followed Grant back to bed. He put his arm around her again, and she rested her head on his shoulder. This time, she fell asleep and when she dreamed, it wasn't of Julie for the first time in weeks.

SEVENTY-ONE

"THE ESTATE WILL BE PROTECTED by both private security and a pair of Dallas PD officers stationed at the main gates. The event itself is taking place in the ballroom of Senator Newport's mansion. He's expecting upwards of a hundred guests, which will make infiltration easier," SAC Harris said, standing at the end of the conference table and looking around the assembled group. Behind him, the wall-mounted monitor displayed a highly detailed satellite photograph of the senator's property that showed the house sitting amid lush landscaped grounds and surrounded by a fortress-like wall. A driveway meandered through the several-acre property and ended in front of the mansion. The entire property was set within a sprawling woodland with no neighbor for at least a mile in either direction. The senator had clearly picked this location for maximum privacy.

It was Thursday afternoon and one day before the fundraiser. They were all back in the nondescript office going over the details of their plan to bring in the senator and his underlings. Patterson had spent the last forty-eight hours collecting her thoughts, mentally preparing herself for the task at hand, and spending time with Grant. It was hardly the romantic weekend away that she had imagined the previous week when they spoke on the phone, but they were together, and she would take it. Maybe after all this was done, a quick trip back to New York would be in order. Not only would she be able to spend more time with Grant, but she could visit her father. After the events of the past month, during which time she had been drugged, handcuffed inside a car to die a slow death, and attacked by a knife wielding maniac, she could use a little family time. She was still sore from her ordeals and some time away might leave her refreshed to continue her search for Julie once this was all over. If this was ever over.

SAC Harris was still talking and referencing the monitor. "Special Agent Blake will breach the perimeter wall from the eastern boundary of the property. There's a woodland trail that runs close to the wall in that sector, but not so close that her van will be detected as she arrives."

"What about that security you mentioned?" Grant asked.

"None outside the compound except the police officers at the front gates, but she'll approach from the other direction. Dallas PD will not have a presence inside the grounds, but the senator's private security personnel will presumably be making regular circuits of the inside perimeter, so she'll need to time her entry over the wall to account for that."

"Do we know how many of them?"

"No." Harris shook his head. "We can assume at least four and they will be armed."

"As will I," said Patterson. She had spent considerable time thinking about the best way to achieve a surprise audience with Newport and had spoken with Walter Harris at length on the matter that morning by telephone. "The biggest risk is right after I breach the wall. I won't exactly fit in with the rest of the guests and will be far away from the party in a remote area where I could be easily spotted. As far as we know there are no security cameras covering that area, but we can't be one hundred percent sure. I'll have a cocktail dress with me in a backpack. Once on the grounds I'll find a way into the house, change into the dress so I can enter the ballroom without drawing undue attention, and confront the senator."

"And the wire?" Phoebe asked.

"My dress will be equipped with an audio and video device that transmits in real time and should capture the entire exchange. Once the senator incriminates himself, I'll make my exit. Leaving should be easier. I'll walk right out the front door."

"You make it all sound so simple," Bauer said. "Newport isn't going to be happy you crashed his party. Getting out in one piece might not be so easy."

"Which is why I'll have the figurative dead man's switch."

"The fake email that will supposedly be sent within hours of you entering the property if it's not canceled. The one that will go out to the press and authorities."

"Yes. He won't want to risk all his underhanded dealings coming to light for the whole world to see. I'll walk out of that estate without a scratch on me, and hopefully, we'll have everything we need."

"I hope you're right," Bauer said.

"Yeah . . . So do I."

Bauer observed Patterson for a moment, maybe trying to gauge her level of apprehension. Then he sighed. "What time are we putting this operation into action?"

Harris cleared his throat. "The function starts at seven with a cocktail hour. After that a meal will be served. At nine o'clock, the senator will give a speech and no doubt try to pry open the wallets of those in attendance, even though everyone will have already paid a grand each to be there. Once the speech is over there will be a band and dancing until midnight. Patterson will go over the wall and enter the house during the speech when everyone is guaranteed to be in their seats. She'll bide her time and approach him afterward. With any luck, she'll be in and out in under thirty minutes."

"I don't like this," Bauer said. "It's too risky."

"It's the only way," said Patterson. "I'm fed up with being on the defensive. It's time to bring out the offence. One way or another, we're finishing this on tomorrow night!"

SEVENTY-TWO

ON FRIDAY EVENING, a little before nine, Patterson turned the van off the road leading to Senator Newport's lavish estate on the outskirts of Dallas and steered up a bumpy dirt trail into the woods. She approached from the west, avoiding the compound's front gates where a Dallas PD cruiser sat guarding the entrance. As she left the road, she could see the glow of its lights in the darkness.

The dirt trail she found herself on was rutted and bumpy, hardly suited to her van's aging two-wheel drive. At times, the leafy corridor became so narrow that she barely squeaked through, with branches raking each side of the vehicle. But then, after a jarring ride, the wall surrounding Senator Newport's home came into view.

She pulled over and stopped the van in an area near the wall where the trail widened. When she cut her headlights, the darkness rushed in like a tidal wave. It was a clear night, but the canopy above her blocked all but a few slivers of the moon's glow.

Patterson was prepared for this. On the passenger seat next to her was a tactical flashlight, which she scooped up and clicked on before stepping from the vehicle and quietly closing the driver's door. The flashlight's beam lit up the trail ahead of her in a crimson glow thanks to its red filter. There were a few reasons Patterson had chosen this over a standard flashlight. The first was simple. Red light diffused quicker than white, which would make her less obvious as she picked her way toward the compound. Another reason was self-preservation. The light would not interfere with her night vision the same way a normal flashlight would. If anything happened to the light, she wouldn't be momentarily blinded as her eyes adjusted to the gloom. There was one more important reason. It would also minimize her profile if she was spotted. Her dark clothing helped with that, too.

Normally, she would have worn combat gear and a tactical vest for an operation such as this, but she was supposed to be on the run, which was why she wore dark blue jeans and a long-sleeved polo shirt to cover as much of her body as possible. The cap was back on her head, too. Completing the outfit were a pair of hiking boots. A backpack was slung over her shoulders, inside of which was a red cocktail dress, neatly folded. She wasn't carrying her Glock service weapon. It was too bulky, especially when she changed into the dress. Instead, she had her backup piece, which was lighter and smaller. Right now, it was in a holster at her hip, ready to be drawn at a moment's notice, but when she changed into the dress it would sit in a concealed carry thigh holster where no one would see it.

She was also equipped with two recording devices. The first was a button sewn onto the placket of the shirt she currently wore, within which was a miniature camera with night-vision that would transmit HD quality audio and video at a range of up to a mile. The second identical unit was concealed in the bust of her dress and disguised as an ornamental button. Both transmitted to a receiver located in the surveillance van parked a safe distance down the road out of sight and would record the entire incursion from start to finish.

"I've reached the insertion point and I'm proceeding on foot," Patterson said, seemingly to herself, in a low voice that she knew the placket button would pick up and transmit to Bauer and Grant, almost a mile down the road in the surveillance vehicle. There was no response because there didn't need to be—they already knew the equipment worked—and also because the communications were strictly one way.

She picked her way forward with the flashlight illuminating the trail. When she was almost at the wall, a sound reached her ears. A rustle of leaves off to her left in the woods.

Patterson froze, sweeping the flashlight across the undergrowth just as the sound stopped.

When they were planning this operation, she had decided it was unlikely the outer perimeter would be patrolled. But they couldn't be certain. Now she half expected to see one of the senator's private security team, or even a Dallas police officer, step out onto the trail ahead of her, weapon drawn. If that happened, she would either have to talk her way out of the situation—unlikely, given what she was wearing and where she was—or attempt to flee into the woods and hope she could lose her pursuer. Drawing her weapon was out of the question. She had no intention of firing on anyone except for self-defense if her life was in danger. What she could not afford to do was to get captured, which would lead straight to a jail cell given her fugitive status. SAC Harris would then be in the uncomfortable position of securing her release and revealing the investigation into Senator Newport before they were ready.

The rustling came again, louder this time.

It didn't sound like a person.

Patterson reached for the Glock and slipped it from its holster. She scanned the darkness beyond the trail, wishing that instead of a paltry red-beam flashlight she was wearing night vision goggles, which would instantly alert her to any threat. The noise had stopped now, and she saw nothing out of the ordinary . . . until a slight movement at the corner of her eye—a barely perceptible shift in the spectrum of darkness like black slipping against darker black—drew Patterson's attention.

She tensed, feeling suddenly vulnerable, just as a large coyote stepped out on the trail ahead of her.

It was a magnificent animal standing about two feet at the shoulder and probably weighing fifty pounds, with dark brown fur and a long brush-like tail tipped in black. It observed her, obviously curious about this interloper within its domain.

Patterson didn't dare to move. If she backed away and retreated, it could trigger the creature's prey response. If she turned and ran, it certainly would.

The pair stood ten feet from each other—coyote and human —neither one giving quarter.

Patterson knew what she should do. Make herself big. Wave her arms and shout. Convince the creature that she wasn't worth the bother. But that was the last thing she could do under the circumstances. Likewise, a gunshot would alert the senator's security to her presence—not that she had any desire to shoot the majestic animal anyway. But if the need arose . . .

The coyote sniffed the air. It took a tentative step toward her.

Patterson's gut tightened. She tensed, raising the gun, and waited for the animal to lunge.

But it didn't. With a disinterested snuffle, the coyote turned and padded back between the trees and was soon lost in the darkness.

Patterson's shoulders slumped with relief. She holstered the Glock with shaking hands, then stood on the trail a moment longer, composing herself. Once her racing heart had slowed, she continued on to the wall. A seven-foot-tall barrier protecting the senator's estate. But it would not stop Patterson.

Here, thanks to a break in the tree canopy, the moon's faint white glow provided enough light for her to see. She turned off the flashlight and slipped it into her pocket.

Then she flexed her knees and jumped, swinging her arms up at the same time. Her outstretched fingers found the lip of the wall and closed on it. For a moment she hung there, gathering her strength, then she heaved herself up and swung a leg over until she was straddling the wall. She glanced left and right, making sure there were no security personnel coming her way, then she swung the other leg over and dropped silently down into the estate.

SEVENTY-THREE

HITTING THE GROUND, Patterson crouched and studied her surroundings. She had landed on a bed of red mulch in a wide and well-maintained landscaping feature that ran the length of the perimeter. Shrubs and trees were placed at intervals between flowering plants and statuary. A couple of hundred feet away she could see the side wall of the house, and to her left a splash of light across the back lawn, probably from the ballroom windows. The faint sound of a blues band playing drifted on the breeze.

She looked around one more time to make sure none of the Senator's security team were close by, then slipped from behind a large bush laden with red berries and made her way across the lawn to the house. Once there, she followed the mansion's side wall to the corner, ducking under windows, and peered around.

The ballroom did indeed look out over the back lawn. Soft yellow light spilled from floor to ceiling picture windows that spanned the fourteen-foot height of the first floor. She could not see inside from her vantage point, but the band was louder now, and she could hear the faint murmur of laughter and conversation from the guests. Nearby, closer to Patterson was an open door through which more sounds emerged. The clink of plates and whoosh of heavy extractor fans mixed with more voices. A kitchen. That would be her way in.

Patterson glanced around again, scanning in all directions to make sure she was still alone. Satisfied, she lowered the backpack from her shoulders and unzipped it, extracting the cocktail dress. She stripped down and pulled the dress on, then took the concealed carry holster out of the backpack and strapped it to her upper thigh so that it would be hidden above the hemline of the knee length dress, then transferred the Glock to it. After repacking the bag with her old clothes and the flashlight, she left it by the wall hidden behind a shrub. Finally, she checked to make sure the tiny surveillance device was still attached to the dress, looking like nothing but a small button holding the garment closed between her breasts.

She reached for the backpack one last time, taking her cell phone from the front pocket, and dialed Bauer in the surveillance van waiting a mile down the road.

"Everything working?" she asked in a low voice.

"Sure is. We have great audio and video from the dress. Everything checks out," Bauer replied. "We also had a fantastic view from the other device just now when you switched outfits."

Patterson's cheeks burned. "I don't know what Phoebe sees in you."

"Me either." Bauer chuckled. "Seriously, be careful in there and get out as soon as you have what we need, okay?"

"That's the plan," Patterson said, then she hung up, put the phone back in the bag, and started toward the kitchen door.

SEVENTY-FOUR

WHEN PATTERSON REACHED THE DOOR, she stopped and peeked inside.

The kitchen was large. An island ran down the middle of the space. A commercial range stood against one wall, with a wide copper vent hood over it. There were pots and pans everywhere. An industrial sized fridge stood next to an equally impressive freezer. Fluorescent lights painted everything in a stark white glare. Even though the meal was over the air was redolent with the scent of cooked meats and spices.

The whole place bustled with frenetic yet ordered activity. Wait staff in pressed white shirts and black pants scurried back and forth carrying silver trays stacked with dirty plates and cutlery that they deposited near the biggest dishwasher Patterson had ever seen.

Other staff wiped down counters and scrubbed cookware in a deep copper sink.

Patterson took a deep breath, pulled at the hem of her dress to make sure the Glock concealed beneath was still out of sight, and stepped over the threshold.

She was noticed instantly.

"Miss, you can't be in here," shouted a portly man who looked like he might be one of the chefs. He strode toward her, wiping his hands on a stained apron.

"I'm so sorry," Patterson replied, doing her best to look small and helpless. "I stepped outside for some fresh air—it's so stuffy in that ballroom—and I must have gotten turned around. I went for a walk and couldn't find my way back inside."

"Well, you shouldn't be in here. It's not safe." The chef waved vaguely toward a set of double doors on the other side of the kitchen. "Go through there and turn left. The ballroom is at the end of the corridor."

"Thank you." Patterson hurried past the man and followed his directions. When she entered the ballroom she stopped, momentarily awed by its grandeur. The room was enormous, with a waxed maple floor and coffered ceiling inset with crystal dome lights. More crystal sconces adorned the walls. Rows of finely detailed columns separated the dance floor from the seating areas around the walls. To her left arched windows rose all the way to the ceiling, beyond which she could see the manicured back lawn as it fell away into darkness.

The band—a six-piece ensemble—were playing on a raised stage at the far end of the room. A few people danced, but most were either sitting at their tables or mingling. She checked her watch, a slim gold Gucci with a two-tone band that Phoebe had loaned her because Patterson's own timepiece, an older model I-Watch, was hardly suitable for such an affair. It was Nine-forty-five. The senator must have already delivered his speech.

She looked around but didn't see him.

Until she glanced toward the bar located off to her right. She recognized him immediately from photographs provided by Bauer that she had studied over the last few days. He was clutching a whiskey glass and talking to a woman dressed in a flowing red gown that probably cost more than Patterson made in a year. Standing at a discreet distance were a pair of burly men in identical black suits, white shirts, and black ties, that Patterson assumed to be the senator's private security. A slight bulge under each man's jacket confirmed they were armed, probably with Glock 19 pistols or similar weapons. Their gaze roamed the ballroom for any threat to their boss, unlikely as that might seem.

She waited until the woman walked away, a fresh glass of champagne clutched in her hand, then sauntered toward the senator, doing her best to look casual.

"Senator Newport," she said quickly when she reached the bar. "We need to talk."

The senator looked momentarily taken aback. "I'm sorry, do I know you?"

"You should." Patterson kept her eye on the senator's security detail. They didn't appear to be paying much attention to him, but she knew they were. "You're framing me for murder. I'm Special Agent Patterson Blake."

A look of alarm flashed across the senator's face before he regained his composure. "How did you get in here?"

"That's not important."

"You're right. It's not." The senator's gaze slid toward his security detail.

As if an unspoken signal had passed between them, both men started toward her, their hands slipping instinctively toward the guns hidden under their jackets.

SEVENTY-FIVE

"I WOULDN'T DO THAT, if I were you," Patterson said. "You'll want to hear what I have to say, I promise."

The senator considered this, then waved his security off.

They studied Patterson for a moment before returning to their previous positions.

The senator placed his glass on the bar. "Alright, Miss Blake. I'll listen to what you have to say. But not here. My study."

"Lead the way."

The senator straightened his jacket and stepped past her toward the ballroom. "Follow me."

The security detail trailed at a discreet distance.

They skirted the edge of the ballroom and made their way to a set of double doors, beyond which was a wide foyer with marble floors and a stunning chandelier hanging down between a sweeping staircase. He led her to a second set of doors, which he opened and allowed her to step through before instructing his security to wait outside and following, closing the doors behind him.

Patterson found herself in a study with dark oak bookcases lining all four walls. The floor was laid in the same oak, with an expensive looking Persian rug over it. An executive desk stood in the middle of the room upon which a desk lamp glowed.

Senator Newport walked past Patterson and took up a position standing on the other side of the desk, perhaps thinking it would make a good barrier should she become suddenly violent. He folded his arms. "You have one minute, after which I'm calling my men in here and having you escorted out to those police officers at the front gate who will be more than happy to take you into custody. Better make it count."

"You're not going to call your men in here."

"And why not?"

"Why do you think?" It was time to play the dead man's switch. "You must know I have insurance. That I wouldn't approach you unless I was confident in my ability to walk away free and unharmed."

"And how do you plan to do that?"

"There's an email scheduled to be sent in one hour to every newspaper and TV station in the state, not to mention the Attorney General and your colleagues in the Senate. That email will contain all the proof they need to bring you down. You'll be exposed as the crook you are. I'm the only one who can stop it going out."

Senator Newport let this sink in for a moment. Then he shook his head. "You're bluffing. I'm not a crook, and I've done nothing wrong."

"That's not exactly true," Patterson said, then she laid out everything she knew about the shady land deal and use of public money, the shell companies, the brownfield site, and blackmailing an EPA official.

When she was done, the senator observed Patterson with narrowed eyes. "Okay. Let's assume I believe your claim, and that I'm willing to play along. What is it that you want?"

"I want my old life back. You fabricated these charges

against me, or at least, it was on your orders. You can make them go away."

"I don't know what you're talking about, and even if I did, that's not something I have the power to help you with."

"You're lying. Leo Galinsky was killed by that pet cop of yours, Detective Sergeant Ortega. I didn't kill anyone, and you know it."

The senator shrugged. "What I know is that you're wanted for murder and on the run from your own people, Special Agent Blake. If you could prove your innocence, you would have done so already. Likewise, if you had enough evidence to prove any of what you claim I've done, you would have used it before now in an attempt to clear yourself. You have nothing and we both know it."

"I have more than you—"

"How about we drop the charade? You're a desperate woman clutching at straws. You should have stayed away from Mark Davis. This mess is of your own doing, and now you have to live with the consequences."

Patterson needed more, and she sensed the senator was about to end their conversation. She took a step toward the desk. "At least satisfy my curiosity. What happened to Alexandria Rowley? What did you do to her?"

Newport locked eyes with Patterson. "Alexandria Rowley was too clever for her own good. She could have walked away with enough money to get herself out of that hovel of a women's center she was living in. But she got greedy. Wanted more. A lot more. Threatened to say that Mark Davis was innocent and that he was set up if we didn't pay her more money."

"Mark Davis is innocent," Patterson said. "Just like me."

"Knowing something and proving it are two different things, Special Agent Blake. And you can't prove a damned thing. Alexandria Rowley is dead. She left us no choice. What's more, the man who killed her is also dead, and you're the one who murdered him. At least, so far as everyone else is concerned. Detective Sergeant Ortega did a good job of putting you in the crosshairs for that."

That was all Patterson needed. She just hoped that Bauer and Grant back in the van had gotten it all. Now she had to extricate herself. "You made a big mistake refusing to help me tonight, senator. But I'm going to give you one more chance to think on it. I'm leaving now, walking out of here. You have twenty-four hours, and then I'll be in touch again. Hopefully, you will have come to your senses."

Patterson turned and started toward the door.

"Wait just a minute, Special Agent Blake."

Patterson stopped and started to turn back toward the senator. Sensing danger, she reached down toward the Glock on her thigh at the same time.

"I wouldn't do that, if I were you." The senator already had a gun pointed at her.

Patterson recognized it as a Sig Sauer P239 semi-automatic pistol, because she had used the same model on the range at Quantico, except this one was equipped with a suppressor. He must have slipped it from the desk drawer when she turned her back on him. A stupid mistake.

The senator looked at her over the barrel of his gun. "Take it off. The dress."

"What?"

"You have at least one weapon about your person. You were reaching for it. I need to make sure you don't have more. Now take the dress off."

SEVENTY-SIX

PATTERSON SUMMED UP HER OPTIONS. It was unlikely the senator would shoot and kill her right there in his study. That would leave him with a lot of explaining to do. But that didn't preclude him putting bullets in her shoulders or kneecaps and then have his men take her somewhere else to finish her. And with the suppressor his shots would not be heard over the band playing in the ballroom.

She reached up and tugged at the dress, letting it fall to the floor and exposing more than just her body. The Glock in its thigh holster was clearly visible.

The senator smiled. "Only the one weapon, after all. Remove the gun . . . slowly. Place it on the floor, and kick it over here."

Patterson complied.

"Excellent." The senator observed her for a moment more, clearly enjoying her discomfort, then sighed. "You can get dressed again now."

Patterson quickly pulled the dress back up and stood with her arms folded across her chest. "What happens now?"

"You go away, for good."

"Have you forgotten about that email? Kill me and it all comes out. How you schemed to offload that brownfield site to the company developing the stadium, even though the land is toxic. How you used taxpayer money to make sure the project went through and then lined your own pockets into the bargain by becoming a silent partner. How do you think the public will react to that? Or your colleagues in the Senate for that matter. And what about the murders you've committed. The attempt on Mark Davis's life."

The senator chuckled. "Please. You have no proof I was involved in any of those murders. And as for the rest of it, so what? I'll take my chances. Assuming that email even exists, which I don't think it does."

"You won't get away with this," Patterson said. "Any of it."

"I already have." The senator pulled a phone from his pocket with his free hand. He dialed and put it to his ear. "It's me. I'm in the study. Get in here. That FBI agent crashed the party and is trying to blackmail me. We need to get rid of her, once and for all."

SEVENTY-SEVEN

A MINUTE PASSED during which neither Patterson or the senator moved. Then the study door opened and Detective Sergeant Ortega strode in. He was wearing dress pants and a white shirt with a black bowtie. He held a pair of handcuffs in one hand, no doubt borrowed from one of the senator's security team standing on the other side of the door, and a Glock 22, also equipped with a suppressor, in the other.

He closed the door and looked at Patterson. "This is an unexpected surprise."

"I don't know why," Patterson said. "You must have known I'd come after you."

"On the contrary, I figured you wouldn't be so stupid." Ortega looked past Patterson to the senator. "What do you want me to do with her?"

"What do you think I want you to do? Put those cuffs on her, take the damn woman back to Amarillo, and make sure she meets an untimely end resisting arrest."

"Right now?"

"Yes, right now. I'll tell Jennifer you had to leave on urgent police business and head back to Amarillo. She can stay the night. You can come back and pick her up tomorrow after this is taken care of."

"Right." Ortega didn't look pleased but he didn't argue further.

"And don't let anyone see you with her. Got it?"

"Sure." Ortega nodded, then he focused his attention back on Patterson and stepped forward. "Put your hands behind your back."

With two guns on her, Patterson had no choice, so she complied.

Ortega slipped the cuffs over her wrists and snapped them shut. Then he yanked her around and pushed her toward the door, gun pressed against her back.

SEVENTY-EIGHT

THE TWO MEN guarding the senator were gone, probably dismissed by Ortega himself. He led her out of the study and away from the party. They reached the expansive entrance hall, but instead of going out the front door, he guided her left to a formal sitting room. As they passed through it, Patterson said, "You killed Leo Galinsky, didn't you."

"Shut up." The gun pressed harder into the small of her back.

Beyond the sitting room was a dining room with a long table and ten chairs. Ortega kept moving.

"I'll take that as a yes," Patterson said as they rounded the table toward another door on the far wall. "Still, seems like a waste. You must have spent a long time grooming him to do your dirty work."

"If you must know, he was a liability."

"Right. Because he killed Alexandria Rowley on your orders. You were afraid he might get caught and talk."

They exited the dining room and entered a small kitchen that probably served the house when the commercial kitchen off the ballroom wasn't needed.

Ortega shoved her along. "I doubt he would have talked, but it seemed prudent to be proactive. He was a loose end, and it was a good opportunity to get you out of the way."

"By framing me for his murder."

"Exactly."

They entered a short corridor on the other side of the kitchen that housed a second set of stairs, narrow and utilitarian. Patterson surmised this must have been how the servants moved between floors out of sight back in the day.

"And what do you get out of all this?" Patterson asked.

"Me? I'll take early retirement and enjoy my cut of the proceeds from that entertainment complex. Senator Newport was very generous after all I've done for him."

"What makes you think he'll let you live that long?"

"Because we're family. I'm married to his niece. You don't turn on one of your own."

At the end of the corridor was another door which led out the side of the building to a gravel parking area where the guest's cars were parked, probably by a valet at the front of the house.

As Ortega pushed her outside, Patterson said, "You sure about that?"

"That's enough talking out of you."

Ortega steered her across toward a red quad-cab truck that she recognized from her previous encounters with the detective. The damaged front fender left little doubt who it belonged to.

He pulled the door open and prodded Patterson to climb up onto the rear bench seat. "Get in."

She put her foot on the running board and tried to step up, but it was difficult with her hands behind her back. In the end, Ortega guided her up and pushed her onto the seat.

He disappeared to the rear of the truck for a moment, and returned with a heavy-duty zip tie, which he wrapped around her ankles and pulled tight. Then he slammed the door, climbed into the driver's seat, and started the engine.

But he didn't head for the main driveway, where Patterson figured Grant would have an FBI team waiting to intercept him and free her. Instead, Ortega went in the other direction and followed a narrow dirt road near the perimeter of the property toward the back of the grounds. Patterson was enveloped by a sudden sense of dread. There must be another way off the property. Which meant she was in a heap of trouble.

SEVENTY-NINE

"WHERE ARE WE GOING?" Patterson asked, as much for Bauer and Grant's benefit as her own. They would be expecting Ortega to exit through the front gates.

"We're going out the back way," Ortega said. "You got a problem with that?"

"No."

"Good. Then shut up." Ortega picked up speed. The large quad-cab truck easily handled the dirt road, which Patterson figured was probably used by the gardeners who maintained the grounds. She was right. He flew along, bumping over ruts and potholes, heading toward the rear of the property, until a metal workshop loomed out of the darkness near the back wall, illuminated in stark chiaroscuro by the twin beams of the truck's headlights. As they drew closer, more came into view. There was a riding mower parked in front of the building, next to a small tractor with a bucket attachment. A huge pile of red mulch was heaped nearby waiting to be spread wherever it was needed. Beyond the building was a gate that led out onto the road. A service entrance.

Ortega brought the truck to stop, hopped out and opened

the gate, then drove through. Out on the road, he stopped again and closed the gate, before climbing back into the cab.

He glanced into the back to make sure Patterson was still behaving herself. "Just sit tight back there, okay." He grinned. "Once we get back to Amarillo, I'll make sure to finish you off clean and quick. You won't feel a thing."

"I can hardly wait," Patterson replied, hoping Bauer and the others in the surveillance van had been paying attention.

"Me either," Ortega said, turning frontward once more and starting the truck. "To be honest, this whole affair has been more trouble than I expected."

"Sorry to hear that."

"Yeah. I bet you are." Ortega started off again, gathering speed.

But then his headlights picked up a vehicle barreling in the other direction. Seeing the truck, it swerved sideways and screeched to a halt blocking the road.

It was Special Agent Bauer's Dodge Charger. Patterson breathed a sigh of relief. They had got her message and circled around to the back of the property in record time.

Two figures climbed out and raced behind the car, using it for cover as they drew their guns and pointed them at the oncoming truck. Patterson recognized Marcus Bauer and Jonathan Grant as the beams from the truck's headlights splashed across their faces.

But Detective Sergeant Ortega had no intention of stopping. Instead, he cursed and jerked the steering wheel to the side. The truck bumped down off the road moments before it reached the stationary car and tried to veer around it, smashing through undergrowth and bushes on the verge. But there wasn't quite enough room. The truck's front fender clipped the Charger's nose, and as it did, Patterson caught a glimpse through the windshield of Bauer and Grant jumping out of the way.

The back of the truck shimmied and spun around.

Patterson was thrown sideways across the bench seat. Her head smacked into the passenger side door leaving her dazed. Then the truck tipped sideways and teetered on the edge of flipping over.

EIGHTY

THE TRUCK BALANCED at an angle for a moment on two wheels as if deciding which way gravity wanted to take it, then the vehicle righted itself and dropped back onto the road with a jarring thud that sent Patterson flying across the bench seat into the other door. She landed on her back with her legs in the air. Realizing her opportunity, she stretched her arms as far as they would extend to bring them up past her legs and to the front. The handcuffs dug into her wrists, but there was no time to consider the pain.

Ortega was distracted and didn't realize what was going on in the back seat. His focus was on Bauer and Grant, who were already running toward the truck with guns drawn, shouting at him to exit the vehicle.

Instead, he spun the steering wheel and slammed his foot down hard on the accelerator, figuring they wouldn't shoot with their colleague in the cab.

The back wheels spun for a moment, but soon they found purchase, and the truck shot forward with a screech of tires. This was the momentum that Patterson needed to complete the task. She felt herself rolling sideways, and as she did so, her rump and thighs slipped past her manacled arms. With a final effort, she threw herself forward and sat up, bringing her wrists past her knees, stretching so far, she thought her shoulders might pop from their joints. But then with one final heave, her wrists slipped past her ankles.

Ortega was speeding away from the Dodge Charger at a dangerous pace, totally focused on the dark road ahead. He still hadn't noticed that Patterson's arms were no longer behind her back.

She needed to stop the truck before he escaped and could think of only one way to do it. She raised her arms and looped them past the driver's seat and over Ortega's head. He noticed the movement at the last moment and tried to duck out of the way, but it was too late. Patterson's handcuffed wrists dropped around his neck. She braced her feet, still zip tied together, against the back of his seat and leaned back so that the handcuffs were digging into his neck in a chokehold.

Ortega let out a gurgling cry and thrashed in the seat, twisting and bucking in an attempt to break free. One hand left the steering wheel and grabbed frantically at her wrists and the handcuffs pressing against his neck.

The truck veered to the side of the trail, first one way, and then the other, as he struggled to control the speeding truck with one hand and free himself with the other. When it became obvious that he was not going to succeed, the detective let go of Patterson's handcuffed wrists and reached down. He came up with the gun, suppressor still attached, and aimed it clumsily over his shoulder into the back of the cab before pulling the trigger.

A bullet whizzed past Patterson's head and shattered the rear windshield inches from a kill shot. Ortega swung the gun blindly sideways and fired again as Patterson shimmied away from the line of fire. This bullet smacked into the back of the bench seat where she'd been sitting a moment before.

She might not be so lucky with the next shot.

Patterson dug her knees into the back of the seat and pulled back on the handcuffs with all her might. The pain in her wrists was almost unbearable, but she persevered, even though she could feel the sharp edges of the cuffs slicing into her skin. It reminded her of another traumatic situation weeks before, when a depraved killer had shackled her in a car and left her to die. Those wounds had only just healed, now she was reopening them.

Ortega removed his other hand from the wheel, desperate to free himself. He clawed at his neck, but there was no strength in his efforts. His foot must have slipped from the accelerator, because the truck was slowing down now, even as it charted a meandering course toward the side of the road.

Patterson could see Ortega's eyes bulging in the rear-view mirror. His mouth was opening and closing like a fish out of water as it struggled to breathe. His index finger curled back over the gun's trigger even as the muzzle swung toward Patterson. But he didn't fire this time. Instead, he went limp and his arm drooped. The gun slipped from his hand and dropped into the seat well.

With more than a little relief, Patterson released the pressure on Ortega's neck.

The truck was still veering off course and losing momentum as it did so. An oak tree loomed large ahead of them, its thick trunk materializing out of the darkness as if it had been hiding until the last moment, eager to surprise her. Patterson realized what was about to happen, but before she could even think about trying to lunge over the seat and grab the wheel, the truck bounced off the road, tore through the underbrush on the verge, and smacked nose first into the tree with a jarring thud.

Patterson was thrown forward. Her forehead cracked against the hard plastic of the driver's seat headrest before she flopped back onto the rear bench, dazed and hurting. Blood trickled from her nose. More blood ran down her arms from her damaged wrists, still held by the handcuffs. She tried to focus, but everything was a blur. And then she heard voices. Two of them. Through the haze she realized it was Marcus Bauer and Jonathan Grant. They were at the truck, pulling the door open. Gentle hands reached inside and lifted her to safety.

"Patterson. Are you alright?" a worried voice asked, piercing the fog that rolled over her senses.

It was Grant.

She tried to answer but the words wouldn't come, so instead she relaxed into his arms and let herself drift away into unconsciousness.

EIGHTY-ONE

FOUR HOURS LATER, Patterson sat in an examination room at the same hospital where Marcus Bauer had been treated for his gunshot wound a few weeks before. They had patched her up and she was now itching to leave. It was almost two in the morning, and she was beyond exhausted.

The door opened, and Jonathan Grant entered. "Doc says you're free to go."

"About time. All I had was a mild concussion and a few scrapes." Patterson stood up. The handcuffs were gone, and her wrists were bandaged. She had sliced them up pretty badly during her attempt to subdue Detective Sergeant Ortega. "It was hardly anything."

"A concussion is not something to take lightly. The truck hit that tree pretty hard," Grant said. "Besides, you've had more than your fair share of knocks in recent weeks. I'm starting to think this search for your sister isn't a good idea."

"Too bad. I'm finishing what I started."

"Could you at least take a week off to get healthy?"

"I'll consider it," Patterson replied, giving him a weak smile.

"You might not have much choice. Right now, you're still

officially wanted for murder, at least until the DA scraps the charges, which probably won't happen until tomorrow at the earliest. Same for Mark Davis. When he's sufficiently recovered, he'll be able to go back home to his wife. There's no way the DA will prosecute after Senator Newport's admissions to you tonight."

"Speaking of which, where is the senator now?" Patterson asked.

"He's enjoying a jail cell downtown. Ortega, who you half strangled to death, will be there right alongside the senator just as soon as he's released from the hospital. Between being choked and the impact with that tree, the erstwhile detective sergeant is not feeling so hot right now."

"He deserved it."

"No doubt. The pair of them will be arraigned on charges of kidnapping, conspiracy, murder, and anything else we can throw at them. I'll hazard a guess that neither man will be seeing the outside world again anytime soon."

"Which means it's over." Patterson's shoulders slumped with relief. She hadn't realized how much stress she had been under. She felt lighter, as if a huge weight had lifted.

"It will be, just as soon as the DA does her job. In the meantime, you're still officially under my supervision as per SAC Harris which means I'm not letting you out of my sight."

"I can think of worse situations to be in," Patterson said, heading for the door. "How about you take me back to the safe house where you can supervise my aches away with a back rub, and maybe even a nice hot shower."

"I take my job seriously, so that shouldn't be a problem." Grant held the door open for her.

As she reached it, Patterson turned to Grant and put her arms around his neck, giving him a quick kiss. "I love you."

"Love you, too." Grant waited for her to step into the

corridor and then followed behind. At the other end was a mostly empty waiting room.

Bauer and Phoebe jumped up and rushed forward when they saw her.

She embraced each of them in a quick hug and then glanced toward the door. "I hate this place. Can we get out of here?"

EIGHTY-TWO

A FEW DAYS LATER, Patterson sat in another hospital room, but this time it wasn't for her. Since the district attorney had dropped the charges against Mark Davis, he had been transferred from the prison infirmary to a regular facility where he was still recovering from the wounds inflicted upon him during the attack in the rec yard.

Patterson sat in a chair next to his bed.

"I can't believe they tracked down my deposit in that sperm bank and broke in just so they could use it to frame me," Davis said after listening to Patterson's explanation of the events that had led up to his arrest. "It was so long ago that I did that. I'm surprised it was even still there."

"It was, at least until Leo Galinsky took it," Patterson said. "And they had the perfect person to set you up. Alexandria Rowley had been arrested a couple of times for prostitution. She was using it as a way to supplement her meager wages at the convenience store. It was easy for Detective Sergeant Ortega to strong-arm her into going along with the scheme to set you up in exchange for a few thousand dollars courtesy of Senator

Newport. Galinsky even roughed her up a bit to make the whole thing look more convincing."

"But then she decided the money wasn't enough and wanted more, and so they killed her."

"Yes. Unfortunately. She tried to blackmail them but didn't realize just how dangerous they were. Neither did Leo Galinsky. He might not have been so amenable to do the detective's dirty work if he'd known that Ortega viewed him as dispensable. When he killed Rowley, it made Galinsky a liability and Ortega decided to kill two birds with one stone by silencing Galinsky and framing me for his murder."

"Which wouldn't have happened if I hadn't asked you to look into the circumstances of my case," Davis said. "I'm sorry you ended up in so much trouble."

"If you hadn't asked, we might never have uncovered the senator's scheme and you would have ended up spending the rest of your life behind bars."

"And all because of some stupid land-use report."

"The senator had to make that report go away. He suspected as far back as the early 2000s that the land might be contaminated, but he didn't know for sure and probably figured it would just sit there doing nothing forever. But then the opportunity to make a fortune with the stadium project came along. He sold the land to the developer for millions under market value in exchange for becoming a twenty percent partner through a shell company. He also used his position to give them millions in tax breaks and other incentives that made the land too good to pass on and build elsewhere, even with its history. It was a gift courtesy of the taxpayers that would make them all filthy rich."

"The only problem was the site contamination," Mark Davis said.

"Yes. The senator hoped that after so many years, the ground wouldn't be contaminated anymore, but he didn't know for sure. The developers needed a clean site report in order to build. They hired you to produce a preliminary study, probably to see what they were dealing with before the EPA got involved. When the report was unfavorable, they did the only thing they could."

"Made me go away so that I wouldn't question the speed with which they were moving forward on the project."

"Exactly." Patterson nodded. "But there was one more thing they needed. That clean site report from the EPA. We did some investigating after the senator was arrested. With no other way out of the situation, he used his position to coerce a junior inspector with the state's EPA office. He found a skeleton in the man's past—an affair that would ruin his marriage—and used that as leverage to get him to fake the tests and issue a clean report."

Well, I guess they got what they deserved in the end," Davis said. "They won't be building that stadium now."

"They certainly won't. The DA is also looking at charges against the board of the development company."

Davis nodded. "This whole thing is crazy. Who would've thought that one little piece of land could cause so much trouble? Thank you for figuring it out. I really thought I was done. Everyone was so convinced that I raped that woman, even I started to wonder if it was possible."

"Your wife never believed it for a second," Patterson said. "She stood by you all the way."

"She's a keeper, and that's for sure." Davis chuckled, but then he winced and clutched at his side under the sheets, obviously still in a lot of pain. "Sorry. They have me on pain meds, but they only go so far."

"Been there, done that," Patterson replied.

"Yeah. I'm looking forward to my evening top up." This time he smiled, but didn't laugh. "And now I think it's time to complete my end of the bargain and tell you about Julie."

EIGHTY-THREE

"I HADN'T REFLECTED on that time in my life for years until you came along and asked about Julie," Mark Davis said with a wistful look in his eye. "We all thought we were going to be rock gods. But we weren't really that good. I think we knew it by the time we played TexFest. That was our last gig. We'd all finished college by then and everyone went their separate ways. Martin and Karissa stayed in Dallas, at least until their relationship broke up. Then Martin died, of course. That really hit me hard. We'd always been good friends and I guess it rammed home the fragility of life for the first time."

Patterson nodded but said nothing.

"Trent and Julie traveled back to Amarillo with me, and we hung out for a few days. They had a little thing of their own going and I felt a bit like a spare wheel, but it was fun." Davis nodded toward a small box sitting on the hospital nightstand. "I think you'll be interested in what's inside. I asked Carol to go through the closet and find that stuff. She brought it in this morning."

Patterson took the box and opened it. Inside was a pack of photos and a folded up sheet of paper with curling edges.

"Go on. Take a look at the photos," Davis said.

She took them out with shaking hands, sensing that she was about to discover something about her sister. The first photo was of the band. There was a stage behind them. She guessed it was TexFest. Julie wasn't in it. Patterson looked up at Davis.

"She was behind the camera," he said. "Keep going."

She flicked to the second photo and there was Julie, smiling at the camera with her arm around a lanky guy maybe twenty-one or twenty-two years old. He had long, straight black hair and wire-rimmed glasses.

"That's Trent."

"I figured as much," Patterson said, flipping to the next photo. In this one she was in front of a line of cars buried by their noses in a field and sticking straight up as if they'd been planted there by some celestial hand. She recognized the strange monument because it was a place her father had always wanted to visit. He'd read about it in some travel magazine years before Patterson and Julie were born and it had stuck with him, even though he'd never actually made it there. The cars were a well-known sculpture on the outskirts of Amarillo, built by a local artist in the 1960s. Visitors went with spray cans and wrote messages on the cars or just simply sprayed random patterns and other graffiti. Julie had a spray can in her hand. She was looking up at one of the cars and standing in its shadow.

The next several photos were taken in the same location. They showed Julie, Trent, and Mark having fun with their spray cans. In one photo Julie had written the word *Queens* across the door of one of the vertical cars. In another she had sprayed the message *For you, dad!* in bright red lettering across the roof of another car. Around the words, she had sprayed a heart.

Patterson swallowed a lump that pushed up into her throat. She hadn't seen so many new pictures of Julie in a long time.

She looked up at Mark Davis and wiped away a tear. "Thank you for this. Can I make copies?"

"I'll do you one better. You can keep them. I have the negatives. Julie and Trent both took copies before they left town."

"Julie had a set of these photos?" Patterson looked through them again, overcome by a sudden feeling of connection with her sister.

"Yup."

Patterson slipped the photos back into their protective envelope. "Where did Julie and Trent go after this?"

"Trent wanted to keep the band going. At least, what was left of it," Davis said. "He had gotten a gig at some bar in Santa Fe because his cousin worked there. He begged me to go there and join him. For a moment, I considered it. But I had a job lined up here, and the band was never going to make the big time. We all knew that. I didn't want a life trailing around after Trent while he played at being a rock star."

"But Julie went with him?"

"Yes. She was heading out west anyway, so I guess she thought it would be fun. Besides, like I said, they had a bit of a romance thing going by then."

"What happened next?"

Davis shrugged. "Don't know. Trent called me once after they got to Santa Fe, still pestering me to keep the band going, then sent me a note he'd written on a flyer for some place he'd gotten a gig—one final attempt to change my mind maybe—but that was it. We were never best buddies or anything. I joined the band because I was friends with Martin, and he said they needed a bass player. Talked me into it. After Trent left, we never really kept in touch."

"Is this the note?" Patterson asked, holding up the folded sheet of paper.

Davis nodded. "I thought it might be relevant."

Patterson unfolded the sheet with trembling fingers. It was a flyer for a bar called Amy's Roadhouse advertising their lineup of bands for July 2005. She didn't recognize the bands playing the first weekend, but 'Singer/Songwriter Trent Steiger' was listed as the entertainment for the second weekend. A ring had been drawn around the Saturday evening performance in black marker. There was a handwritten note at the top of the sheet.

Come see me play.
It's not that long a drive and maybe you'll change your mind about the band.
Trent

The note didn't mention her sister. Patterson folded it back up. "Did you go there and see him play?"

"No. It's not that short a drive. Four and a half hours each way."

"Do you think Julie was still with him?"

"I have no idea, but it wasn't long after they left Amarillo and she was with him then, so probably."

"Can I borrow the note?" Patterson asked. "I promise I'll send it back to you when I'm done."

"Don't bother. I have no sentimental attachment to it. The note's all yours. I hope it helps you find out what happened to your sister."

Patterson sensed she had gotten about as much information out of Mark Davis as she was going to, and he looked tired. Actually, he looked like the pain had gotten worse. She slipped the note back into the box alongside the pack of photos, then stood up and thanked him.

When she left the room, Patterson saw Grant leaning against the wall, waiting for her with his arms folded. She took a step toward him as a nurse hurried the other way and disappeared through the door she had just exited. With any luck, Mark Davis was about to get his pain meds.

"Well?" Grant asked as she approached. "Did you get what you needed?"

"Yes. I think I did." She looked down at the box still clutched in her hands. "I'm going to Santa Fe." Then, when she saw the look on his face, she put her arms around him and smiled. "But first, I'm taking a week off and flying back to New York to spend some time with you and dad. How does that sound?"

Grant returned the smile and wrapped his arms around her. "That sounds perfect."

Read the next book in The Patterson Blake FBI Mystery Thriller series.

Dark Road From Sunrise
Pattterson follows her sister's trail to Sante Fe.

Buy Now!

READY FOR MORE PATTERSON BLAKE?

The next book in The Patterson Blake FBI Mystery Thriller series.

Dark Road From Sunrise
Pattterson follows her sister's trail to Sante Fe.

ABOUT THE AUTHORS

A. M. Strong is the pen name of supernatural action and adventure fiction author Anthony M. Strong.

Sonya Sargent grew up in Vermont and is an avid reader when she isn't working on books of her own. They divide their time between Florida's sunny Space Coast and a tranquil island in Maine.

Find out more about the author at
AMStrongAuthor.com

Made in United States
Orlando, FL
22 August 2024

50656227R00221